WITCH FINDER

What Reviewers Say About
Sheri Lewis Wohl's Work

Drawing Down the Mist

"Vampires loving humans. Vampires hating vampires. Vampires killing humans. Vampires killing vampires. Good vampires. Evil vampires. Internet-savvy vampires. Lovers turning enemies. Nurturing revenge for a century. Kindness. Cruelty. Love. Action. Fights. Insta-love. This one has everything for a true drama."
—*reviewer@large*

Cause of Death

"I really liked these characters, all of them, and wouldn't say no to a sequel, or more."—*Jude in the Stars*

"*CSI* meets *Ghost Whisperer.* ...The pace was brilliantly done, the suspense was just enough, and I'm not ashamed to admit that I had no idea who the serial killer was until almost the end."—*Words and Worlds*

"*Cause of Death* by Sheri Lewis Wohl is one creepy and well-written murder mystery. It is one of the best psychological thrillers I've read in a while."—*Rainbow Reflections*

"[A] light paranormal romance with a psycho-killer and some great dogs."—*C-Spot Reviews*

"There's a ton of stuff in here that I enjoy very much, such as the light paranormal aspect of the book, and the relationship between our two leads is very nice if a bit of a slow burn. The case was engaging enough that I didn't really set this title down once I started it."—Colleen Corgel, Librarian, Queens Public Library

"Totally disturbing, and very, very awesome. ...The characters were amazing. The supernatural tint was never overdone, and even the stuff from the killer's point of view, while disturbing, was awesomely done as well. It was a great book and a fun (and intense) read."—Danielle Kimerer, Librarian (Nevins Memorial Library, Massachusetts)

"This thriller has spooky undertones that make it an intense page turner. You won't be able to put this book down."—*Istoria Lit*

The Talebearer

"As a crime story, it is a good read that had me turning pages quickly. ...The book is well written and the characters are well-developed."—*Reviews by Amos Lassen*

She Wolf

"I really enjoyed this book—I couldn't put it down once I started it. The author's style of writing was very good and engaging. All characters, including the supporting characters, were multi-layered and interesting."—Melina Bickard, Librarian, Waterloo Library (UK)

Twisted Screams

"[A] cast of well developed characters leads you through a maze of complex emotions."—*Lunar Rainbow Reviewz*

Twisted Echoes

"A very unusual blend of lesbian romance and horror. ...[W]oven throughout this modern romance is a neatly plotted horror story from the past, which bleeds ever increasingly into the present of

the two main characters. Lorna and Renee are well matched, and face ever-increasing danger from spirits from the past. An unusual story that gets tenser and more interesting as it progresses."
—Pippa Wischer, Manager at Berkelouw Books, Armadale

Vermilion Justice

"[T]he characters are so dynamic and well-written that this becomes more than just another vampire story. It's probably impossible to read this book and not come across a character who reminds you of someone you actually know. Wohl takes something as fictional as vampires and makes them feel real. Highly recommended."
—*GLBT Reviews: The ALA's GLBT Round Table*

Visit us at www.boldstrokesbooks.com

By the Author

WITCH FINDER

by

Sheri Lewis Wohl

2023

WITCH FINDER

ISBN 13: 978-1-63679-335-1

This Trade Paperback Original Is Published By
Bold Strokes Books, Inc.
P.O. Box 249
Valley Falls, NY 12185

First Edition: August 2023

Credits

Editor: Shelley Thrasher
Production Design: Susan Ramundo
Cover Design By Tammy Seidick

Dedication

For Zoey

And the light shineth in darkness;
and the darkness comprehended it not.

John 1:5
The Holy Bible
King James Version

PROLOGUE

1855
Cornwall, England

"Mama, he is coming." Tamsin walked to the fire, where her mother sat bent over a charm she had prepared for the sailor with a deeply lined face and sad eyes. A troubled soul who had shown up at their door the night before. Like many who knocked on their door late when darkness fell and the moon rose high in the sky, he came in search of the kind of help and protection they alone could give.

Her mother, known by all as Tammy Blee even though her birth name was also Tamsin, lifted her head as her hands stilled. Their eyes met, and she saw sadness. "We always knew he would."

Neither of them spoke of the sailor who traveled their way and would soon burst through the heavy wooden door that kept the cold from the small room where the fire blazed and her mother shared with her the lessons of the witches and diviners who came before them. She had learned from them how to harness the magic and the healing powers gifted to each of the first daughters of the first daughters.

"I thought we would have more time." She did not believe her moment had arrived. It could not be. Too soon. She was not ready. She needed many more lessons before she stepped into her destiny.

Tammy set aside the charm, now ready and waiting for the sailor. She stood and put her hands on Tamsin's shoulders, her touch sending warmth throughout her. "Time is not ours to control, child of mine."

Their powerful legacy had brought them much, yet now it all seemed for naught. Despite the many lessons, she had chosen to believe her mother would be the one to end it. That they would be a family that lived out their lives together. "It is not fair."

Her mother shook her head. "My beautiful daughter, have I taught you nothing? Fairness has never been ours. One day it will be, but not during the years we walk this land. This I have seen." Her hands dropped away, and a chill replaced the warmth.

She would not argue. That she had the power to divine the future could not be disputed. Her mother possessed the power of ten white witches and the sight of a hundred. Women like them—not just like them, all women—lived in the shadow of the men who ruled the world. The Witch Finder came, and nothing she did would change that one fact.

"I understand." And, she did. All her life, she had prepared for this day. Her destiny had been sealed on the day of her birth, as it would be in the future for a daughter that she too would one day give life to. Like her mother, she could see through the veil that separated the past, the present, and the future. While not as powerful as her mother, impressive in her own right. Their birthright would carry forward for many generations. Her wish for it to be different this night fell into ashes. She had no power to bend the will of the universe. She opened the door and stared out into the darkness, searching.

The legacy of the Witch Finder General, Matthew Hopkins, meant the latest generation of Witch Finders would hunt them as though they were nothing more than criminals, just as they had done for over two hundred years. They killed every witch they found, and it did not matter that the witch practiced white magic, that they healed and helped. They destroyed each one, all in the pursuit of the grimoire beneath the boards of the floor she stood on now.

Her mother knelt and began to pry up the planks, her fingers bleeding as splinters from the wood pierced her skin. "You must hurry."

From beneath her bed, Tamsin pulled out the prepared bag and a pile of men's clothing. She set them on the table before sitting on a stool in front of the fire, willing herself not to weep. After her mother tucked the grimoire into her bag, she took a pair of shears from her sewing basket and began to cut off Tamsin's hair. It fell in long strands to the floor.

Once her beautiful tresses lay in a pile, her mother gathered it up and threw it into the fire. The small house filled with the stench of burning hair as she slipped out of her dress and into the trousers, shirt, and overcoat. With a hat on her nearly shorn hair and the bag slung across her body, she no longer resembled the lovely young witch known to the village as a powerful healer.

Her mother put her hands on either side of her face and stared into her eyes. "Stay strong, and follow your path. Keeping the world safe is in your hands now. Hide as a man until you are safe, and only then finish your destiny and bring forth a daughter. The universe has called to you this night to take your place as the Keeper."

"I will do my duty." She understood the importance of the journey she was about to undertake. She would not fail her mother or the ancestors who came before.

"I love you, my daughter, very much."

She kissed her mother on the cheek, a single tear escaping despite her best intention to stay strong. "I love you too. You will forever be in my heart." She hugged her for only a moment.

She walked out into the darkness and did not look back. There would be no point. She would never return, for she would have nothing to return to.

The Prophecy

She shall come under the dark of the moon,
with curls of sable and eyes that reflect the blue sky.
Her step will be light.
Her power will be mighty.
Her sight will be true.
She will find her,
and the power of touch will bring the cleansing fire.
So it is written in the stars.

CHAPTER ONE

Present Day
Eastern Washington State

The cold wind that blew over Tamsin Chaney's skin made her drop the half-gallon bottle she carried to the workbench. It hit the floor with a thunderous bang, the cap flying off and olive oil spraying over her legs, the cupboard doors, and the slate tile she'd installed herself. A mixture of glass and pale-green ooze spread around her feet like an incoming tide. She stepped out of the way. "Damn it." She should have bought the brand that came in a plastic bottle. Or not. The plastic part violated her sustainability beliefs.

She grabbed a microfiber towel and threw it on the floor in a halfhearted attempt to staunch the flow of slime creeping across the floor. It would be an absolute bitch to clean up. She'd be lucky if she didn't break her freaking neck on the slick tiles in the process.

Instead of working on the mess, she leaned against the counter and sighed. It wasn't like she hadn't expected it. She'd really thought she'd have more time. The idea of being forced to pick up and move didn't land well. This place suited her more than anywhere else, and that said a lot, given she'd lived in six different states and three countries in the past eighteen years.

Not to mention that sooner or later, she'd have to get serious about the daughter thing, and that damned clock kept ticking in the background. Hard to do while moving around all the time. Hard to do for other reasons too, but she preferred not to get caught up in those. They might matter to her heart. They didn't concern her when it came to her duty to the greater good.

Duty first.

"Jesus, Tamsin. What the hell happened?" Her friend and assistant, Holly Klein, walked into the workshop, grabbed a bunch of paper towels, and dropped them onto the floor. The spread of olive oil stopped.

"Hit my elbow and the container went flying," she lied. As close as she'd become to Holly during the several years they'd been working together, she wouldn't understand the truth of the unseen force that touched her soul and caused her to drop the bottle. Of course, Tamsin didn't plan to share her secrets, which would make it impossible for Holly to get it, and so she came up with a story she could understand. They were secrets for a very good reason. Centuries of them.

Holly, bless her heart, didn't push, and for all of fifteen minutes they worked side by side to clean the oil from the floor and the cabinets. A bit of earth-friendly green cleaner wiped away the last remnants, returning the tile to a walk-safe state once more. A bag full of towels to wash and a roll of paper towels to recycle. At least the workroom sparkled, which was never a bad thing. Out of every dark cloud came a ray of sunshine, or so her mother had liked to say.

Wow. How long had it been since she thought of one of her mother's quirky sayings? A shadow passed over her, and a twinge of pain hit her heart. A loss that couldn't be measured. One of those continually bright lights, even in the face of the darkness that had surrounded her the entire course of her life, Mom had never allowed reality to dampen her spirit. Tamsin always wished she could be more like her. Instead, she'd inherited the seriousness that defined her father. What she could remember of him anyway. Their brief time together had resembled a flash of lightning, and every little piece of memory that stayed with her, a treasure she held tight.

"Well," Holly said with her hands on her hips. "Shall we start this batch again since you decided to throw the most important ingredient all over the floor?"

She smiled at the tall, slender woman with her long braids hanging over each shoulder and dark eyes always seeming to sparkle with life. "Yes. I suppose we should."

"Think you can work on not throwing anything else on the floor? Particularly given the price of olive oil these days. I hate to put my accountant hat on, but it really hurts our bottom line."

This time she laughed and put a hand to her heart. "I promise to do my very best not to dump any more olive oil on the floor, or anywhere else, except in the soap pot." The laughter helped dispel some of the darkness that had wrapped over her since the cool wind whooshed over her. It would take time to make plans and, thus, important to maintain normality in the interim. She'd learned one thing during her life, before and after: everything must be done with purpose, intention, and care. Nothing hasty. The responsibilities that lay on her shoulders were too important to risk a single mistake. No way would she be the one to jeopardize the centuries-old legacy she'd inherited. However, an idea whispered in the back of her mind, and no matter how hard she tried, she couldn't ignore it. For the moment, she shoved those whispers aside.

Six hours later, they managed to wrap up four batches of goat's-milk soap, and cut and wrap another forty-eight bars for shipment, plus feed and water all the animals. Pretty good, considering a timer had begun clicking in the background. When Holly drove away from the farm, the sun had started to drop behind the mountains to the west. If she suspected that anything bothered Tamsin enough to make her drop that bottle of olive oil, she didn't let on. Accidents happen even to the most careful. From all appearances, a normal day at the Seven Sisters Farm.

Tamsin left the workshop and returned to the house, where she made herself a cup of green tea and took it to the library. In the room with floor-to-ceiling bookcases filled with her passion, she centered herself while her mind raced. So much to do and it must begin now.

In her favorite chair, she took a few minutes to sip her tea, which flowed warm and wonderful down her throat. A comfortable routine. Nice to have that for a few minutes anyway.

When the bone-china teacup grew lighter, she set it aside. From the table drawer, she picked up a small cell phone and turned it on. She had only one number in the contacts list, and it rang a single time before someone picked it up.

"Are they coming?"

She closed her eyes. "Yes."

❖

Morrigan James jumped when the alarm on her smartwatch both buzzed against her wrist and screeched. She'd set it to do just that, but the noise still jarred her. Rather than call from the watch's speaker-phone function, she pulled her cell from her pocket, punched in the number, and put the phone to her ear. Some conversations didn't need to run the risk of being overheard. That she didn't currently have company didn't affect her sense of caution.

"They're on the move."

"Damn."

"We need you."

"How close?"

"Other side of the state. You're about six hours away."

"Give me the location." She wrote it down. No texts. No electronic record. Not safe. Even writing it could be risky. She never knew the strength of the magic she'd face, and with the kind of power that had taken hundreds and hundreds of years to develop, combined with the darkness that amped it up, danger always lurked.

In the bedroom, she shoved clothes into a bag. Jeans, T-shirts, a hoodie. In the bathroom, she grabbed her small, zippered bag and tossed it in on top of her clothes. A spare pair of boots was already in the car. It didn't take long to clear out her things. She traveled casual and light. Easier to move fast that way.

"You're leaving." Ginny stood in the doorway, watching, frowning, arms crossed across her chest. A petite, pretty woman with green eyes and pale hair, and a quick mind, she was, in many ways, Morrigan's polar opposite. Ginny was as emotional and demonstrative as Morrigan was reserved.

"Yeah. Sorry." She didn't look at her.

"That's it? Yeah, sorry?"

Morrigan zipped her bag, put the strap over her shoulder, and turned to face her. The truth always worked the best. It always wounded too. "I don't know what else to say. You knew from the start this would be temporary." She'd never made promises. Not to Ginny or anyone who came before her. In her life, long-term didn't exist.

Ginny's eyebrows rose. "Seriously? That's what you say to me after all this time? Pretty shitty."

Morrigan took a deep breath before she answered. Her fault really. Though she'd chosen to ignore the warning signs, she'd known for a while that Ginny wasn't adhering to their original agreement. Fun. Sex. Laughter. No commitment. That had been their arrangement and the path of her life. Every relationship began with those ground rules, and this one hadn't been any different. She liked Ginny and enjoyed the months they'd shared. A little normality in a life with zero chance of ever qualifying as normal. Today, it ended.

She tightened her grip on the strap of her bag. "It might be shitty, but you knew from the get-go how it would end. You can't say I haven't been honest with you because I never made any promises. Not once."

Tears filled Ginny's eyes and spilled down her cheeks. "That's not just shitty. It's mean. Just because something starts off with no strings doesn't mean it can't change. Life does that, you know, and people adjust. Especially if they care about each other."

Morrigan stepped close and put a hand on her damp cheek. Guilt did tap at her heart. It didn't change what she had to do. "I am sorry, Ginny. I really am. You're a beautiful, caring woman, and you deserve more. I can't give it to you, and I've tried to be clear about that fact."

"I thought you'd changed your mind. I thought you loved me."

She'd never have the luxury of enjoying love. Not in the destiny she could neither ignore nor outrun. Not that she wanted to. She took her legacy so seriously she'd never be able to explain it to Ginny or anyone else. Even in her own ranks, few understood the intensity that defined her "I like you, I do." It wasn't a lie, and she hoped the truth rang in her words.

"Fuck your *like*." She jerked away from Morrigan. "Just go, and don't ever come back here."

She stepped close again, kissed her on the cheek, and then left. She didn't look back. No point, and really, the moment she stepped outside, her focus shifted. Between her and duty stood three-hundred-plus miles of freeway and a mountain pass. No time to delay.

The traffic on the freeway lightened up by North Bend, and she took the main exit routing her past the outlet stores. Time to fuel up and grab a coffee at the Starbucks half a block away from the gas station. It would be nice if she had company on the long drive, someone from her own ranks who would be able to strategize with her. Given she happened to be the only one in the Pacific Northwest at the moment, she'd be on her own. Not a big deal. She'd handled similar situations before by herself, and she'd be fine this time too.

Well, not exactly a situation quite like this one. A call to protect the Keeper came once in a lifetime. They all trained and prepared. Only a chosen few were ever called. It was an honor and a mission that demanded zero failure.

Her phone rang right as she merged back onto I-90 East. "Yeah."

"Another one down."

Her heart sank. Over the last few years, the Black Faction had grown increasingly bold. Right from the start, beginning in the seventeenth century with the Witch Finder General, Matthew

Hopkins, they'd been ruthless. Lured by money and a sense of holy righteousness, many joined him in a mission to keep the world safe from witchcraft, at least until it grew clear the journey Hopkins embarked upon had become less about good and more about power. It was then the Witch Finders fractured into two distinct groups: black and white.

The darkness embraced by Hopkins and his devotees blossomed over the centuries in the Black Faction, while her family, and others like them, formed the White Faction. They not only possessed their own magic, but they also understood that most executed for supposed black magic crimes were, in fact, innocent victims. Hopkins and his followers looked not to keep the world safe but to destroy it with the help of the *Book of Darkness*. The grimoire had been in the possession of a white witch known only as the Keeper for hundreds of years. Morrigan, and the rest of the White Faction, had worked nonstop to keep the Black Faction in check ever since, to keep them from exploiting what could be found in the *Book of Darkness*.

Today wasn't much different.

❖

Freddi smiled as she looked down into the slack face of the dead witch. "Nice try, girlie." A spunky little bitch, she'd give her that. Spunk didn't cut it against the refined skill of someone like her.

For her entire life, they'd underestimated Freddi, which wasn't necessarily a bad thing. She considered it one of her superpowers. Most saw a tiny woman with dark hair and green eyes, a second-born witch overlooked by everyone in favor of a sister bigger, prettier, and outwardly more talented. By the time anyone realized Freddi might be a threat, it was already too late. This one had made that same fatal mistake.

With the toe of her boot, she nudged the body, which didn't move much. Not exactly a little witch. The whole encounter disappointed her in several ways. First, she'd been too easy to kill, and second, as it turned out, she wasn't the Keeper.

Surveillance over the last several weeks had caused her optimism to rise, and as it turned out, falsely. "You stupid, fat bitch." Another kick. Made her feel a little better, and perhaps, as she looked around the living room, she shouldn't jump to conclusions before conducting a thorough assessment.

In other words, she needed to check out the house before she finished here. Make certain that, even if she wasn't the one she sought, fatso didn't also hide important information. Many worked to protect the Keeper, decoys who distracted the Black Faction from the mission: the return of the *Book of Darkness* to its rightful place. For centuries the White Faction had secreted it away with the Keeper. It should never have been with them. It had always belonged to those like Freddi.

Not quite accurate. She'd become more and more convinced that it belonged not with the collective that made up the widespread Black Faction. It belonged with her, and her alone, and the injustice of that truth burned in her soul. Only Freddi possessed the magic and the power of the spirit needed to harness what the *Book of Darkness* promised. With it she would usher in a new era, where witches held glory and all bowed before her as leader of the new world. No longer would those like her have to pretend to be other than what they were. The Keeper and those who spent their lives and their legacies protecting her would perish as well. The world as they knew it would be forever altered, with all whom she spared kneeling at her feet.

It took her more than an hour to search the house. The futility of her actions wasn't lost on her. All the magic had vanished when the witch died. She'd felt it but was nothing if not thorough—a trait that would help her when she ruled the world. She fully embraced a leave-no-stone-unturned philosophy.

The search complete, time to tidy up. Not that she intended to pick up the emptied drawers or sweep up shattered glass. No. She had something much better and more satisfying in mind. She stood over the body and spread her fingers wide.

"In my heart resides the spiritual flame. I am the fire on the darkest night. Mother of the full moon, I draw down your perfect beam, to light the burning cauldron. Fire to slow the deceivers. Fire to bless us."

She brought her arms up as her head tipped back. "So shall it be."

She stepped into the darkness outside, the spit and crackle of the spreading fire fading as she distanced herself from the growing conflagration that filled the night sky with flames.

CHAPTER TWO

Tamsin waited on the porch. Her tea, untouched, grew cold in the antique cup. The delicate blue flowers hand-painted over a century earlier typically soothed her and, earlier, had done just that. Something about the family connection, she supposed. It always helped to touch what all the mothers before had held in their hands. The power came through and steadied her in those times when she felt tested.

The test crashed in bigger this time. One word kept flitting through her mind, though she didn't let it pass her lips: *final*. Her knees buckled, and she nearly collapsed. Generation after generation had succeeded, and she couldn't shake the feeling that she would be the final Keeper. The one who failed. How did one process that, let alone deal with it?

"No!" She straightened and began to pace back and forth, her hands stuffed into the pockets of her jeans. Then she stopped and stared out over the acres of woodland that bordered the land to the east. "No. I will not."

"You will not what?"

Her scream came out strangled. "Holy hell, Mae. You just took ten years off my life."

Mae Mosely stood on the top step looking at her through narrowed eyes. "Where were you? It's not like I came in here like a ninja." She pointed to the bright yellow SUV parked in the driveway.

Tamsin's heart stopped its rat-a-tat pounding. "I didn't hear you."

"No big revelation there, friend. You were miles away."

"Something's in the air." Tamsin waved her hand.

Mae inclined her head over her shoulder in the direction of the acres of tended flowers just beyond the edge of the yard. The rows were long and even and blooming a beautiful shade of purple. "Lavender."

Tamsin slid her gaze to the blooming plants in the north field. She'd planted them all herself, and oh, how they'd thrived. The orders for her soaps filled with the dried flowers were constant. Did her skill with the plants result from her magic or simply a green thumb? She wanted to believe that something about her work belonged only to her. "They do smell nice, don't they?"

"Sure. Whatever you say. How about we talk less about flowers and instead go inside and brainstorm your next move?"

She looked at the beautiful field of lavender for a long time, sighed, and went inside. Mae had a point. "You want some tea?"

"Not really. Got a cold beer?"

"Probably."

"Can't understand why you drink tea all day long. It's like dirty water." Mae made a face.

She laughed. Mae could do that to her. "Fine. Beer it is."

"That's my girl."

She handed Mae one of the two bottles she grabbed out of the refrigerator. "Let's think this through. I'm feeling like we don't have a ton of time, but we do have some, so let's use it."

Mae took the beer and walked out to the living room to sit on the sofa. Before saying anything more, she tipped up the bottle. "Now that's what I call thinking juice."

"More like avoidance juice in my case."

"Works either way because I'm here to make sure you don't avoid." Mae's tone turned serious. "We have to plan your exit strategy."

Tears pooled in her eyes. "I like it here."

"I get that, and I understand. Hard to beat a place like this."

"We have to try." The words came out of Tamsin's mouth without any real conviction.

"You and I both know why we won't." Mae held her gaze.

She didn't look away, her fingers buzzing. "Who is coming?"

Mae served as a Watcher, and for hundreds of years, witches like Tamsin had relied on their strength and wisdom to help keep them safe from the Black Faction Witch Finders. The Watchers couldn't do it alone because they, unlike the women who would be coming, had no powers. Mae was a regular. Pure, unadulterated magic would be needed in the coming days and months. Tamsin would need the power of a White Faction warrior to keep her safe.

"I know only her name—Morrigan James. She's been in the Seattle area for a while now and the only warrior close enough to reach you in a hurry."

"Is she strong enough?"

Mae shrugged. "I don't know. I put in the call, and that's what I got back. I'm sure more will come as soon as they can. For now, it will be you and James."

"It's strong this time." She closed her eyes and relived the power on the wind as it had washed her earlier.

"Right there with you. I can feel it, and we both know I don't have a magic bone in my body."

Tamsin opened her eyes. "I'm tired."

"I know. You've got this though." The expression on Mae's face mirrored what she felt.

She sighed. "I've got this." She didn't have a choice, not until she fulfilled her destiny, and time was clicking away.

❖

As Morrigan passed the first exit into Cheney, her hands began to shake so much she had to pull over. Breathing shallow, she rested her head against the steering wheel and closed her eyes. Good grief. Not now.

Intense heat washed over her, and with a whole lot of effort, she managed to keep the screams inside. Tempting as it would be to let them loose, they wouldn't help. Hot tears stung her eyes. Damn. Damn. Damn. Too late to save one good woman. One good witch. It hurt her heart to lose anyone, even if the Keeper remained safe.

For the moment.

As the intense emotion passed and the wave of heat cooled, she sat up and drew in deep, relaxing breaths. Her hands steadied. She gave it another minute and then hit the call button. From the car speakers, a phone rang. "Are you there?" No need for pleasantries.

"Not yet. I'm close."

"The Watcher, Mae Mosely, checked in, and the Keeper is aware."

"She probably already senses the change." She'd be surprised if a witch powerful enough to assume the role of Keeper failed to pick up the changes that wafted through the air.

"I'm sure you're right."

"What's wrong?" The concern in Hailey's voice wasn't unwarranted. Her role as a White Faction coordinator made her one of the select few who knew the when, where, and why of every white witch, including the Keeper.

"Someone's down."

"We know." Unflappable. Coordinators tended to be that way. Always the steadying voice at the end of the line.

"Who?"

"Belle."

"Crap." She'd met Belle several times—beautiful, talented, and full of bright magic. She didn't deserve to die, and not at the hands of one of *them*. She tightened her grip on the steering wheel as she maneuvered back into traffic on I-90 East.

"We have to surround her, quickly. Belle was about fourteen hundred miles away. That's too close. Makes me nervous, and I don't like nervous."

Morrigan's mind raced. "Where?"

"Just outside of Lincoln, Nebraska."

Damn. Hailey wasn't kidding. Way too close. "That's what? A twenty-hour-or-so drive?"

"Something like that. We have to hope she's still in the dark. Belle didn't know the Keeper's location. Outside of the council, you and a Watcher are the only ones who do."

Her fingers tightened on the wheel. "I'm getting there as fast as I can."

"Go faster." Hailey didn't give instructions lightly. If she said go faster, that's exactly what she'd do.

"I'm on it." She pushed harder on the accelerator. Probably end up with a speeding ticket.

Morrigan ended the call and focused on the freeway. Heavy traffic had her passing semi-truck by semi-truck moving the goods that kept commerce flourishing. She had a special place in her heart for drivers. Her father, now resting in the arms of angels, had been a long-haul trucker, and her few memories of him were filled with hugs and laughter, and sitting behind the wheel of his big truck pretending to drive. A mere six years together hadn't been enough.

"Not now," she murmured. Her sad life didn't rate the time or the energy of reflection. The past couldn't be changed, and dwelling on it, a waste of time and energy. Better to look forward, as in saving the life of a very important witch. Most had no clue how their lives and their world depended on the very women who were prosecuted in centuries past and looked down upon as eccentrics now. It never occurred to anyone that they kept them safe from an unimaginable evil.

She needed to release the bitterness of that actuality too. Her work happened in the shadows of life, a necessary reality. No thanks would ever come her way, although she would welcome a kind word now and again, especially after the nastiness of the departure from Ginny's. It wasn't Ginny's fault, and she didn't begrudge her the need to unload on Morrigan. She deserved it, and she'd take it. Still, her spirit could stand to hear an "atta girl" once in a while, or even once in a lifetime.

That wouldn't happen, and wishing it to be otherwise wouldn't change a damn thing. She'd inherited this legacy and been trained since birth to deal with that truth. For the most part, she felt okay about it. What she did, and those around her as well, held importance beyond explanation. Though she could never share with others, it provided her with a sense of fulfillment. It wasn't necessarily bad that the world might not know what the sisterhood did for it. That way people could go about their lives oblivious to the danger that lurked right beyond their sight. She would keep them safe.

Of course, first, she had to make certain the Keeper remained safe. That task came as her birthright, and she did a damn fine job, her few stumbles aside. She didn't really want to think about those. Best to leave them in the past, where they belonged. The future belonged to the Keeper, as long as she kept her alive, anyway. The call had been made for her to step up, and by Goddess, that's what she planned to do. She pressed the accelerator even harder and zipped past half a dozen more semi-trucks. Definitely a speeding ticket in her future.

❖

"Give me a minute to fill you in." Freddi wondered, not for the first time, why men found it so hard to shut the fuck up and listen. Aldo did his sex proud. Always had something to say. Never took the time to listen. Always believed himself right regardless of the issue. The fact that his advice typically turned out to be wrong never seemed to impact his grandiose sense of self-importance.

If she didn't have to go through him to get to his sister, Abba, she'd never talk to the jerk again. She breathed in and counted to ten. Then, twenty. If not pressed for time, she'd take it to fifty, just to make sure she didn't say what she meant.

"My intel indicated she would know the location of the Keeper."

If he'd heard her, he didn't give any indication. His words continued to spew out unfettered by any actual reliance on facts.

"And I'm telling you your intel was shit. She didn't know."

"You should have tried harder."

Fuck him. "I watched her for two weeks before I went in. And when I did, she told me everything she knew, which turned out to be jack shit."

"We'll never know for certain now, will we?"

The snarky edge to his words made her want to go through the phone and choke the life out of him. Years of his arrogance wore away any patience she might be able to afford him. "I know, and you're being intentionally obtuse." That remark would probably come back to bite her in the ass. She didn't care. Enough of his crap. "I need to talk to Abba. Now."

"She's busy."

"I'll wait."

"It will be a while." She could almost see him smiling, and her fingers flexed.

"I'll wait." Two could play his game, and with her motivation, the win would be hers.

"Fine."

Aldo didn't take well to being challenged, which, of course, made it more fun for her. She'd make a healthy bet Abba would be more than willing to take her call, and he simply wanted to block access because he could. Most were afraid of him and the power he wielded as the second-in-command of the Black Faction. Freddi wasn't one of them. Confident in her own powers, she didn't hesitate to take him on. Anywhere. Anytime. Bastard.

The wait didn't turn out to be long. Less than three minutes later, Abba picked up the call. Made her smile knowing that it also would make Aldo angry that she hadn't been forced to wait longer. "Frederica, explain to me about the witch and why you didn't get the Keeper's location from her."

Good old Aldo, painting a picture of incompetence before allowing Freddi to talk to his treasured sister. He made sure to get his digs in even if he failed to prevent her from talking with Abba. "She didn't know." The truth served her in this instance. Quick and to the point.

"You're certain?" Her question held none of the disdain she got from Aldo. Abba asked for clarity because, unlike her brother, she had confidence in Freddi's skills. Abba had been a champion for her since her induction into the elites known as the Witch Finders.

"One hundred percent." She'd squeezed that witch for every bit of knowledge she possessed. And it had been fun.

CHAPTER THREE

Mae hadn't wanted to leave Tamsin alone, but she needed time by herself to think through her next steps. Hard enough to be in her position. Harder still to concentrate when the whole world weighed in. At least the whole world of witches. Mae might be a regular, or non-magic person, but she understood the gravity of who and what Tamsin was.

They all knew that a Keeper existed after the *Book of Darkness* came into existence and its true potential became known. A coveted few knew the identity and location of each successive Keeper. Beyond those at the highest level of the White Faction, only Mae was aware of Tamsin's real identity, and if confronted by any from the Black Faction, she'd die silent. At least one Watcher kept track of every Keeper. They were able to move in the world of the regulars easier than the witches could. If discovered, it wouldn't matter what magic the faction tried or what pain they might inflict. The spell Tamsin herself had placed on Mae would ensure they'd never get anything useful. Another of her little secrets.

The Keepers held those close. The knowledge moved from mother to daughter through oral history. For hundreds of years, they'd protected their mysteries as they'd safeguarded the *Book of Darkness*. How much easier life would be if they could simply destroy the grimoire that held the power to end life as they knew it. The black magic between the pages of the ancient book almost too powerful to comprehend and nothing yet brought forth enough to destroy it.

Tamsin did comprehend its power. All the Keepers before her had as well because they could see it. In their dreams came the screams and the blackness with the power that could blank out the stars and the moon and the sun. She'd seen flashes of the face of the one who would unleash its power if she failed at her job. The one she felt certain came for her now. She'd not allow that to happen.

Though she kept close to home in her day-to-day life, she nonetheless scanned every face in every situation and everywhere she went. If she saw her, she'd know it at an intuitive level, even if her visions hadn't brought her a crystal-clear look. If she did see her, or rather, when she saw her, she'd kill her. The Keeper prepared for more than simply protecting the grimoire. The Witch Finders were a constant threat, generation after generation and, like her mother and grandmother, were trained to take them down. Violence didn't come to her naturally. Certain situations called for it nonetheless, and if put in the right position, she'd do what she needed to.

Her location now compromised, the decisions forced upon her left a bitter taste in her mouth. Despite everything, she wanted to stay here. This felt like home, and for a person who'd moved all over the world her entire life, that said a lot. More than that, when she'd come here, she'd been body-and-soul tired, and this place had gifted her with a peaceful, fulfilling respite. She'd communed with nature that brought eagles flying over her house and moose walking through the pastures. Hummingbirds gathered at the feeder and owls hooted from the trees. No, she didn't want to give up any of it.

Right now, did she have a choice? According to her mother, one always existed. But what was the right one? Should she stay and fight? Should she leave and start again somewhere new? Her heart said stay. Her mind said run. Decisions. Decisions.

She spun at the sound of a car coming down her long drive. One of the reasons she'd picked this piece of property centered on that driveway. Easy to hear someone approach, unless of course, her mind wandered, and they drove right up unannounced, as Mae did earlier. She wouldn't let that happen again. Mae came to protect. Others would arrive with motives far less noble.

The magic she'd been born with burned inside her, ready and waiting for release. Her fingers tingled and her nerves hummed. Given the current situation, she stood prepared with more than her magic. She unsnapped the strap on the small holster at her waistband. A little real-world protection in the form of a Smith & Wesson, air weight.

Her feet shoulder-distance apart, she stood on the porch and stared at the black SUV approaching the house. Unfamiliar, although she knew the look. Odds were the leader of the White Faction had sent the driver her way with orders to sweep her up and run. Those who would be coming to harm her wouldn't be bold enough to drive straight at her, even if daylight had made its exit. Stealth and surprise were more their style. Cowards of the worst kind.

Her breath caught as the woman stepped out of the SUV. Power rolled off her like a giant ocean wave that Tamsin wanted to catch and hold. Until this moment, she'd believed her mother to be the most powerful witch she'd ever been around. This mystery woman had just demonstrated that Mom had competition in that department.

"You're the Keeper." Her voice held a low, husky vibration. Beautiful. Sexy.

She nodded without hesitation. "You are?"

"Morrigan James."

"White Faction."

"Of course."

Of course. She'd stated the obvious. Members of that group gave off a vibe she'd been able to pick up on as long as she could remember. She supposed the legacy she'd inherited made her more sensitive. A blessing and a curse. The first warrior she'd met had come to protect her mother, whisking them away to safety in a strange land that never quite felt like home. She'd not been sad when they'd been forced to move yet again.

Most wouldn't be able to grasp the power of the woman who stared at her with eyes so blue they were like the sky on a gorgeous sunny day. Given the intensity that came from her, Tamsin would have expected her eyes to be black. Funny how the universe worked. A bit of camouflage, she supposed. No one would suspect a woman this attractive and with those pretty blue eyes to be lethal.

"Come in, Morrigan James." She moved her hand from the little Smith and Wesson and walked to the door, opened it, and motioned toward the interior. Regardless of what Tamsin might want in her heart, the appearance of Morrigan signaled a coming change to her life.

She didn't move. "You should check on me first."

"I already have."

Her eyes narrowed. "What do you mean?"

"I'm the Keeper." Did she really need to explain anything beyond that?

For a moment Morrigan said nothing and didn't move. Then her head dipped just a fraction of an inch, and she walked up the stairs and into the house.

❖

Morrigan wasn't sure what she expected to encounter when she met the Keeper. Given the gravity of the Keeper's duty, she supposed her to be a woman, old and wise. Powerful, without question. The image in her mind definitely didn't match someone close to her own age, tall, smoky, and with curves that made her heart pound. The long black hair streaked with white that fell to her waist made her all the more intriguing. The sharp mind tied it all up in an impressive package. Nope, not at all the picture she had in her head. The universe had a funny way of twisting expectations and delivering one hell of a surprise.

After the initial shock faded, Morrigan managed to regroup and refocus. The task to get the Keeper and the secret she guarded to a new and safe location took center stage. A couple of places occupied top spots on a list she kept only in her mind. It would be a matter of feeling the Keeper out to determine which one would work the best.

All the plans in the world didn't mean shit if the one chosen didn't fit the spirit of the person she came to protect.

For Morrigan, it came down to instinct. For as long as she could remember, it had guided her well, except for a single time, and she didn't like to think about it. That one needed to remain a part of her past and far away from the future. She understood that everyone made stupid mistakes when they were young, but her mistake whizzed right past stupid. Stop. That memory had no place intruding here.

Her focus back on the here and now, she followed Tamsin into the large house and stopped to breathe in deeply. Lavender wafted over her, gentle and soothing. Not for a minute did she believe its presence to be unintentional. The Keeper controlled her environment, top to bottom. Gotta say, she liked her approach. She immediately relaxed.

The interior also spoke to her. Clean and comforting, with subtle touches that referred to the magic she possessed. It didn't scream "most important witch in the world." Instead, more like "peaceful oasis." A person who took care of herself and leaned upon the bounty of nature to do it. Natural colors and fabrics. A Keeper not only beautiful, but thoughtful too. In a subtle, pleasing way that Morrigan appreciated.

"Come on into the kitchen." Tamsin kept walking toward the back of the house. She followed.

Once there, she watched Tamsin turn on the teapot and take bright mugs out of the cupboard. The very domestic and polite actions sent her anxiety skyward. So much for the calm she'd experienced when she first walked into the house. "We don't have time for a tea party." They had plans to make and actions to put into motion.

"We have time."

"I beg to differ."

Tamsin didn't pause in her tea-making. The electric tea kettle steamed, loose tea spooned into two diffusers. "You need to trust me. She's not that close." Her voice remained calm.

"On the move, regardless of the distance, is always too close." One thing she understood—the Witch Finders could not be trusted to do the expected.

"I've been around this since I was born. Have you?" Now she paused and put her hands on her hips. Her dark eyes were intense as they met hers, and an edge sharpened her tone.

"In a manner of speaking, yes. I'm a James, and my family has been White Faction since the split." *Take that.* She had no idea of the legacy Morrigan carried with her. They were one of the oldest, if not the oldest, family in the faction. Her ancestors had been hunted, driven away from their homes, hanged, and burned. They were also tough and confident witches who never took the names of their husbands. The history of the James family ran straight from woman to woman to woman.

Tamsin stared and then nodded. The lightbulb came on. Recognition shone in her eyes. "I know of your family and of the incredible service you have provided to the Keepers for hundreds of years. My family and I owe you a great deal."

"Then you know that you need to listen to me." Maybe now she'd stop wasting time and get on board with taking action. Gather up her shit and get out of this place.

As if reading her thoughts, she said, "I will absolutely listen to you. I will not, however, be forced to flee my home."

"It's not about you." Wrong about not wasting time. Wrong about getting on board with quick action.

"I disagree. It's about me as much as anything. At this point, I'm the Keeper, and I will not make any move without great care and great thought. Mistakes occur when you hurry. It's not my way."

Morrigan looked around the kitchen. Like what she'd seen thus far, a great space. Bright cabinets and gleaming countertops. Various kitchen appliances that spoke of a love of cooking. Processed foods were not found in the kitchens of true believers, and she'd be shocked to find any here. Purity kept minds, bodies, and souls nourished.

She returned her gaze to Tamsin's face as she thought, screw her way. "Someone is closing in with a speed none of us have seen before. I suspect she's very powerful."

Tamsin held out her hands. Short nails and long fingers. "I'm powerful."

"No argument there. Doesn't change anything." The family line of Keepers possessed the magic of many witches. Destiny chose them for a reason.

"You're powerful." She pointed one of those long fingers at Morrigan.

"Again. True enough, and together we'd be something. But you have to consider more than anything else that we can't risk a stand-and-fight scenario. Too important to keep you safe. What you protect is too dangerous to risk."

Tamsin poured hot water from the teapot over the infusers. Steam rose, sweetly fragrant. Earl Grey. "I'm not going anywhere until I know exactly what, when, and where. I know the why, so we're good on that front."

The air in the kitchen charged with more than just the scent of excellent tea. "You're planning to be a pain in the ass, aren't you?"

Tamsin set a steaming mug of tea in front of her. She didn't smile. "I am."

❖

Freddi ended the call with Abba and smiled big. Worth the effort to spar with Aldo, the sonofabitch, when the end result rolled in large as a win for her. Abba had blessed her with a wide berth to continue her mission to seek out the Keeper. She got the golden ticket that every Witch Finder coveted. No matter what anyone else said, she had carved out the right path. It thrummed deep in her bones. Both the Keeper and the *Book of Darkness* were within her reach if she maintained her focus, which she could do with ease. Focus should be her middle name.

Unfortunate that she'd been unable to glean anything useful from the fat witch. Going into it, she'd had high hopes. Instead, she'd encountered a witch with an excellent façade, undoubtedly crafted to throw off those seeking the Keeper, and it became clear very quickly that the role wasn't hers because the woman's magic, though steady, had been weak. Those trusted with any kernel of information about the Keeper would not be of the garden variety. Too much at risk to put it in the hands of the average. Decade after decade, century after century, only the very special could hold the role of Keeper, and only the strongest and best protected the Keeper. Neither described that witch.

Thus, her crusade continued. That she embarked upon it because of a motive she did not share with Abba didn't much bother her. Need-to-know, and Abba didn't need to know. In fact, no one did. Not at this point anyway. Once she had the grimoire in her hands and harnessed the power it would gift her with, well, then they'd all know. And they'd all pay.

First, however, she needed to plan for the next leg of the journey. That the now-crispy witch got her no closer to the end goal didn't mean wasted effort. The fun factor couldn't be discounted. Fire held a special affinity for Freddi. The thought alone made her smile again. Her fingers began to tingle as flames flickered through her memory. It never got old.

In her bedroom, she began her transformation. While she loved the tight black jeans and tailored shirt that accentuated her curves, it wouldn't do for where she'd be going. Too clichéd. Abba had tried without success to get her to tone down her evil vs. good look, to blend in better. Hadn't worked before and didn't work now either. Her wardrobe would remain the many shades of black that made her feel strong and untouchable.

Except for the special bag she kept for nights like this. A flowing flowered dress, a pair of clunky, though comfortable, clog-style shoes in an ugly shade of green, and a wide-brimmed hat. For the world to see, a flower-child in tune with the natural universe. It almost gagged her to put on the outfit. The upside to it came in the form of acceptance. No one in the group she'd be visiting would see anything other than a white witch who practiced good magic. Harm no one. Embrace the three-fold law of return, which she knew to be bullshit. They all seriously believed that whatever they put out in the universe would return to them threefold, bad or good.

Well, she'd been putting the bad out there for decades and could confirm the bullshit factor of the law. Another one of those things preached to keep the masses in compliance. Nobody wanted a rogue witch. Nobody except her. She threw her head back and laughed.

At the massive garden on the edge of the city, a small group of women lingered by the fountain, rows of tea lights set around it casting flickering light into the dusk. The scent of roses filled the air, and people wandered through the paved paths taking pictures and talking softly. The beauty of the place seemed to instill a sense of tranquility, and loud voices didn't fit here.

As she approached the women, the air changed. Instead of calm, unease rippled through the soft breeze. Turned out to be hard to hide her smile, given the joy that filled her. Who knew? Had to push through though, for if she were to fit in with this gathering, she didn't dare allow her true feelings to reflect on her face. Delight and pride would have to reflect outwardly as sadness and concern.

"Welcome." A tall, thin woman greeted her. Older than the others who stood around chatting quietly. The crone. Not for the first time she wondered why they all embraced *the look*. Long silver hair, no makeup, a wispy dress, butt-ugly shoes.

Every time she had to do this, it took huge effort not to scream at these women. Stop buying into the folklore and simply be yourself. Be one with the world and enjoy the power it has to offer those willing to grab it. That meant being an individual, not a cartoon character. That's what she saw when she looked at women like the crone: a cartoon that mocked what they really were.

"Hello." She held out her hand. Her gentle greeting hid the building fury.

"Welcome."

Freddi gave her a small nod. "I'm sorry about your sister." She'd dispatched the witch only a few hours ago, but news traveled fast in their community.

The crone's eyes filled with tears. "Senseless."

"Black Faction."

"Yes. The magic still lingers in the ashes, and it's bad."

"Are more coming?" She studied the small group. Not enough to even come close to stopping her. Though the group had magic and it rippled in the air around them, collectively it would fail to rise to a level necessary to affect her.

"I'm passing through but heard the call. I'm here to help however I can." She came to help all right. They just didn't have a clue as to the kind of help she brought.

CHAPTER FOUR

Tamsin already knew she liked this Morrigan James. She couldn't fault her for being overly serious. Her job pretty much demanded it, and she appreciated the dedication to keeping her safe and, more important, alive. That didn't mean, however, she could swoop in and start telling Tamsin what to do. She'd been keeping herself safe for decades, thanks to lessons learned at both her mother's and grandmother's knees. Her own magic had grown along the way to become pretty darned impressive, if she did say so.

"I still believe the best option is to get you out of here. Your location has been compromised." Maintaining her gaze, Morrigan held the cup of tea between her hands as if to keep herself warm.

Tamsin leaned against the counter and considered the offered solution. A little. "Not yet."

Morrigan set the mug on the table and closed her eyes. For a couple of seconds, she said nothing. Then she opened her eyes. "Why not?"

Lots of reasons why not, some more important than others. "Hear me out."

"I'm listening."

How much she'd listen remained to be seen, given that Tamsin figured her mind was already set about the leaving part. Morrigan came across as the type of person who made a careful plan and then stuck to it. "I like it here."

Frowning, Morrigan shook her head. "Not relevant."

Matter of opinion. "It is to me."

"Explain to me how it's more important that you stay than to take the wiser course of leaving."

"I have built-in protections that I've developed over the years. I knew that someday one of them would find me, and I prepared for that eventuality."

"Did you figure on how powerful this one seems to be?"

"Not specifically." She held up a hand to stop Morrigan's rapid-fire response. "That doesn't mean I haven't considered the force they'd use to get the grimoire. I have it safe. You can trust me on that one. I wouldn't risk it."

"Safe enough?" A lot of doubt in those two words.

"I believe so." Not quite right. No belief about it. Absolute conviction with respect to its safety.

Morrigan turned the cup between her hands, round and round. She looked up, her gaze intense. "Let me get this straight. You want to risk the Dark Faction getting their hands on a grimoire that holds the potential to change the world as we know it because you like living here making soap and raising animals. If I'm not getting that right, please correct me."

"How do you know I make soap?" It surprised her that she knew the bill-paying business of the farm.

"Don't change the subject."

"No, really, how do you know what I do for a living?"

Morrigan shook her head. "I'm not blind, and I can read big signs. Seven Sisters Handmade Soaps."

Tamsin shrugged and almost laughed. Kind of a duh on her part. "Well, there's that."

"Did I get it right?"

Morrigan's train of thought wasn't getting derailed, and she sure wasn't giving up. She remained focused on an exit strategy with the same kind of intensity a dog gave a brand-new marrow bone.

Tamsin sat at the table and folded her hands, staring at them for a moment before she spoke. "Yes and no. I actually love living here making soap and taking care of my animals. So, that's the yes part."

"And the no?"

She brought her head up and held Morrigan's gaze as she said, "It's time to stop running from the Black Faction and end this thing once and for all."

Tamsin couldn't pinpoint the moment she'd decided to stay and fight. It came unbidden and yet stronger than she could imagine. She could probably tell this woman how the voices on the wind spoke to her, and Morrigan would understand. One nice thing about talking to others with a legacy similar to her own. They got it. Those who came from the non-magical population would look at her with the you-need-serious-help expressions.

Still, she held back from sharing everything that rattled around inside her head. Morrigan wouldn't want to hear it because she came here with a time-tested plan. Those tasked with the protection of the Keeper always had one. Her mother had emphasized the need to follow the witches that came to protect them. They were trained. They were dedicated. They were powerful.

Yeah, well, that had worked for centuries, and good for them. Sometimes, things had to get shaken up, and suddenly, it occurred to her that she was the Keeper to do it. She looked around her kitchen where she'd made many meals and opened some great bottles of wine. Why should she have to leave? Why had her ancestors been forced to flee century after century? Time for that shit to stop.

❖

Morrigan tapped her fingers on the table. She didn't like where Tamsin appeared to be going with this whole conversation. It went against everything she'd been taught her whole life. "The *Book of Darkness* matters more than the fact that you like your house." Might be blunt but she spoke only the truth. Not enough time to worry about hurting feelings. Feelings could be soothed. Dead Keepers couldn't be brought back.

Tamsin shrugged, and if she took offense at Morrigan's directness, she didn't give any hint. "No argument there." Smooth and unruffled as though the fate of the world wasn't at risk.

Oh yeah. Pain in the ass without question. "Then why are you so resistant to getting the fuck out of here?" She didn't feel bad about her choice of words. Harsh and to the point is exactly what the situation and this woman warranted.

"Because these witches have been terrorizing my family for hundreds of years, and I'm sick of it. Time for us to turn the tables on them. Make them run instead."

In theory, she didn't disagree. In the real world, a different story. "Not a good idea."

"Why not?

"Because they could destroy everything if they get their hands on *it*."

Tamsin shrugged. "Easy enough to solve that problem. We don't let them."

"Let them what?'

"Get their hands on it."

Morrigan stood and started to pace. "You're making this more difficult than it needs to be. We get you and the grimoire safely out of here and let the Black Faction fail, just as we've done forever. No need to make this harder than it has to be."

"I think I want to go with option number two."

"There is no option number two."

"Oh, then they didn't train you very well, did they?"

Nothing too insulting about that. "What the fuck are you talking about?"

Tamsin smiled. "My mama taught me well, and one particular lesson resonated with me the first time I heard it."

"And that would be." This better be good.

"The Prophecy."

Morrigan stopped her pacing and stared. "You are fucking kidding me, right?"

Tamsin stared back. "I am fucking not."

❖

It took a whole lot of effort not to laugh. Freddi didn't dare. Imperative to maintain a nice, somber demeanor throughout the ritual. Blending in would be the only way she'd get what she needed from this pathetic group of losers. Not that she actually needed *them*. Their energy belonged to her, and that's what she intended to grab. A sort of turbo boost, as it were.

Now, as the moon rose full and golden, the park emptied of visitors, and only the group of witches remained when darkness fell. They formed a circle, hand to hand. Contrary to a lot of the drivel written about the rituals performed by witches, a full moon wasn't a prerequisite. It just happened to coincide with this particular event. They also didn't drop their clothes and scamper around a fire naked. Made for titillating reading but had zero to do with reality.

When her fingers connected with those of the women on either side of her, a current of electricity rumbled through her. That's what she'd come here for, and they were delivering, bless their little witchy hearts. The Crone led the prayer, although Freddi tuned her out. Under her breath, she whispered her own prayer, drawing in the power from the other women as each word passed her lips as quiet as a breath.

One by one the women in the circle dropped to the grass, leaving Freddi the last woman standing. Her fingers tingled, and she turned her face to the sky with her eyes closed. The wind picked up and swirled around her, a lullaby that sang to her of magic. Many called it dark magic. She didn't see it that way. In her mind, dark and light were the same. No good or bad. Only what belonged to those powerful enough to grab it. Someone just like her.

Her mother's face flashed before her, and her eyes snapped open. A momentary ripple in the euphoria. She would not dwell on her. It didn't matter what she thought of Freddi or her mission. She wouldn't understand. Had never understood anything about Freddi. Nor did she ever try.

She shook her head and cleared her vision. No more thoughts of the mother who tried hard to mold her into something she'd never been. The path she traversed now spoke to her destiny. Every vision that came to her kept her journey true. The naysayers like her mother were nothing more than irritants. Ignore them and carry on.

"Well, ladies." She stepped back and looked at the crumpled bodies, a jumble of young and old, colorful dresses, and tangled hair of varying shades of red, black, brown, white, and silver. "Anybody cold?"

She laughed as she held out her arms and spread her fingers wide. As she'd done earlier, she began to call upon her own magic. "In my heart resides the spiritual flame. I am the fire on the darkest night. Mother of the full moon, I draw down your perfect beam, to light the burning cauldron. Fire to bless us and fire to slow."

She brought her arms up toward the star-filled sky as her head tipped back. "So shall it be." Flames rose in a perfect circle of tendrils that reached out to the night. By the time she got back to her car, nothing would be left but ashes.

As she clicked her seat belt, she stared out the windshield, seeing far more than a dark sky and sparkling stars. Those bold enough to take what they needed, regardless of the cost, were the chosen ones. Her body buzzed and her fingertips tingled. "I see you, and I'm coming for you," she whispered.

CHAPTER FIVE

This wasn't the first time Tamsin had considered the take-a-stand course of action should the Black Faction discover her location. It was the first time she'd allowed the idea to be spoken out loud. Tamsin's mother, her grandmother, oh, hell, her great-grandmother would scream at her for even thinking of going up against the Black Faction. In her defense, she didn't want to buck tradition as much as she wished to stand up against bullies. Because, really, that's what they were. Granted, if they got their hands on the *Book of Darkness*, they could take bullying to a level never before seen, but that didn't change her opinion. Time was up, a stand locked in on her agenda as the only course of action. Add the potential brick wall the Prophecy promised, and why the hell not take a risk? The odds in her favor looked better than ever before.

Morrigan shook her head. "You and I both realize that the only one who knows the true nature of the Prophecy is the Keeper, and really, it doesn't matter. If it could be helpful, then it wouldn't be shrouded in secrecy. The rest of us have heard nothing but rumors, which leaves me with a zero level of comfort."

Some truth in her words. Not all the story though. "To everything there is a purpose."

Morrigan blinked, and to Tamsin it looked like an effort not to roll her eyes. "Whatever. I'm not relying on something vague and unhelpful. I'm leaning toward the tried and true."

"Look," Tamsin said. "We've been doing the same song and dance for hundreds of years. The Keepers stay in one place for a while, the Black Faction finds them, witches like you swoop in and whisk us away to a new, secret location. We stay safe for a bit, and then boom—it happens all again. We've been on every continent, every culture, and the circle never gets broken."

"That's because it's tried and it's true, and most important, it works."

"It's the definition of stupidity…doing the same thing over and over and expecting a different result."

"I still maintain it works. The world has stayed safe from the Black Faction, and we can't risk what they could do if they got their hands on the *Book of Darkness*."

She could be as stubborn as Morrigan. "It's not rocket science. We just don't let them."

"Great, so you're on board to get the hell out of here."

Clearly, she read Tamsin wrong. She hurried to correct her. "Nope."

"You're driving me insane. Nobody told me the Keeper would be totally unreasonable."

Tamsin shrugged. "I prefer to think of myself as far more pragmatic. I'm actually a very reasonable person, and what I'm proposing isn't that far out there." The more she got into it, the more right it seemed to her and not unreasonable at all.

"Stay and fight."

"Yes."

"Fall back on the Prophecy."

"Absolutely." She could almost see the words in her head, and yes, it all fit.

"You're nuts."

Tamsin tilted her head and studied Morrigan. Frustration and disbelief shone from her eyes. She met her gaze with an equal amount of determination. "But am I?"

❖

Just fucking wow. Nothing in the years of training had prepared her for this woman—this witch of unique beauty and, damn it, character. Morrigan had come here expecting urgency and, well, a whole lot of frenzied packing. Nothing so far came even close to her expectations.

"Here's my proposal." Tamsin carried on without waiting for Morrigan to respond. "We hunker down for tonight, given there's no immediate threat, and tomorrow we make more concrete plans."

Un-freaking-believable. "A slumber party."

"More like a convergence of kindred souls with a common purpose."

Clearly, she had a way of twisting words to create an advantage. "I don't know about how common, given our polar-opposite views on what to do here."

"Sleep on it, and we'll revisit the issue in the morning."

"I don't want to sleep on it. You're wrong about all of this."

"So says you. Remember, I'm the Keeper, and the women of my family have been safeguarding the grimoire for centuries. Don't think for a minute I'm shirking my duties. I'm not."

"Feels like it."

"I repeat, I'm not."

This conversation was, as they say, going nowhere fast. As much as she wanted to continue to argue with Tamsin, perhaps they should give it a rest for a few hours. Maybe if Tamsin slept on it, she would see the danger more clearly, along with all its potential threat. Morrigan would see everything exactly the same in the morning as she viewed it today, though she didn't believe telling the Keeper that fact right now would make one iota of difference.

"Fine. Show me where to sleep, and we'll take this up in a few hours." Outside, the night had grown deep and dark as they argued strategy. The air stayed quiet, and that, at least, gave her a little peace. They would be safe for a while longer. In the morning, she'd be able to talk sense into her, or so she hoped. Finesse might not be her strong suit. Didn't mean she couldn't summon the skill when needed.

Warrior, on the other, came as natural to her as breathing, and if she had to, she'd fall back on that. Throw the woman over her shoulder and run like hell. Old school and not exactly politically correct these days, even for a witch with her particular task. Still, she'd do whatever she had to in order to protect the Keeper and the *Book of Darkness*. She'd been born to the job, and she'd be damned if she'd fail. Her family had never fallen short, and she'd not be the first.

"This way."

The room Tamsin showed her to contained a comfortable-looking bed, a dresser, and a private bath. "This is nice. You have a lot of company?" A great setup for guests, but not a good idea for any Keeper. The job she'd inherited required a healthy dose of isolation.

Tamsin shook her head. "Not many. I'm a bit of a hermit. My circle of friends is small."

"Good." At least she understood that part of her duty. High profile made for a poor Keeper and a whole lot of work for witches like Morrigan attempting to keep them safe. There'd been a few along the way, or so the stories were told, who put themselves too much in the public eye. It didn't end well for those Keepers.

"Look." Tamsin stood in the doorway with her hands on her hips. "I know you don't approve of me, and I can live with that. Thing is, I was groomed from the moment of my birth to be the Keeper. I've been taught to think and pivot and, most important, fight. I might be coming across to you as flippant and unprepared. I assure you, I am not."

Everything about Tamsin screamed sincere, and she appreciated that. No getting around the fact they'd be forced to spend days or even weeks together, and honesty would be critical. From all appearances, they were on that honest path. She might as well extend the same sincerity. "I think you're planning an unwise course, and like you, I've been tutored in my job since my first memories. I'm not suggesting anything to you that I haven't gone over a thousand times."

"Noted."

"I hear a *but* in there."

"But, regardless of anything we've both been prepared for, I believe it's time to look at options. Just because it's always been done that way doesn't mean there isn't a better way to do it now."

For a few seconds, Morrigan said nothing. She studied Tamsin's face. Despite not agreeing with her, she glimpsed steel in in her eyes. From her body rolled energy that could knock all but the strongest off their feet. She finally gave a tiny nod. "Let's talk in the morning."

"Excellent." Tamsin shut the door, leaving Morrigan alone.

"Well," she said to herself. "This promises to be pretty fucking interesting."

❖

Freddi didn't bother to look back at her handiwork as she drove into the night. Within seconds, nothing would be left except a circle of ash anyway. Fire had always been one of her superpowers, and she'd used it freely. Her mother would chastise her for the risks she'd take, and none of her scolding ever made a bit of difference. When she was a child, the flames filled her heart with joy. As an adult, she'd harnessed fire as a weapon both destructive and cleansing. Who, in their right mind, would walk away from using magic like that? A gift from the universe she treasured.

As the last witch had dropped to the ground, Freddi had begun to fill with energy—exactly the boost she needed. A path became clear. A direction of travel that would take her to the one who held the key to her future.

As much as she'd wanted to jump into her car and charge west as fast as she could drive, she knew better. No need to hurry and risk a mistake. She'd been on this journey her whole life, and now that the pot of gold lay within her reach, she wanted to savor every moment of her impending victory. Everything needed to be perfect. In her head, she could see it all with delicious clarity.

She stopped at a lovely hotel in St. Cloud. No dives for her. Someone with her skills and power didn't do cheap. All about comfort, baby. Scrambling their security cameras required a touch of finesse because she also didn't do video capture. Her movements were not to be tracked. The cyber piece didn't require much, only a little magic to push the glitch into cameras so that if anyone were to look later, they'd see only a blurry figure. Combine the useless security video with an identity cloaked by ghost accounts, and no one would be able to place her here.

Once in her room, Freddi showered and slipped into comfortable clothes. As much as she'd love to burn the flowery dress, she folded it neatly and put it back into her bag. Could be she'd need to use it again. She plugged in the tea kettle that traveled with her and, once the water boiled, poured it over the leaves. Cup in hand, she stood at the window and sipped the tea until only a teaspoon or so remained. Holding the handle in her left hand, she closed her eyes. "Goddess of Power, I call on you to assist me now and show me the way. Light my path that I may find the Keeper of the secrets that rightfully belong to me."

For a few moments, she swirled the cooling tea and then quickly tipped the cup upside down on the saucer. When she turned it right-side up again, she studied the pattern of the tea leaves as they appeared on the inside. Sometimes the leaves liked to shroud their message in ambiguity. Not tonight. She smiled.

"Thank you, Goddess of Power." She walked away from the teacup and to the bed. She lay down and closed her eyes. Sleep came easy and deep.

CHAPTER SIX

Tamsin wasn't accustomed to having anyone in the house with her. She'd spent her adult life by herself, so to have another person down the hall, another really attractive fellow witch, kept her from dropping off to sleep. The last time she glanced at the clock it showed a little after midnight.

Her body clock didn't care what time she went to sleep. Wake-up time still came as scheduled. She didn't try to fight it either, given her animals wouldn't care if she got eight hours or ten minutes. Faint dark circles under her eyes told the tale of a short night. Oh, well. Wasn't the first one and wouldn't be the last. At the back door, she slipped into her knee-high rubber boots and then walked outside. Cool air brushed against her skin, and early morning sunlight kissed her cheeks.

As she poured grain, hauled hay, and checked water troughs, her mind whirled through all possible defense strategies for her position on stay-and-fight. That Morrigan would dig in her own heels and insist they leave tracked with her sense of the woman. Nobody could or would blame her for that strategy. For centuries it had been used in one version or another to maintain the safety of the Keeper. To date, all highly successful. Why would they want to change anything? A solid argument.

From her side, things looked a whole lot different. Lately, the Prophecy played in her mind when she least expected it. Every Keeper knew of it, and they spoke of it often as the lessons were passed along to each Keeper's daughter. What it failed to reveal to even a single one of the Keepers, however, was when it would come to pass. The mystery of that question became the piece she pondered the most. She couldn't get past believing the time had arrived.

"You know we have to leave this place."

Tamsin screeched, jumped, and whirled. The handful of carrots went flying, landing like orange raindrops on the ground. "You just took five years off my life." Her heart pounded. The alpacas trotted over and began to snack on the dropped carrots.

Morrigan leaned on the top rail of the fence around the corral. "And, if I can sneak up on you like that, what do you think a witch from the Black Faction would be able to do?"

Direct hit. "I would have felt her." She hoped.

"Or him."

"Or him." Though the majority of both factions consisted of women, witches were an equal-opportunity bunch.

"Maybe. You want to take that chance?"

Truth would serve them both better than pretense. If she wanted to recruit Morrigan to her way of thinking, she needed to be straight up with her. "No."

"Here's the other thing to keep in mind. You have no daughter. Or have I missed something here?"

She'd been waiting for that one since their conversations last night. Like it didn't weigh on her daily? "I can fix that easy enough. I need only nine months."

"You have a man in mind?"

"Oh, God, no."

Morrigan raised an eyebrow. "A donor? IVF?"

"Why not? It's the twenty-first century. Lots of options."

Morrigan shook her head. "And you call yourself the Keeper. Doesn't work that way, and you know it. I mean, from a biological standpoint, yes, it does. For the Keeper, far from it."

Damn it, she got her again. This woman wasn't giving her an inch, and she knew her stuff. "Love match." The two words were bitter on her tongue.

This time Morrigan nodded. "Love match."

Another of the quirks applicable to the Keeper only. The first daughter of a first daughter, generation after generation. And, only the daughter born from a true love match. The universe had rules even with magic. Or, more likely, because it involved magic.

Her parents had been gone a very long time now, the Keeper role passed to her at the ripe old age of nineteen. Despite the passing of years, she could still remember the way her mother and father gazed at each other. After her father's death, her mother never looked at another. Everyone should be lucky enough to experience love like that. In her case, nothing even close, and she didn't expect it would ever grace her life in the same way. Another reason to take a stand and end it once and for all. Not just for herself either. The Black Faction had killed both of her parents, and she'd vowed to make them pay. She'd make good on that promise.

She held Morrigan's gaze. "Direct hit."

"I don't make the rules."

Not quite time to concede. She still believed. "The Prophecy provides an out."

"Maybe." It didn't appear that Morrigan planned to give up on her stand either.

Ready for just this argument. Her turn for a direct hit. "Have a little faith."

❖

If anything, sleep hadn't softened but rather hardened Tamsin's resolve for such a bold and foolish plan. She sounded ready to go a few more rounds with Morrigan, and for that, she needed coffee, really strong coffee, and she told Tamsin as much.

"Give me five more minutes to finish here, and then I can fix you up. Fred and Ralph have been patiently waiting."

"Fred and Ralph?"

She smiled. "My boys." She pointed to a pair of cats sitting on a bale of hay, tails swishing. One black with a single spot of white in the middle of his chest and the other gray with black stripes. "Their patience will come to an end if I don't fill their bowls soon."

"Familiars?" It wasn't common these days for witches to keep familiars. It happened, just not often, and she couldn't remember the last time she encountered one.

Tamsin let herself out of the corral and walked over to the cats. She rubbed the head of the gray. He leaned into her touch. "No. Mere barn cats. They do a darn good job of keeping the mice away. And they're pretty good fellows."

Morrigan waited while Tamsin scooped kibble from a bin into two stainless bowls. The cats stood, stretched, and made their way to the bowls. No hurry, just a leisurely stroll to the breakfast table. A cursory sniff and both walked away, tails twitching.

"They don't seem too interested in their food."

A smile crossed Tamsin's face. "Their morning game of snobbery. As soon as we leave, they'll be back to clean out their bowls. God forbid they let me think I've done something nice for them. One of the things I love about cats, their attitude."

"I'm more of a dog person." Not that Morrigan considered bringing a pet of any kind into her life. Not with the way she moved around. Wouldn't be fair to the pet, though to be honest, she'd like the company. Her lifestyle tilted toward lonely. She could picture herself with a spirited Malinois, whip-smart and athletic. She admired the breed. One day. Maybe.

"I like dogs too. I lost Simon last year. He was a senior rescue, and the old man made it to fourteen. Pretty good for a German shepherd. Miss him a lot."

Why did it not surprise her that Tamsin would adopt a senior dog? Or that she seemed to be guiding the conversation into mundane subjects like pets. Okay for a few minutes, and those few minutes were up. "About leaving here."

Tamsin pointed her toward the house. "Not in front of the children."

"Seriously?" She glanced at the goats and the alpacas that, like the cats, were paying not the least bit of attention to the humans.

"Seriously. Vibes matter." Tamsin continued walking. "We'll talk over coffee."

At least she'd get her total attention once they were back in the kitchen. Or so she thought. That strategy failed a few minutes after they'd returned to the house, when the back door flew open and an energetic young woman with long, shiny, black hair almost skipped in. "Good morning!"

With effort, Morrigan managed not to groan. It was beginning to feel like everything that could go wrong was going wrong. Her hands were quivering as she held the mug of coffee given to her before Tamsin offered one to the most recent intruder.

"Good morning, Holly. This is my friend Morrigan. She's staying with me for a few days."

White lie or another way of telling her that she had no intention of leaving her farm anytime soon? Not a question she could ask in front of the stranger. Critical to keep the details of the situation between only her and Tamsin. Outsiders would create a messy complication. She aimed for a clean, tidy extraction.

"Hey." Holly turned her attention to Morrigan. Not model pretty, but with those eyes, she would turn heads. She shifted her gaze back on Tamsin. "You didn't tell me you were expecting company. For that matter, you never told me you had friends. Besides me, that is." Her laughter was warm and genuine. She pulled a mug from a cupboard and filled it with the offered freshly brewed coffee.

Tamsin shrugged. "Morrigan's a very old friend who happened to be passing through."

The look in Tamsin's eyes almost challenged her to contradict the story. Not to worry, little bird. She didn't intend to reveal the real reason her *old friend* happened to be in town. She turned a smile on Holly. "True enough. I'm passing through and thought it would be great to spend some time with Tamsin. We have a great deal to catch up on."

"Cool. Cool." Holly sipped her coffee. "I'll tell you what. I'll go do the cuts on the batches from yesterday, package the orders we have waiting, and then head to the shipping office. You two can visit up a storm, and I'll stay out of your hair. Sound like a plan?"

Tamsin smiled at her. "That would be fantastic. Enjoy the rest of the day yourself. You've been working super hard lately and deserve time off. Morrigan and I are just planning to hang out and talk about old times."

"We've both been hauling ass. You have some fun with your friend, and I'll see you next week. It was nice to meet you, Morrigan." Holly put her mug in the sink and breezed back out the door before Morrigan could say a word.

Tamsin put her finger to her lips as she shook her head. Interesting. It would come as a big surprise to find out anyone the Keeper allowed in her world turned out to be untrustworthy. Holly didn't have that kind of aura either. Harmless enough, or so it seemed to Morrigan, and she had a good sense of people. Well, she'd developed a good sense of people. Not exactly something she'd been born with, and that lapse had almost cost her everything.

For close to an hour, she sat with Tamsin drinking coffee and talking about the farm, the weather, and the business Tamsin had built from the ground up. At least that's what they did until they heard Holly's car heading down the driveway toward the main road. Only then did Tamsin open the floor for topics of more interest to Morrigan.

Tapping the top of her mug with a finger, she started with, "She's a good soul."

Morrigan believed it. "I could feel that about her. No darkness there."

"She doesn't know."

"Yeah. I pretty much caught that too."

"Whatever happens, I want her to be safe. This fight has nothing to do with Holly. Only Mae knows who I am, and I don't want her involved either. She's done her work as a Watcher, and her safety is important. I sent her away and told her not to come back. This fight is for witches only, and she'll do as I ask without questioning."

She couldn't agree more, except for an unavoidable catch. "I can't guarantee anything if we stay here."

❖

The three-o'clock wake-up didn't surprise Freddi. She'd fallen asleep easily enough, and the hours she'd managed were deep and restful. It wasn't her way to sleep for any significant length of time. She didn't mind and never did understand those who wasted so many hours in bed. Gave her a lot more time to get things done, or scratch an itch, as it were.

Hadn't been hard to catch his attention at the all-night diner. Never was. Men like him were easy. Fucking him in the sleeper section of his big rig got her off, and he wasn't bad at the job either. She'd set the bar low, and he'd zipped right over it. The man had some skills she'd been quick to put to good use.

He did talk a little too much for her taste, and she'd had to tune out his constant jabbering. After she'd gotten off, she'd taken the rest of what she'd needed from him and left. The small vial in her pocket, she'd walked back to her car parked in a dark corner of the massive lot. Someone would find him later, and a subsequent investigation would surely uncover the fact that he'd returned to his truck in the company of a lovely woman. They'd try to find the woman who'd climbed into the big sleeper with him, to no avail. A futile search because no one would be able to remember her face. A beautiful thing to possess her level of skill.

Back at her hotel, she lay down again, staring at the shadows dancing on the ceiling. One issue continued to weigh on her: the lack of clarity even with the resources she'd been able to garner. The witches of the night before, particularly the crone at the head of the circle, should have amplified her vision to the point of a high-definition television. As it turned out, she'd gained enough sight to keep her on the right path, but not enough to let her see the face of the Keeper.

Irritating as it might be, it shouldn't really come as a shock. The Keeper held powers unmatched and, thus, the reason for her continued survival century after century. That kind of magic came only to those with a lineage that traced back to the origin. Like the big bang, their worlds split apart between the dark and the light. Power against power for generations. Only the Keeper continued to stop those of the Dark Faction from obtaining what rightfully belonged to them.

Freddi planned to change that situation real soon. Those before her who had embarked upon the quest to secure the *Book of Darkness* had failed every single time. They didn't possess her level of skill, and they sure as hell didn't have her drive. In truth, the world had not quite been ready for someone like her, until now anyway. The thought buoyed her, and she threw off the covers. After a shower and a cup of the awful coffee brewed in the single-serve coffeemaker in the room, she left the hotel. As she guided the car onto the freeway on-ramp, the sun began its ascent.

She groaned when her phone rang. Aldo. "Yeah." Would he ever give it the fuck up?

"Abba wants a status report." Snippy. Must not have had any coffee yet this morning.

"I'm on the road. Nothing else has changed since last night."

"Going?" The arrogance rolled off him, and she bit her lip, the taste of blood metallic in her mouth.

"West."

"A little more detail." The wanna-be-king didn't like her one-word answer.

"Still working on the specifics." He didn't rate any more detail than that.

"So, you're saying that you have nothing." Snippy turned to self-righteous. He really did get on her last good nerve.

"I'm saying that I'm working on it, and as soon as I have specifics, I will let Abba know." *Take that, you little fucker.*

"Not good enough."

"Yeah, it is." She ended the call. "Fuck off," she muttered and kept driving. "I have places to go and people to see." Too early in the morning for Aldo. Especially given she hadn't had a decent cup of coffee yet. Or a drink. Could go either way right now regardless of the time of day.

CHAPTER SEVEN

Tamsin understood Morrigan's concerns more than she realized. Most likely, Morrigan thought her to be reckless and clueless about the trouble headed her way. Wrong on both counts. She got it. The danger that rolled toward her didn't pass her by mentally or physically. Every nerve sang a dark warning.

A must to convince Morrigan of her sanity if they were to face the coming threat as a united front. "I'm really not crazy." Nothing too weak about that statement.

Morrigan leaned back in her chair and laced her fingers behind her head. The move pulled her button-down shirt open to a "V" that revealed flashes of intricate ink. Morrigan got more interesting by the minute. That little voice in the back of Tamsin's head whispered for her to pay attention, and she did.

"Crazy, no. I don't believe that for a minute. In fact, just the opposite, which is why I'm still sitting here listening. If I thought you needed a good psychiatrist, I'd have called for reinforcements."

Tamsin gazed up at her eyes. Dark and serious. "You've considered making me leave through force?" For the first time since she'd arrived, Morrigan surprised her.

She shrugged. "It's a lot bigger than you. I have to look at everything. Consider everything."

"Point taken. At the same time, it is about me, and I should have a say in how this goes down. Nobody has the right to force me to do anything." Did that last part make her sound like a five-year-old?

"Oh, you have a say. At least to the extent we can keep you and the grimoire safe. If we believe, for even a minute, either is in imminent danger, you'll get overruled. Clear enough for you?"

That statement leaned an awful lot in the direction of insulting. "I would never risk the grimoire. I will die protecting it." Did the woman really not realize what family she descended from? They'd put their lives on the line for the *Book of Darkness* for centuries.

"It will stay safe, whatever it takes to keep it that way."

"Of course." She understood. No need to beat the crap out of the point.

"And there'll be no dying until you have an heir."

Well, damn. Way to take a perfect shot, and one she'd been thinking about more and more even before this latest development. A daughter had always been part of what defined her destiny, and actually, the thought of an heir made her happy. In some ways. To have a child would fill her heart. It would also create a new burden, and she didn't mean the task of raising an offspring. The thing about it that no one could possibly understand came with spending every day of her life carrying the knowledge that the only thing standing between darkness and light in the world was her. Not even the woman across from her, who no doubt spent her own lifetime preparing for the day she'd be called on to save the Keeper, could possibly understand the true weight of it. The enormous burden changed them all.

It was also what made her reach out and grab something different. "Or, we end it."

Morrigan let out a sigh and shook her head. "Why are you so focused on the end? No one has been able to even get close to that. What makes you think you're different? That this time it can be brought to an end?"

How to make her understand? "I feel it here." She tapped her chest.

"Sorry to burst your bubble, but that is not reassuring. For me to even get close to considering your option B, I need something more concrete, and so far, you haven't delivered."

Tamsin tapped the table. At this point, even trying to sort it out in her own head took work. To verbalize it for Morrigan proved even harder. "Give me a little time."

Throwing up her hands, Morrigan blinked. "Time for what? I have proof there's a Black Faction Witch Finder on the way. You have zero proof that we can use a different tactic to keep you and the *Book of Darkness* safe."

"All true." She couldn't refute any of it. She knew only what she felt more and more firmly as they talked about what to do.

Morrigan sighed louder this time. "You're killing me here." Her eyes met Tamsin's. Still dark. Still intense. Still sexy as hell. Off topic.

"I've felt them coming for several days now. There are voices in the wind. A chill to the air. I know we're on borrowed time here." Back on topic. No time to drown in the beautiful eyes or reach out to run her fingers over the hint of ink showing above the collar of her shirt.

"Then I don't know why you're fighting me. We need to move, and we're wasting valuable time. The sooner we get you and the grimoire out of here, the better."

Tamsin's turn to shake her head. "It's different with this one. You have to remember, I've been through this kind of situation before. Both as a child when they came for my mother and twice since I've been the Keeper. I know what it feels like, and trust me. Whatever is coming for me now, it's different. If that doesn't call for a new approach, I don't know what does."

❖

Morrigan wanted to argue more, to pound her hands on the table and make Tamsin understand the importance of getting the hell out of here. The thing about it that kept her from doing any of those things, she felt the change too. Of course, this would be her first time guiding and protecting the Keeper, so she had nothing to compare it to. Didn't change the fact that the vibe washing over her wasn't anything she'd prepared for. Quite simply, it felt off.

Her entire life, her mother had taught her to be ready for every imaginable situation. To pivot when necessary. To always keep a mind open to alternate plans. She'd taken to the calling to be a warrior as if she'd been born to it, which, in fact, she had. Her family's history of protecting the Keeper went back to the beginning. Without question their ancestors had met along the line. She doubted any of her lineage had dealt with the kind of resistance she encountered with Tamsin.

"All right." A continued fight wouldn't benefit either one of them, and her mother had pushed judicious thinking in critical situations. "Give me your pitch."

Tamsin nodded, and a light came into her eyes. Such a beautiful face, filled with strength and intelligence. It made her want to listen, even if that little voice in the back of her head screamed for her to move her ass. "There's more to the *Book of Darkness* than the spells to release evil into the world."

Tamsin spoke of the Prophecy. She had a vague knowledge of it. Any witch worth her salt did, because the whispers about it had been going on forever. Didn't change anything right now because it wasn't relevant or helpful. "I know."

Shaking her head, Tamsin stood up. "No. I'm not talking about the Prophecy. Don't get me wrong. It's important, and I also believe it's at play here. It's not the only thing behind my push to stay."

Something in her voice made Morrigan listen closer. Maybe something more did lie behind Tamsin's stubbornness than just not wanting to leave her farm. Didn't hurt to give her the benefit of the doubt. For a couple minutes anyway. Show her that she could be open-minded. "I'm listening."

Tamsin turned toward the doorway and waved for her to follow. "It will make more sense if I show you."

Her breath caught in her throat. Show her? Could Tamsin be saying what she thought she was? No one except the Keeper had touched the *Book of Darkness*, let alone read a single page, since put into the hands of the first Keeper. Her voice came out wispy. "What? Are you suggesting what I think you are?"

"I could blabber on all day, and you won't get where I'm coming from. You can't, or won't, really hear me, so the only way to get you on board is if you see it with your own eyes."

"The *Book of Darkness*?" That Tamsin wanted her to see it had her trembling and her heart racing.

"Yeah. The bad boy itself."

"You don't really know me." The risk defied explanation. She didn't understand how Tamsin could take the leap to share it with her. It wasn't a smart move. Tamsin took her hands. Electricity shot up her arms, and she almost snatched them away.

Tamsin raised a single eyebrow. "Feel that?"

"What the actual fuck?"

"Pure and simple connection, and we have it. I can almost hear what you're thinking. I'm crazy. I'm taking a critical risk. It's too dangerous. Morrigan, you're not wrong, yet you are. I'm the Keeper, and you need to trust me."

"No shit." The sarcasm spilled out unbidden.

"Come on. I'm not stupid, and I understand where you're coming from. I'd be more concerned if you didn't think I was about to do something seriously nuts. I'm not. The one thing that's kept me and my ancestors safe has been our ability to distinguish good from bad. Black from white, if you will. You are White Faction through and through. Beyond that, you are a good and kind person. You can be trusted."

She didn't know about the good and kind. Ruthless would be more accurate. Not to mention that she'd spent so little time with Tamsin, that for her to make that call fell on the side of super foolish. "I'm definitely White Faction."

"You could have been a mile away from me and I'd have been able to discern that fact about you. All the Keepers can see beyond the veil, giving us a distinct advantage when it comes to reading people. I view you as straight-up worthy of the trust I have in you. I feel it in you with the mere touch of our hands."

That put a little better spin on the confidence Tamsin seemed to be throwing at her. And, yeah, the touch thing, a new twist. She'd never had that happen before. She straightened her shoulders. "You can trust me."

Tamsin squeezed her hand, the buzz intensifying. "I know."

❖

Freddi pulled off the interstate and drove down a dirt road leading to an outcropping of rocks that caught her interest. Not hard to do in a relatively flat landscape. The sun shone bright, the sky a gorgeous blue. Trees swayed in a gentle breeze, and wildflowers created a blanket of blue and yellow. The day held great promise. Yes, a perfect spot to perform a bit of magic.

The car parked in the shade of a stand of trees, she grabbed her bag and hiked to the top of the rocks. The air had warmed, and she watched her step as she climbed. Just the right conditions for a rattler who might feel like sunning itself, which wasn't the kind of surprise she wanted to encounter, though she wasn't certain rattlesnakes made this place home. A stay-alert mentality nonetheless. She didn't need to encounter reptiles anytime, anywhere.

Nice and empty at the top of the outcropping, as if it waited for her alone. Probably did. Even the creatures knew when their superior approached and acted accordingly. All hail the queen. She laughed and dropped her bag.

Facing the rising sun in the east, she created a circle with small stones she'd gathered and dropped into her pocket as she'd walked up from her car to the top. From the big leather bag she withdrew four bay leaves, a small wooden bowl, and a bottle of water. She put a leaf on the rocks at each point of the compass. North, south, east, and west. The bowl she placed in the center of the circle and filled with water. The final item pulled from the bag was a vial of blood. *Thank you, Mister Trucker.*

On the ground with her legs crossed and the bowl in front of her, she held the vial between her palms, closed her eyes, and tipped her head back so the sun shone on her face. The warmth kissed her skin, the air sweet with the scent of wild grass. Nature speaking to her.

"Great Mother, I come to you, daughter of your light, seeker of your wisdom. Here rock and soil are alive with your words. Your power seeps up from the earth, rising potent and illuminating."

A whoosh of wind blew across her face, making her skin tingle. It picked up her hair and whipped it around her face. The Great Mother was listening.

She opened her eyes. Holding up the vial, she uncapped it and poured the crimson blood slowly into the bowl of water. After she emptied the vial, she set it aside. "Sacred water, body of the Great Mother—rich, wise, and powerful—I call on you to show me the way. To show me the face of the one I seek."

The water began to swirl, streaks of red fading slowly to pink. The wind picked up even more as the water circled. Hands clasped, hair whipping around, she breathed in and out with slow, even breaths. The wind stilled and so did the whirling water. Inside the bowl the surface turned to clear glass, and when it did, a face appeared. Not as defined as she'd wished for, but she knew better than to second-guess the Great Mother. All things in their time. It would be enough for now.

Freddi let out the breath she'd held while gazing upon the face in the water, then picked up everything and packed it into her bag. Back at the car, she sat behind the wheel and looked out into the distance. A long ray of morning sunshine shot westward, and she smiled. Oh yes. The Great Mother had her back. She started the car and drove toward the sunshine.

The words she sang as she drove were old and lovely. "She's only a bird in a gilded cage, a beautiful sight to see…"

The Prophecy

She shall pull back the weave
to reveal flames and wings.
Color and beauty and magic.
Her power will be mighty.
Her sight will be true.
She will find her,
and the power of touch will bring the cleansing fire.
So it is written in the stars.

CHAPTER EIGHT

Tamsin's heart sang. Despite the danger that lurked beyond the horizon, everything had dropped into place. Even more so after the glimpse of the ink revealed by Morrigan's open shirt. Though she'd not recognized it at the time, the signs had been coming to her for weeks now, and that beautiful ink arrived as one more. Definitive and hopeful. It made so much sense when taken all together.

Every word of the Prophecy was chiseled into her mind. Not that she'd needed to read it from within the pages of the *Book of Darkness*. Nor had any other Keeper before her. The time-old practice of oral history provided her with the knowledge without the necessity of opening the grimoire. Word for word, it had been repeated to her until she, too, could recite it from memory. That was how things were done.

The more she pondered the meaning of the Prophecy, the more she questioned her role in its coming to pass. Amazingly, a grimoire that had the power to unleash evil into the world also included what felt like a caveat directed at those not inclined toward darkness. It offered an out for a book that had defied destruction. A way to save the world instead of destroying it. Simply put, the *Book of Darkness*, in the wrong hands, would destroy the world, and the Prophecy, in the right hands, would save it. Her heart was telling her that now was the time to put it to the test.

She looked at Morrigan, and those blue eyes sent a whoosh through her. "Do you believe in destiny?"

Morrigan raised one eyebrow. "Seriously? Me, of all people, you ask about destiny? Sister, isn't that the whole reason you and I are here together right now?"

Tamsin nodded. She did have a point. "It is, but it's even more than that. It's the whole picture. Think of it this way. We take away the *Book of Darkness*, and what does the Black Faction have left? Nothing, right? It's got to be worth the risk to finally end this war."

"And if they get their hands on it before it can be destroyed? What then? Don't forget. No one has ever been able to annihilate it, and I'm not inclined to think we'd have any better luck."

"I have to believe it's worth the risk to try."

"It's not."

Tamsin couldn't fault Morrigan for her stubborn stand on the issue. Centuries worth of training wouldn't be undone in less than twenty-four hours. Didn't mean she planned to give in and run. Her own finely developed intuition told her the time had come. White and black would become one as they had been in the beginning, and the threat to the world would end. Yes, the time fell upon them.

"Let me show you why I'm so confident about this situation, and then tell me what you think."

"I won't change my mind."

Tamsin walked out the door and toward the workshop. Over her shoulder she said, "We'll see."

❖

That woman, Keeper or not, irritated the bloody hell out of Morrigan. Mama hadn't prepared her for someone who resisted a very logical course of action. The *only* course of action if she would take a breath and look at it with an honest eye. How she wished she could pick up the phone and call Mama. Bounce this twisted situation off her. She'd have some great ideas on how to work with Tamsin and guide her to the right path. No such luck. Mama had been gone for a long time now, leaving Morrigan to figure this out for herself. Another piece of her destiny, she supposed. Being alone at the most critical point of her life. Karma was a real bitch.

The immediate issue revolved around getting Tamsin to understand the sky-high stakes here. Hard to plead a case after she'd crossed the yard and disappeared into a small structure with tan siding and a dark brown metal roof. The workshop, she surmised, and hurried after her. Not much else she could do unless she just stood here.

Tamsin had left the door open, and Morrigan took that as an invitation. She stepped inside. Her assumption hadn't been incorrect. The workshop turned out to be a large, cheerful space with long counters, an industrial-sized stove, and two refrigerators. A packaging center at the far end of the room butted up against a built-in desk with a computer docked to a dual-monitor setup. No hobby here. This had all the makings of a sophisticated business. A little clearer as to why Tamsin resisted leaving. Not that it really changed anything. The threat didn't diminish because of the professionalism of her business.

"What? Are you planning to make soap?" Okay, sarcasm wouldn't help, but she didn't get why Tamsin had hot-footed it out to the workshop and gave in to a knee-jerk reaction. She'd made it sound like there'd be something here to change Morrigan's mind, except that didn't appear likely. Amongst all the soap-making supplies, the pans, the boxes, and the scales, what could or would alter a single thing about what headed this way?

Tamsin shook her head. "Not today. I want to show you something else, far more important than what I do with my business."

"I can see your setup, and I get why you don't want to leave." Clear that a lot of time, money, and effort had gone into the establishment of Seven Sisters Handmade Soaps. No one would want to bail on a thriving business. "It doesn't change anything. We need to go."

Tamsin walked to a counter near the back of the building. On the wall behind it, a large painting of a wolf running through the forest hung with prominence. A beautiful piece that she must have paid a fortune for. "Shush."

Did she just shush her? "Sister, this better be good."

Tamsin held up her hands, her head bowed.

Fine, she'd give her five minutes, and after that, done. Morrigan would take control. And they'd do things her way. That throw-her-over-her-shoulder idea started to gain weight.

"Great Mother, hear me…"

Those four words snapped her lips shut. At the sound of them, she'd earned at least ten minutes. The rest of Tamsin's words were too soft to hear. Not that she needed to because she could see their impact. The painting began to shimmer and shake until it turned into a darkened blur, like a flat-screen TV without power. What it ultimately revealed almost sent her into cardiac arrest. A carved box, old and beautiful, hung suspended within the dark panel. Tamsin reached in and took it out. She turned, and her eyes met Morrigan's. Her hair floated around her face, strands of dark and light, charged with the electricity that gathered in the air.

"Is that what I think it is?" Her fingers tingled, and the hair on the back of her neck stood up.

Tamsin's eyes sparkled. "Yes."

❖

The clouds replaced the sunbeam Freddi had been following for a great many miles, and it kept her going in a westerly direction. Once she cleared the big city, the traffic thinned out, making it an easy drive. Heading toward the Dakotas, she shifted to more autopilot. Not exactly hazardous roads. She'd spent a lot of her life in major cities, and the vast nothingness that she encountered in this part of the country would, for most raised in the urban environments, induce a sort of panic. Not for Freddi. For her, it calmed.

More than that, the openness all around spoke to her as if the universe whispered to her alone. A sisterhood with the unseen world. Everything about this journey felt right. More so than anything else she'd done to date. When her phone rang, she flinched. Nothing like the jarring sound of a ringtone to return her to reality. And here she'd been enjoying the respite from the normal routine.

At the name appearing on the screen, she ground her teeth and forced a pleasant greeting, or as pleasant as she could muster. "Yes, Aldo. What do you need?" Not as sharp as it might have been if she'd let out her true feelings. Good on her. Not the time to poke the bear.

"I need you to stop in Fargo." No pleasantry or even acknowledgment through use of her name. Typical Aldo.

How in the fuck did he know her route? She'd told him nothing, yet he somehow was informed that she was headed directly for the best-known city in North Dakota. "Why?" Something about his request wasn't passing the smell test.

"I'm sending you reinforcements." He blathered on as if she hadn't even spoken. A dick, through and through.

"What the fuck for?" If she wanted to stop in Fargo, she would, on her schedule and for her reasons. That he demanded she do so had her thinking of an alternate route.

"Abba wants this."

The game began again. Big surprise that he played the Abba card. "Abba?" Not for a minute did she believe it came from her. It smelled one hundred percent of Aldo interference.

"Yes, Abba. Did you want to speak with her and confirm it?" Challenge issued. Challenge accepted. "Yes."

He didn't pause and fired back. "Too bad. She's unavailable. You have to take my word for it."

"You're fucking with me, and taking your word for it just doesn't roll." Bold words, given his power complex. He didn't like defiance.

"I'm doing what must be done. You will pick up Ian at the Residence Inn in Fargo. Understood?"

Fuck off, she wanted to say. "Understood."

As her mother would have advised her, "Pick your battles." She'd already pushed back one step. It had to be enough. This wasn't the time to go to war with Aldo. That moment would arrive, and when it did, she'd drive the sword through his crispy black heart and smile as she did it.

At least she had a few hundred miles left of blessed silence and time to ponder why Abba had sent in Ian to back her up. Granted, the idea had to have come from Aldo, but Abba must have bought into his argument for some reason. She didn't like it, and for more reasons than the mere fact she trusted Aldo only as far as she could toss him.

The upside to it: she knew Ian. A competent warrior, he had proved himself in the field numerous times. Not as skilled as she, but reliable, a very important distinction. If she were to be saddled with another, it might as well be Ian. Besides, men were inconsequential and easy to ignore. Some witches distracted her, and that she didn't need right now. Later it would hold a great deal of appeal, and at the right time, she'd indulge.

The face she'd seen earlier intrigued her. Even with the blurriness of the vision, both beauty and intelligence shone through. Great power had a way of amplifying natural gifts, and clearly this Keeper possessed something very special. This wouldn't be an easy battle. It would be fun though. A good challenge always got the blood roaring.

She was still smiling at the thought of facing off with the Keeper and destroying the legacy, which centuries of Black Faction witches had dreamed of, when her tire blew, and the car careened off the shoulder. "Damn it," she roared as she tried to hold it steady. It began to roll.

CHAPTER NINE

Tamsin held up her hand when Morrigan reached out. "Don't. It won't end well if you touch it."

Morrigan snatched her hand back. "It's protected."

"Yes." More than she could explain. No one except a Keeper could actually touch the *Book of Darkness* or the box that held it. Not that she'd ever actually opened the box. A few non-Keepers had tried through the centuries to put hands on the grimoire, and their failure turned into the last for each and every one. Not that the spell around it couldn't be released. The critical words had been imparted to her on her tenth birthday. She might have been only ten, but she'd understood the gravity of that particular lesson. To take the step to remove the spell would require a massive leap of faith, and despite her good feelings toward Morrigan, she wasn't close to that particular leap yet.

The magic protecting the *Book of Darkness* didn't extend to her. Not as the Keeper. She took hold of the intricately carved box, pulling it free from suspension within the magic safe she'd just opened. A master craftsman, who also possessed impressive magic, had created the box hundreds of years earlier. As beautiful today as the moment the grimoire had been placed inside. Each time she gazed on it, warmth spread through her. A threat of unimaginable magnitude rested inside, yet the beauty of the box itself demanded appreciation. The dichotomy of the box and the book echoed the mix of good and evil that flowed throughout the world.

After she set the box on the counter, she stepped back and put her hands out. "Great Mother, hear my plea. Show me the way. Keep me safe. Protect us all." A whoosh of air wafted through the workshop. The Great Mother heard and answered.

"Am I all right to touch it now?" Morrigan asked softly from right behind her.

She shook her head. "Look, but don't touch. It's important. Only one spell can lift the protection from the *Book of Darkness*, and it's never been used before. It's too dangerous to lift it unless..."

"Unless what?"

"Let me show you." The last time she'd witnessed the lid of the box opening, she'd been a teenager standing at her mother's side. By that time, cancer ravaged her body, and their time together neared its end. A cancer she always believed resulted from a spell of a Black Faction witch. They thought it would bring them what they sought, but, as usual, they'd been wrong. Even cancer hadn't stopped her mother from fulfilling her duty.

If she closed her eyes, she could almost feel her mother's spirit standing next to her now. Instead of the emaciated, bald woman with pale skin, she saw her as she had been—athletic and tanned, with long, dark hair pulled back into a braid that hung to her waist. That remained the image she preferred to remember.

And that image steadied her now as she prepared to do something she'd never before considered. She lifted the lid and pulled out the grimoire. Her fingers tingled as she laid it on the counter without opening the cover. Not quite ready for that yet. Too big a moment to rush.

"It looks brand-new." Reverence whispered through Morrigan's words.

It did look new. It always did. The leather shone as though the book had been bound only yesterday. Always struck her how something this dangerous could be one of the most beautiful things she'd ever witnessed. "It's never changed since the day it was put into the box."

"Strong magic."

She could hear the awe in Morrigan's voice and understood. She might be the Keeper, but it awed her as well. "Beyond anything else we're able to do."

"The protections stay, even with your prayer to the Great Mother?"

She nodded. "Yes. There's a spell to take them off. By the time I hit puberty, I could recite it in my sleep."

"Pretty big responsibility for someone that young."

She shrugged. Not that she disagreed. "Part of the job. We are what we are, and we carry what we carry."

"You take it well."

Her gaze met Morrigan's. "Tell me it's any different for you."

Morrigan shook her head. "It's not."

❖

As much as she wanted to grab the grimoire and open it, Morrigan stood back. The waves of power rolling off it told her to beware. She also believed Tamsin's words of caution. Only a special kind of fool would disregard a Keeper's warning. Her hands stayed at her sides, fingers twitching.

Not touching it didn't mean she couldn't at least look. She leaned in. "Show me."

Before she opened the cover, Tamsin's hands hovered over it, and her lips moved without making a sound. More magic of a very special kind. Then she slowly touched it with her fingertips. The air turned icy.

"This is what I wanted you to see." A loose piece of folded parchment lay inside the front cover. Tattered edges gave it an almost cloth-like appearance. She unfolded it to reveal the words written there. "This is important and what, I believe, affects us right now. Me and you." Her head came up, and she stared at Morrigan.

Adrenaline shot through her the moment their eyes met. With a breath to steady the sensations rushing through her, Morrigan looked down, her hands clasped behind her back. She began to read and, when she finished, looked up as her hand drifted to the neckline of her shirt. "Am I reading what I think I am?"

Tamsin's eyes moved to her hand, which still rested at her neck. "Did I glimpse what I thought I did?" She reached over and placed a hand over Morrigan's, her touch featherlike, thrilling.

Unfreaking believable, yet the words were right there in front of her. "You did," she murmured. Morrigan hesitated for only a second before she grabbed the hem of her shirt and pulled it over her head. The sports bra she wore underneath hid only a fraction of the ink.

"Are you starting to understand why I'm against running?"

Belief remained a bit elusive despite the words before her. Her fingers whispered across the images on her chest. "It's a coincidence."

"The universe doesn't play tricks like that." Tamsin nodded toward Morrigan's body, where art and color blended in what she'd thought, until this moment, to be nothing more than her family's display of dedication to their craft.

"It might."

"If you really believe that, I have some ocean-front property to sell you."

"Ha-ha." Tamsin touched the color on Morrigan's chest. For some reason it felt particularly warm.

❖

Freddi opened her eyes slowly, painfully, and she fucking hated pain. A stranger's face peered through her broken driver's-side window. "Don't move," the man said. "An ambulance is on the way."

The deployed airbag pushed into her face, and she remained buckled into her seat, the belt locked against her body. Beyond the light that stung her eyes, her chest hurt. Felt like she'd been through twelve rounds of one of those no-holds-barred cage fights. "What happened?" Her thoughts were a blur.

"I was right behind you. Looks like one of your tires blew, and you flipped like an aerial acrobat. Amazing your car landed upright. Pretty lucky you didn't pancake yourself. Emergency response should be here in a few minutes, and they'll be able to help you with injuries."

"I can get out." She felt around for the seat-belt release. Like the stranger said, a good thing the car had landed on its wheels, or she'd be upside down, or worse. The vague sound of the tire exploding echoed in her head, and the loss of control made her fingers twitch. Beyond that, a big blur. Things like this didn't happen to people, rather, witches, like her. Regular people had car accidents.

"Stay put," the stranger urged her. "They're almost here. You don't want to move until they've made sure you haven't broken anything."

She'd know if she had broken bones. Sore without a doubt. Broken? She didn't believe so. Her body felt intact, if a little battered. Even a witch as powerful as she would be certain to feel a bit pummeled if strapped into a rolling automobile. Everything had limits.

Her hand drifted away from the seat belt. Maybe it wasn't a bad idea to wait for an EMT to release her. This accident would put her behind in her mission, and if she hurt herself trying to get out of the car, it would delay things even more. While she might be very self-sufficient, she wasn't stupid. There were times that warranted caution.

Three hours later, she walked out of the small regional hospital. The ER doc wasn't super happy with her, as he'd wanted her to stay the night just to be on the safe side. She hadn't taken that grain of advice. The only surprising thing turned out to be two broken fingers. She hadn't realized they even hurt until she'd been sitting in the mandatory ambulance. A sore neck and a few bruises were minor and would clear up quickly. The broken fingers would take a little longer. At least she'd suffered no concussion or whiplash. The doctor called her extremely lucky. No reason to school him that luck had nothing to do with it. The powers around her wouldn't allow major injury. Her place in the great plan of the universe was too important for a freak accident to slow it down.

The Uber she called took her to a fairly nice hotel for a town this size. Once she reached her room, she checked in with the shop where they'd towed her car. The news about the bent frame didn't piss her off too much, given her car didn't have the same level of protection she did. She'd fully expected bad news on that front and sweet-talked the tech into dropping her bags by the hotel on the way home so at least she'd have her things.

Next up involved locating an alternate vehicle. As much as it galled her to do it, she called Aldo. After all, she might as well leverage the fact she was on Black Faction business. The one thing that came through the accident without so much as a scratch turned out to be her phone. Saved her a lot of time not having to find a store to get it replaced. She might be a powerful witch, but she relied on cell phones just as much as those without magic. A piece of modern technology she quite appreciated.

Aldo snapped the second he answered. "Why haven't you picked up Ian? You should have been in Fargo by now."

"Hello to you too." Goddess, how she'd love to pinch his head off.

"Answer my question. If you're planning to go rogue, I would urge you to think again. I won't have it, and it won't end well for you. That's a promise."

Talk about obsessive. The guy got on a one-train track, and he never got off. "Give it a rest, Aldo. I don't need your shit right now."

"I'll give it a rest when you do what you're supposed to. I don't want to have to go to Abba." Threats. Always threats.

A pounding began behind her right eye. She rubbed her temple. "Shut the fuck up and just listen."

"Don't you dare—"

"*Shut up.*" For a change, he did. "I had an accident. A tire blew and my car rolled."

"What? Are you okay?" If a sincerity meter gauged the concern in his voice, the needle would have barely moved, though he managed to utter the right words.

Like he really cared. What he cared about had more to do with the mission and zero to do with her. Had she died in the accident, it would have been a mere hiccup to him. "I'm basically fine. I need a new ride."

"What?"

Did the man know anything else to say? "I said I need a car. The accident totaled mine, and if you want me to pick up Ian in Fargo, then get a car sent to me."

"I can't do that." All pretense of concern vanished. Aldo back to being Aldo.

"Of course you can. Or do we need to bring Abba in?" If he could use Abba as a threat, so could she. Tit for tat.

A sudden change in attitude. He didn't like his own bluff getting called on him. "I can handle this. Tell me where you are."

After she filled him in and ended the call, she lay down on the bed with her hand propped up on a stack of pillows. She'd taken the small bottle of pain pills the hospital gave her, but she hadn't ingested any of them. Throbbing fingers aside, she chose not to have her senses dulled in any way. Elevation did a pretty good job of lessening the pain to a tolerable level.

Aldo had agreed to have a replacement vehicle delivered tomorrow, which gave her time to sleep. Or, if not to sleep, time to think through her next steps. The unplanned delay clearly bothered him. Not so much in her case. More like an opportunity to improvise, adapt, and overcome. The universe always brought her what she needed, and maybe now, she needed to slow down for a few hours and listen more closely to the whispers on the wind. Given she'd been lead-foot driving toward the west, the accident only slowed her progress.

The drapes pulled to block out the light, she watched the shadows dancing on the ceiling. Soothing. Her mind moved away from the aches, pains, and throbbing fingers. Her thoughts turned to the shadowy face she'd seen in the bowl.

"I'm still coming for you," she whispered as her eyes closed and sleep slipped over her.

CHAPTER TEN

Three hours later, Tamsin's pulse continued to race. When Morrigan had pulled her top over her head and revealed the ink beneath, she almost dropped right there. The designs that spread across her shoulders and down toward her breasts were breathtaking. Until she'd bared herself to Tamsin, long sleeves had hidden the art flowing down her arms, its color, form, and movement as fascinating as it was sexy. Her fingers itched to reach out and trace each image. With effort, she'd managed not to embarrass herself by acting on the urge.

After she'd returned the *Book of Darkness* to its hiding place, the protective spells back in full force, Morrigan left to go for a run. She told her she'd need the exercise to clear her head and help her think. Tamsin got it. She had her own ways of doing the same. Running wasn't one of them.

Rubbing her hair with a towel, Morrigan walked into the kitchen. "Amazing what five miles under the shoes does for concentration. I'm thinking a lot clearer now."

With all the ink once again covered by long sleeves and a high-necked shirt, so was she. "And?" Dare she hope Morrigan would start to see things from her perspective?

Morrigan draped the towel over the back of a chair and shook her head. Morrigan's version of combing her wet hair? Or an effort to keep Tamsin off balance? It almost worked. "And, that was pretty fucking weird." She draped the towel over the back of one of the chairs.

Tamsin tipped her head and shrugged. "That's pretty much our world. Or, at least compared to that of the regulars."

"The regulars?"

She laughed. "That's what my mother always called those who were not of the magical variety."

"The non-witches."

"The unfortunates." She could still see the sad look on her mother's face as she talked about those not blessed. She'd have wished a bit of magic on everyone if she'd had her way.

"You know, when you put it like that, I have always felt a little sorry for those who don't have magic in their lives. It's got to be very flat, if you know what I mean."

She did. "It's hard to even imagine. Being a witch has defined me. Of course, it's all I've ever known, so there's that."

Morrigan nodded. "And being the Keeper on top of that makes you even more special."

"I don't know about special. I just know my job and what I was born to do." She figured Morrigan would get it. She'd been raised, or so she assumed, in a manner not that dissimilar from her. Magic weaved throughout their entire lives. She'd been trained to protect the *Book of Darkness*, and Morrigan had been trained to protect her. Well, not specifically her, but whoever held the role of Keeper.

"Trust me. Special it is, accept it. Not to change the subject, but what are we doing about the Prophecy? I mean, I'll be straight with you, I'm a little freaked out by it. I'm also kinda pumped. I've never even considered that there might be an option besides the tried and true."

Warmth flowed through her yet again. That seemed to be happening frequently. God, she hoped her face didn't do something awful like flush. It would be freshman year of high school all over again, and nobody wanted to see that. Especially not Bailey Green, even though she'd been pretty cool about the whole thing, and that said a lot for high school.

"When I first felt them coming, I immediately thought of packing up and getting out of here because that's the way it's always been done. A knee-jerk reaction to a threat."

Morrigan nodded. "Smart, and don't misunderstand me, but regardless of what I read today, I still believe we need to get the hell out of here."

Tamsin heard her and at least on some level understood her. The trick would be to get Morrigan to do the same for her. "Then I looked around and it pissed me off. It's not fair. I get everything about being born into this life. I also understand about being born different, and that changes everything."

❖

Though Morrigan wouldn't admit it out loud, reading the Prophecy had sent her mind in another, and very unexpected, direction. The shock of the words came as more than reading something no other warrior had seen for centuries, if ever. It hit in a really personal way. As in heart-and-soul personal.

The tattoos that decorated her skin weren't something she'd picked out herself. She liked them, quite a bit, and wore them with pride, as did all the women in her family throughout the generations. Not something they ever talked about outside of their home. Yet, from mother to daughter again and again, the designs graced their skin. A rite of passage each first daughter anticipated.

Now, she thought she understood why. One day the right woman would fulfill the Prophecy, and she would be a member of Morrigan's family. Possibly even her daughter. The way Tamsin had looked at her when they read the words together, she'd swear she thought the woman might be her. Despite everything Tamsin had thrown at her since arriving, she couldn't quite embrace that one. While she felt comfortable saving the Keeper, she didn't have the same comfort level when it came to saving the world.

She could, however, concede a tiny bit. "I think you're right that at some point, the stand-and-fight option could come into play."

No denying the Prophecy did read that way. It wasn't hearsay any longer or a thing of the stories warriors spoke of as they sat around fires.

Tamsin put her hands on her hips, her shoulders square. "I think it's now."

"I don't agree." It didn't feel like now to her, and if Tamsin accused her of being afraid, she'd deny it.

"You know what the *Book of Darkness* promises. You and I both know it's so valuable because it holds verity and power."

Again, Tamsin spoke truth, just not all the truth. "It's also about potential and not an absolute. Besides, if we're getting right down to the nitty-gritty details, the Prophecy isn't part of the *Book of Darkness*, is it?"

Tamsin's brow furrowed. "I'm not following you."

"Think about it. The *Book of Darkness* has the potential to unleash a horrible evil into the world, if those spells come into the wrong hands. It's not an absolute. It will happen only if someone with evil intent gets their hands on it."

"Of course, I understand that."

It was all very clear in Morrigan's head. All she had to do was make it super clear for Tamsin. "Good. We're getting there."

"Not really. I'm still not following." Tamsin's brow wrinkled.

"Two things. The Prophecy isn't actually part of the *Book of Darkness*. Someone just slipped it between the pages. Second, the Prophecy is only a potential. It could go right, and it could go very, very wrong."

"I don't see it that way."

"How can you not?" Geez, it felt like teaching a bunch of middle-schoolers who stonewalled everything.

Tamsin's expression cleared, and she put her hands on the table. "It's not a spell. Everything else inside that grimoire requires magic to make it happen. The Prophecy just is, and that means, my beautiful soldier, it waits only for the right people to make it happen."

A valid point and she had a valid counterpoint. "The right woman and man." And from the looks of it, that hadn't happened for Tamsin yet. Sure would never happen for her. Neither here nor there. This became more about Tamsin than Morrigan.

Tamsin took a big breath and let it out slowly while shaking her head. "That's so old school. Look, here's the thing, and let me be brutally honest. I'm not into men. Never really have been, and I don't see that changing."

Explained her level of attraction to Tamsin. Didn't change any of the facts. "You have to produce an heir. An heir produced from a love match, don't forget."

Tamsin chuckled. "Yeah, yeah, yeah. Again, don't need a man to make that happen. I mean, clearly, I need something from a man, I just don't really need the actual guy in my life. I can produce a daughter on my own."

"It doesn't sound like that's in your plans." Morrigan would have to be both blind and deaf to miss the subtext here.

The shrug echoed the tone in her voice. "Never say never. I don't think it's our only option."

"Our?"

Now she rolled her eyes. "Seriously? You think I don't know?"

Good that they were on the same page. "Okay, okay, you get me. Still doesn't change who you are and what you need to do. Like find a man to love and produce a baby girl."

"Again, I can do it on my own. I also don't think a love match and children are exclusive to a straight relationship. I have options."

"So you keep saying."

"So it's written."

She had her there. Morrigan had seen the words with her own eyes. Written centuries ago, it did seem to fall back into her lap. Or, rather, her chest and arms. The words described her ink at a frightening level. Not that she should be scared. She'd never doubted for a moment the magic of her ancestors. There had been some powerful witches years ago, and while many had been killed through the centuries by the holy and the so-called righteous, fortunately for both her and Tamsin, many more had survived.

Their numbers might have been seriously damaged. Their power had not.

She brought her gaze up and met Tamsin's eyes. "Yeah, so it is."

❖

So fucked up. Freddi's most considerable magic didn't seem to be useful when it came to mending her physical body, and that made about zero sense. With her skills, she could turn a man to dust with a simple spell. Make a circle of witches burst into flames. Yet her own body resisted her most powerful magic, as evidenced by the unhealed fingers and a body full of aches and pains. Pissed her off, and all she could do was hang out in the stupid hotel room and wait.

The nap she thought would be a welcome doorway to healing magic didn't quite manifest. Oh, she slept for a couple hours all right, except she felt worse once she woke up. Her whole hand throbbed, sending pain up her arm as though her broken fingers wanted company. Not going to break down and open the pill bottle. Nope. No way. Nada. Nyet.

That said, au naturel wasn't cutting it either. She swung her feet from the bed and began to pace the room. While it afforded her plenty of room to move, the walls closed in just the same. Staying in here until the car arrived didn't feel like a good option. She'd pull her hair out. If nothing else, a little air would do her good.

Once she stepped outside, her shoulders relaxed. Like usual, her instincts were on point. The fresh air and blue sky dotted with clouds made such a difference. The air, fresh and clear, filled her lungs, and while the throbbing in her hand didn't abate, it became easier to ignore when the stimulation of the natural environment flowed over her. Power, pure and energizing. Exactly what the doctor ordered. The doctor, of course, being her. The one at the hospital had been full of shit. Stay overnight for observation? Not likely.

The clouds moved out, and the afternoon faded as she walked. Streetlights began to blink on in the tidy urban park not far from the hotel. The deeper she walked into the park, the more the pain ebbed.

Far more effective than pharmaceuticals. Any witch with any level of skill knew much better how to heal injuries than any arrogant hospital doctor. Sure, her neck hurt, and her back might be a touch sore, in addition to the fingers. It would all heal, and much quicker than with the average person. The magic couldn't be ignored.

"Are you all right?"

The footsteps behind her didn't come as a surprise. She'd heard them from some distance away. Smelled the light scent the woman wore. Pleasant. Intriguing even. The sensations flowing through her let Freddi know she might have been hurt, but she wasn't out of commission.

She held out her injured hand, complete with splinted fingers. "A little fender bender today."

"Looks painful."

"A bit. More annoying than anything else."

"I'm Cathy." She held out a hand.

Her long, blond hair glittered in the fading sunlight. A sign. "I'm Freddi." She shook the outstretched hand with her uninjured hand.

"Short for?" Her smile lit up her face. A great deal of promise there.

"Frederica. I arrived a miniature version of my mother, and so my father insisted upon me being named after him. A girly version of Frederick."

Her laugh was as light as her blue eyes and blond hair. "I like it. Suits you."

"You don't know me." People assumed they knew her, another testament to her skill at creating the perfect façade.

Cathy's lips lifted into a smile. "We should maybe fix that. You know, there's a lovely little bar just on the other side of the park. What do you say? Up for a drink and a bit of get-to-know-you conversation?" Her blue eyes were bright.

Given she had some time to kill and Freddi liked what she saw, why not? Not that she drank much. Didn't care for dulled senses, even when a beautiful and willing woman offered up the invitation.

No problem with her new friend getting a little loose though. Could make things even more interesting, and a few sips from day-drinking wouldn't hurt her either. "Lead the way."

Much later, after Cathy's third glass of wine and an impressive orgasm, Freddi stood at the window looking out. Cathy snored softly. Kind of cute. Not that she'd want to listen to that every night. Not so bad right now.

The air brushed cool and refreshing against her naked flesh. At least for a few hours, she'd managed to banish the pain, and it was worth it. As she stood staring out as the day faded into night, the pain eased back in, although not as bad as hours earlier. The fresh air and sex had combined to become the perfect healing remedy. That and a little magic.

She turned and stood over Cathy's sleeping body, whispering a quick spell. Then she went into the bathroom and turned on the shower. When she came back out, Cathy was gone.

CHAPTER ELEVEN

"What are you doing here?" Well, didn't that sound bitchy? Tamsin backpedaled. "Sorry, Holly. That didn't come out right."

Holly waved her hand in the air as she sat down at the kitchen table with a cup of tea held between her hands. "No worries. You wouldn't expect to wake up to find me rummaging around your kitchen on a Sunday morning. Sorry for not giving you a heads-up. Sort of a compulsion to get here and I went with it."

After a light touch to the kettle and finding it still hot, she made herself a cup of tea and then sat across from Holly. Much gentler this time, she asked, "What are you doing here?" Only then did she notice how pale Holly appeared, and given her skin tone, that sent a surge of alarm through her. Why hadn't she noticed it before? Some friend she'd turned out to be.

Holly sighed and stared down into her tea. "I thought about doing what you said and enjoying a little time off. I mean, we've had a big year and worked super hard. It was kind of nice to take some downtime to cherish the free time. In fact, yesterday turned out to be a pretty darned good day, and then I woke up this morning and knew it wouldn't last."

"I don't understand." Not only did her appearance alarm Tamsin, so did the tone in her voice. She'd not heard it before.

Holly's fingers tapped against her teacup. "No reason you should."

This conversation had her lost so far. She wasn't usually this cryptic. "Holly, seriously, what is going on?"

She finally brought her gaze up and met Tamsin's. "After I left here the other day, I got the call I've been waiting for. You remember my doctor's appointment about a week ago."

"Yeah, of course. You told me it was a routine physical." A whisper of alarm ticked at the back of her neck.

She grimaced. "A bit of a white lie. More than routine. A bunch of tests."

"What kind of tests?" She didn't like where this seemed to be headed.

"The kind that tells you that you have terminal cancer."

For at least a full minute, she simply stared at Holly. "You're joking, right?"

"Who jokes about cancer?"

Good point. "How? Why? I, I…"

A single tear slid down Holly's pale cheek. "I haven't felt good for a while now. My grandmother is a healer, and she's helped me, but this grew even beyond Grandmother's powers. I needed help of the more twenty-first century kind."

She'd met Holly's grandmother, Grace Two Wolf, and been duly impressed. They'd bonded quickly, recognizing the magic that lived within each other. Every time she visited with Grace, she came away feeling renewed and even more powerful. That she'd sent her granddaughter to a medical doctor came as the worst kind of news.

"What did the doctors tell you?" She almost hated to ask that question.

Holly stared down into her cup for a few moments, her voice quiet when she answered. "Six months tops. Pancreatic cancer and it's stage four."

She almost threw up, and she slapped a hand against her mouth. "No."

"I wish." A wry smile pulled up the corners of her mouth as her eyes met Tamsin's.

"What can I do?" Life could sometimes be incredibly unfair, and despite all the magic she possessed, she felt helpless in this situation.

"Be my friend."

She took Holly's hand. "I've been your friend since we met, and I'll always be here for you." She well remembered the day she'd walked into the workshop. Goodness shone from her as bright as a photographer's light. Not a hard decision to work together. Even easier to become friends and one more reason why she fought to stay here.

Holly's gaze grew intense and the smile faded. Her fingers tightened around Tamsin's as if to ensure her attention. "You've been a good friend. You haven't been an honest friend."

She pulled her hand free, sat back in her chair, and stared. "Bullshit." That statement hurt.

Holly stared back without so much as a single blink. "It's the truth, and you and I both know it. If you want to help me like you say you do, I need you to tell me who you really are."

❖

Morrigan walked into the kitchen just as Holly demanded the truth from Tamsin. Though she'd not caught the bulk of the conversation, she took a leap as to what truth Holly asked for. "No fucking way." She stopped in the doorway, legs spread and hands on her hips. This conversation would end right here, right now.

They both turned and stared at her. Apparently, neither one of them had heard her when she stepped into the room. Morrigan wasn't exactly a ninja, so she attributed it to the intensity of the exchange happening between the two women. At least she had their attention now.

Tamsin raised an eyebrow. "Good morning, sunshine." Such a calm greeting, as if she didn't think Morrigan heard any of the intense talk going on between her and Holly.

Bad enough they'd made zero ground last night. Now she walked in to find Holly demanding the revelation of secrets from Tamsin. So damned much danger out there. No room for someone like Holly, and truth came totally off the table.

"I don't know what you two have going on, and sorry, Holly, I don't mean to be a bitch, but no. Just no. Nothing gets said here. You'll have to deal with that regardless of how good of friends you believe you are."

Holly leaned back in her chair and studied Morrigan. The intensity of her gaze unnerved her a little. Sort of made her wonder if Holly had her own kind of magic. Not like they possessed, because she'd be able to sense it if she did. And she figured Tamsin would tell her if Holly was something other than a regular. Since she hadn't mentioned it, she had to believe it wasn't the case.

Folding her hands on the table, Holly said, "Yeah, well, see, here's the thing. I'm not going for just no. I have my reasons."

"Really? And those reasons would be? I'm not trying to come across as coarse or uncaring, but cancer doesn't factor in here." She'd caught the part about her diagnosis right before she made her presence known.

Holly shook her head. "No, it's not that, and I have no plans to play the I'm-dying card. What neither of you is understanding is that I've hit that spot where I have nothing left to lose and no time for waiting or being patient. My truth boils down to I've been patient, and I'm done with that path. If nothing else, I believe I've earned the right to the truth."

Tamsin tilted her head and stared at Holly. "Now, you've got me confused. You've been patient?"

"Oh, please. I've known for a long time that you're something special. I've sensed the magic in your soul. What I don't know is why, and I want to understand. You." She pointed at Morrigan. "Aren't just some random friend showing up to spend time with your buddy. You're here for a reason, and I want to know that too."

"You figured that out?" That feat impressed Morrigan. Most of the general public had no idea of the world that existed side by side with the magic of theirs. Some of them could feel vibrations or glimpse things they couldn't quite explain. That's usually as far as it went. This Holly sounded like she had a foot in both worlds.

"I felt the difference the first time I met her." She inclined her head in Tamsin's direction. "She almost glowed. Some people are like that, and most of the time it means nothing more than the fact they're good souls. After she met my grandmother, I knew how much more. You should have been in the room with the two of them. Indescribable energy. You could almost get high standing next to them."

Damn. Holly did have a freaking clue and, right now, about the last thing they needed. This operation had to be kept low and on a need-to-know-basis, as the saying went. Holly didn't need to know.

Morrigan pointed to Tamsin. "She is different, and that's why I'm here. I'll protect her, and you don't need to know anything else beyond that." Firm and to the point.

"I disagree." Holly stayed just as firm, and she'd give her props for that. Kind of impressive for someone who'd minutes before confessed to be dying.

"I disagree as well." Tamsin's words were calm yet filled with authority.

Talk about being ganged up on. How did her usual control slip so far away and so fast? Her mother trained her better than this. *Come on, Mom. Help me out here.* "No." The one word really did sum it all up. Simple and direct.

Tamsin stood and put her hands on her waist. "Yes."

"Fuck me running." The potty mouth she got from her dad.

Tamsin started to laugh. "Intriguing idea, but we don't have time at the moment."

A little tingle ran through her. Shit. Not only did she have to fight to protect her, but now she'd be fighting her own complicating attraction to this damned fascinating woman. Nobody had prepared her for a Keeper who proved to be smart, stubborn, and beautiful. "I think I'm starting to hate you."

This time Tamsin winked. "Naw. You don't hate me."

"No. I don't." She could lie, but what would be the point?

Holly looked between them, and a slow smile turned up the corners of her mouth.

Morrigan frowned. "What are you smiling about?"

"Nothing." Holly's smile didn't vanish. "Nothing at all."

❖

The energy Freddi had pulled from Cathy helped a great deal. She'd heal better and faster if she could siphon from those like her bed guest. The sex didn't hurt either. It felt good, and that counted for a lot. Helped to pass the time waiting for her ride.

Once again, she paced the confines of her hotel room. It didn't have much to offer in terms of interest or entertainment. While she appreciated the wide-open roads, she'd never been a big fan of the Midwest. Not her style. Truthfully, she liked the South, where they laughed and believed and, best of all, could hold a grudge. She admired that latter trait the most because she embraced it wholeheartedly. A bit of a Black Faction unwritten code. Sort of like the do-unto-others-before-they-can-do-unto-you. Those born into the Black Faction nurtured that philosophy for good reason. It had kept them alive and strong for centuries.

It would be a fool who discounted the White Faction though. They could be as sneaky and dangerous as any of Freddi's fellow Witch Finders. That's why they continued to stand strong on opposite sides of the war over the *Book of Darkness*.

It should belong to the Black Faction and, in her opinion, to her alone. Not to a bunch of jerks who'd waste the potential of that kind of magic. The witches who practiced the goody-two-shoes brand of magic because it wasn't safe to put anything else out there. Never could tolerate the inane three-fold law of return. Chickenshit. Whatever in the hell she wanted out there, she'd put out there, and the only thing that would return to her in triplicate would be three times more power.

That said, while she didn't buy into their particular philosophy, she also didn't underestimate any of them, particularly not the Keeper. The legends around the Keepers came into being for good reason. They were special. Not as talented or unique as Freddi, but perhaps a close second.

Focused on fulfilling her quest, she jerked when her cell rang. She glanced at the display. "Fuck." Aldo. Again. "What?"

"And a lovely morning to you too, Frederica." Sugary sweet. Motherfucker had something up his sleeve.

"Fuck off. What do you want?"

"Ian is on his way to pick you up. He's about twelve hours out."

"That's too long. All I need is a rental and I'm back on the road."

"No. You wait for Ian."

"No. That's too much wasted time."

"It's what Abba wants."

Of course, he'd throw that in. Nobody defied Abba's wishes, and in this case, no doubt Abba's wishes were his wishes. For the moment, she'd let him believe she would play by their rules, despite how very weary she grew of his game. For another day or two anyway. Then it would all change, and that son of a bitch would kneel before her. What a sweet day that would be. "Fine." Bile followed the single word.

"And then you will pick me up in Denver."

"Excuse me." No way did she hear that correctly. What in hell did they need him for? Aldo had been sitting around admiring himself for so many years, he'd be not only a hinderance. He'd be a liability. Fieldwork wasn't in his tool kit.

"You will pick me up in Denver." He said the words very slowly, as if she had a problem comprehending.

"That's off course." Way off course and would cost her days. Not acceptable at any level. Besides, what on earth was he doing there?

"Doesn't matter. Ian has his instructions. Pick you up and then head to Red Rock for me." It made more sense now. Not exactly

Denver. The Red Rocks area where Abba kept her fortress sat near the border between Colorado and Utah. His sense of geography sucked.

"I need to get to the Keeper. I can't afford a side trip."

"The Keeper is sitting still. We have plenty of time." His royal pronouncement.

"You don't know that." Waves of energy roared through the air. Every hour they grew increasingly dense and palpable. Aldo didn't have the first clue about the Keeper and couldn't comprehend how time wasn't on their side. She needed to get her hands on the *Book of Darkness*, and Aldo crashing that particular party didn't work for her. What did she do to deserve a ball and chain like Aldo?

"Ah, but I do. Here's the thing, *Frederica*. I know you are on track to capture the Keeper. My faith in your abilities is strong, and here's where I need you to listen closely. I will be there when you do it, as Abba has charged ME with taking custody of the *Book of Darkness*."

Just no. The two words almost tumbled out of her mouth. What stopped her were options. Not bad ones either. She could work with this. "Fine. I'll be ready when he gets here."

"Good girl."

Her uninjured hand curled into a fist.

CHAPTER TWELVE

Tamsin took control. She appreciated Morrigan and the job she came here to do. More than that, she liked her, and not in the let's-be-friends kind of way. The woman spoke to her soul, and damned if it didn't feel good. Now, however, she had Holly to deal with, and while she couldn't explain why, she understood that she needed to be brought into the inner circle. Another one of those whispers from the universe, and she felt compelled to listen.

She put down her mug and looked over at Holly. "I'm the one they call the Keeper."

"No." Morrigan's protest held a tone of despair. Her face mirrored the same. "Don't do this."

With a quick glance at Morrigan, she continued. No choice. "I'm also a hereditary witch, and born into a centuries-long line tasked with keeping the *Book of Darkness* out of the hands of witches known as the Black Faction. If they got ahold of it, they would use it to unleash evil with the power to destroy everything good and kind in the world." Wow, did that feel good. The first time she'd ever said those words out loud, let alone shared them with a regular. Empowering to speak her truth to the world. Well, a stretch to equate one person with the world but still felt good.

"Shit." Morrigan sank to a chair. "This isn't good." Her shoulders sagged. While Tamsin felt for her, she remained confident in the importance of bringing Holly into this.

Holly nodded and folded her hands on the table. "I had a feeling it was something like that. I didn't know exactly what your role in the universe might be, only that it was critical and magical. This book, what's it do?"

"It's what it *can* do," Morrigan jumped in. "This place." She waved her hands in the air. "This life you all love will go up in flames if the Black Faction gets their hands on it, and they've been trying for hundreds and hundreds of years to wrestle it away from the Keepers."

"The women in my family have been keeping it safe for as long as it's been in existence. I come from a very long line of such women."

"I can help you." Holly brought her head up and squared her shoulders. Light shone from her eyes.

Morrigan slapped her hand on the table and stood. Her expression grew dark. "No. You're putting Tamsin in more jeopardy. I can't get her to leave, and you sitting here demanding to know all the secrets is only making it worse, not helping. If you really care for your friend, you'll walk away."

"I can help." Holly wasn't giving ground, and Tamsin admired her for the confidence she showed. Holly had said that she noticed something special about Tamsin when they first met. Well, the same thing held true for Holly. She'd had an extraordinary light to her as well.

"Tell me." She wanted to understand, her trust in Holly solid. She'd go with that despite the darkness in Morrigan's eyes and the barely controlled anger that rolled off her. Perhaps Morrigan needed a bit of time, and then she'd feel it too. Worth the risk.

"It is said that when one who is on her journey to the beyond touches hands with those with the power to push away the darkness, sparks fly." Holly reached out, one hand to Tamsin and the other to Morrigan.

Morrigan shook her head and kept her hands in her lap. "All of this is crazy, and both of you are driving me even crazier. We know what needs to be done, and hanging around drinking tea and singing kumbaya is insane. We're sitting ducks and even worse is putting this poor woman, already in a fight for her life, into imminent danger. It's irresponsible. It's unkind."

Tamsin disagreed. More and more, her belief about staying and fighting looked to be the exact right thing to do. She reached over and took Holly's hand. No way could she leave her behind. The universe had brought them together for a reason, and she refused to abandon her when she fought for quality of life in the time she had left.

"Morrigan," Holly said. "Please. You've lost nothing by seeing if what I say is true. Please." She motioned with her fingers.

"She's right. Just do as she asks. Two seconds." Tamsin really wanted Morrigan to take Holly's hand. She wanted to know if any truth lay in her words and felt sure it did.

"Fine. Whatever." She grabbed Holly's hand.

The kitchen filled with a flash of bright light.

❖

Not one single thing in a lifetime of lessons had prepared Morrigan for what just happened. She snatched her hand away and stared at the other two women as the light in the room returned to normal. "What in the hell?"

Tamsin smiled. "That was amazing. Deny them all you want, but the signs keep coming."

"Not a sign. Something else." She directed her gaze to Holly.

With her hands folded on the table once more, Holly took a breath. Her face serene, she closed her eyes for a moment. "It is the manifestation of a legend I've heard my whole life. The trinity that will keep the world from descending into darkness."

Nope. Morrigan wasn't buying the simplicity of her explanation. Never before had she ever heard of an outsider being part of their particular war. "You believe you're involved with this? You're just, just..." She still buzzed with the energy that rolled through the room, and the words eluded her.

Holly raised an eyebrow. "What? Just an Indian? Just a woman? Just a what?" Dark eyes in a pale face stared, the challenge clear. Not giving an inch. Fair enough.

Because, yeah, that didn't sound very good. Shame on her. "Sorry. That came out wrong. What I meant is that we…" She waved a hand between herself and Tamsin. "…are witches. We've been in this fight since birth. You're a normal person, and this fight isn't yours. You don't have to get involved, and even you have to admit you've already got a lot on your plate."

Nodding, Holly seemed to accept her explanation for what it was, clarity, and what it wasn't, an insult to her gender or heritage. "All of that is true enough. But you have to understand that we're on the same side. We've fought against darkness in all its forms since the beginning of time. This is not different. Same battle, just slightly different people."

"Why didn't you say something before?" Tamsin asked. Her calm voice soothed the tension.

Holly's gaze softened. "It hit me yesterday when I left the oncologist's office with the news that no more options are available to save my life. The stories I'd grown up with all dropped into place, and the vibes I've gotten from you, Tamsin, dropped into place as well. I suddenly knew, and that's why I'm here and why I'm not leaving."

Morrigan couldn't believe how off track all of this had become. She wasn't prepared and it scared her. No training had ever covered this scenario. Holly made some good points, and yes, she could believe she understood what Tamsin and Morrigan faced because of her own background. It still didn't track for her. An apples-and-oranges kind of situation. "This feels wrong."

"Does it?" Tamsin stared at her with eyes wide. "Somehow it feels pretty right to me."

Morrigan looked down at her hands that only minutes before had sparked with lightning when she'd touched Holly's flesh. Couldn't explain that one beyond the legacy of magic that defined her entire existence. Holly might not be a witch like her and Tamsin, or the witches coming for them, but Morrigan would have a hard time denying that she possessed something otherworldly.

She walked to the window and stared out as she ran her hands through her hair. Apples and oranges worked together, right? The sun outside the window shone, the promise of a bright day. A promise she prayed extended to them as well. "Okay, ladies, what next?"

Tamsin came to Morrigan and stood next to her. She put a finger on her chin and turned her face so they stared at each other. "Now, you're talking. I say we start with the Prophecy." Then she kissed her.

❖

Freddi could swear she heard her smart watch ticking like an old-school wind-up timepiece. The hours passed at the speed of a moving glacier, each minute feeling like a month. Waiting for Ian didn't work for her, yet she didn't dare push the envelope too hard. Dumb-ass Aldo had his limits. He might not be at Abba's level, or hers, for that matter, but the man did have some skills. No need to force him into using them on her.

She almost wished she hadn't cast a spell on Cathy to get her to leave. Right now a little sex would go a long way toward relaxation. All the good feels of earlier had wafted away, and the throbbing in her body resurfaced. That it meant her body worked to heal didn't help her reconcile with it. She wanted everything back to perfect and to be on the road. Like fucking now.

Time to pull out a little magic to keep her energy and spirits high. If she could hijack the power of a couple of local witches, that would be helpful. With a bum hand, she wasn't quite up to the hunt tonight. She'd have to rely on her own skills to make it happen, though not for a little while yet. Her calendar app showed that tonight would be a full moon, and that lone fact would be quite helpful. The boost would be all she needed to recharge at the level required before Ian arrived.

Patience would be a good thing too, and much to her mother's dismay, she'd never had an abundance of that particular trait. In her opinion, only for losers and wimps. Neither described her. Instead, she pulled a little something from her own bag of tricks. A lot of forms of magic existed in the world, and the smart ones didn't discount what others brought to the table. Like the mushrooms a former lover turned her onto. Could be a twofer right now. Her body wouldn't ache anymore, and perhaps she could tap into a vision that would put her closer to the face of the Keeper. Clarity counted for a great deal.

An hour later she reclined against a stack of pillows on the bed, her legs stretched out, her injured hand elevated. Bright colors flashed before her eyes in hues of red, blue, green, purple, and yellow. She relaxed into the softness propping her up. Oh, yes. Just what she needed. Her eyes closed, she let the sensations take her on a wave of pain-free joy.

"Come to me, you little bitch," she murmured. "Show me your face."

She kneeled at the edge of the meadow, yellow and violet wildflowers swaying in the breeze. Their sweet, pleasing scent wafted through the air. Her long black hair, streaked with strands of white, hung down her back, nearly touching the ground. A gentle wind picked up stray strands and whipped them around in a kind of dance.

"You're not welcome here." Her words were firm, almost angry. She didn't turn around.

"I go where I please."

"You don't go here. You don't go near me. Leave."

"Fuck you." Even in a vision she didn't put up with shit from an inferior.

She held up her hands, and petals in shades of violet and yellow scattered on the wind like a snowstorm. "Not here and not with me. Ready yourself, witch. I will destroy you and those you bring with you. Of this you have my promise."

The beautiful field of wildflowers and the bright blue, cloudless sky contrasted with the hardness in her voice. It shouldn't be a surprise. The Keepers were a stubborn bunch, who took their duty to heart. That might have worked in the years that came before her. Times had changed.

"You can give it your best shot." Her own laugh filled the air, loud and heartfelt. No one could stop her. Not even this one who undoubtedly believed herself superior to all others.

"I will." The two words were barely audible yet held a tone of steel.

She replied in kind. "It won't be enough."

The Prophecy

She comes as her time grows short
before her magic wanes.
Of earth and water,
wind and fire,
her power will be mighty.
Her sight will be true.
She will find them,
and the power of their joining will reveal the path.
So it is written in the stars.

CHAPTER THIRTEEN

The kiss roared like fire through Tamsin right before everything went black. She woke up on the kitchen floor to the worried face of Morrigan hovering above her. After a few blinks and a deep breath to get her bearings, she muttered, "Wow. Sorry about that."

Morrigan's hands cupped her face. She kind of liked it. "Holy shit. What just happened?"

"I kissed you." That much she remembered. It had been awesome right up until the point she dropped like a ton of bricks.

"Yeah, well, there's that, but what's with the blacking-out part? You do that often?" The worry hadn't lessened. Nice to have someone care.

She pushed up to a sitting position and brushed her hair out of her eyes. "Can't say that I do, but wait until you hear why I blacked out. This is some kind of crazy." Processing what happened came at lightning speed, and she really wanted to share.

"Okay, we're waiting." Morrigan held out a hand and pulled her up. For a second she wobbled and almost went back down, but Morrigan's grip steadied her. The same spark remained when they touched. Good.

Holly's face was filled with concern. "You know," she said. "I'm the one with terminal cancer, so really, knock that crap off. We only need one patient around here right now. You almost gave me a heart attack when you dropped."

Made her feel guilty for causing any stress to her friend when she already suffered. She placed a hand over Holly's. "Don't you worry for a second about me. If we can figure out how to heal you, trust me, we will. We have skills." She glanced up at Morrigan. "Right?"

"Yeah, we do. Problem is, we can't afford to get sidetracked now, and I'm not saying that to be an asshole. Holly, I think you'll understand when we explain all this to you. Before we get to any detailed explanations on that front, Tamsin, what the hell happened just now?"

This part excited her as much as it scared her. "I was with her."

"Her, who?" Morrigan's words took on a note of impatience.

"The Witch Finder. The one who's heading our way." The explanation seemed obvious to Tamsin, even though both Morrigan and Holly looked confused.

Morrigan's face cleared and her eyes widened. Now she followed. "You were not."

"I swear to you, I was with her." How to explain so they could feel it like she had. "That woman has some serious skills. I don't know how she was able to draw me in, but she did. Absolutely bizarre, and I'm telling you, nobody ever prepared me for that."

Now Morrigan frowned and crossed her arms. "I don't like the sound of this. Way too intrusive. What does she look like? That will help with a heads-up on her arrival, and maybe somebody will have run into her before."

The not-so-exciting part. Tamsin shook her head. "I didn't see her face."

"I thought you said you were with her."

"I did, but my back was to her the whole time, and it all happened very fast." She couldn't explain why she'd been unable to turn and face the Witch Finder. Visions didn't exactly have hard and fast rules, even for a powerful Keeper.

"Damn it. I'd like to know who we're up against. A face would help a ton."

Holly looked between Tamsin and Morrigan. "Would one of you mind looping me in here? A Witch Finder? Sounds medieval."

• 122 •

❖

Morrigan definitely didn't want to loop in Holly any more than they already had. Contain. Contain. Contain. That was the very first lesson her mother taught her. Keep the circle small, tight, and get the Keeper to safety. To widen the circle to include a regular went against everything she'd learned. It almost hurt her to do something different. Unsettling at the very least, and she didn't care for unsettled.

"I don't like this." So far, her protests had done her zero good. Maybe continuing to lodge them would eventually have some effect? She glanced over at Tamsin and decided that hope would be dashed any second.

Tamsin ran a hand over Morrigan's hair, and it took a lot of effort not to shiver. Every time Tamsin touched her, waves of pleasure raced through her. What in the actual hell? "Relax. It feels right to me, and my mother always told me to rely on my instincts. They tend to be pure and true. Surely your mother taught you the same?"

Damn it anyway. Of course, her mother had shared that little bit of wisdom with her too. She'd practically beat it into Morrigan, metaphorically speaking anyway. The problem now came with her gut telling her something quite different from Tamsin's. "No." And she wasn't referring to lessons learned.

"Yes." She knew Tamsin wasn't referring to lessons learned either.

She didn't stand a chance here. Time to shift gears. Her mother had also taught her when it made sense to compromise in order to achieve the end goal. Keep an eye on the big picture. "Fine, but if this goes south, it's on you."

Tamsin smiled. "I'll take it because I swear to you, nothing is going south."

Holly clapped her hands. "Well, then, ladies. Loop me all the way in. I'm dying, literally speaking, to know what's up in your world."

Morrigan threw up her hands. "You guys are impossible, and I clearly don't stand a chance with either of you." She looked at Tamsin. "Go ahead. It's your show. Might as well bare it all."

Tamsin nodded and put a hand on Holly's shoulder. "Welcome aboard."

For a situation quite a few centuries in the making, Tamsin did an excellent job of boiling it down to the essentials. Perhaps Holly's own heritage gave her more of an open mind than any of the regulars she'd been around. She could almost see the wheels turning in her head as Tamsin explained both their legacy and their current situation. Her admiration for the woman had jumped up quite a bit in the last thirty minutes.

After Tamsin wound down, Holly leaned back in her chair. "Of earth and water, wind and fire. There's a lot of meaning there, and I need to think about all this for a while. Something is whispering in the back of my mind, and I have to coax it forward. Some of the drugs I have to take these days dull my processes, and things don't move as quickly as they should. I'll get there. Just need a little time."

"I believe the answer is within our grasp, and I'd love to hear your thoughts. Take whatever time you need. We'll be right here." Tamsin shot a meaningful glance at Morrigan.

Morrigan could appreciate the mindset of the two women. Sort of. Every instinct she possessed screamed, RUN! She didn't bother to share her feelings. No point. Tamsin wasn't about to budge, and her last words to Holly reinforced that belief. Morrigan gave in and officially arrived at the if-you-can't-fight-em, join-em stage.

Grudgingly, she told Holly, "If Tamsin is right, and I'm telling you it's a really big *if*, then we need to make plans, and quick. Not a lot of time to think things through. I don't mean to push you, particularly given your health situation, but it is what it is."

"The Witch Finder." Holly tapped her fingers on the table. "They sure sound like a pain in the ass for you guys."

"Yes, the Witch Finder. She, and I'm leaning toward a she, given what Tamsin saw when she blacked out, will be moving fast to get to her. They only send the best when they believe they've targeted the Keeper."

"It's a she," Tamsin told them. "That much I know for a fact. I didn't see her face. I did hear her voice."

Holly tapped her fingers on the table for a moment. When her fingers stilled, she looked at them both. "My grandmother. I've got to share this with her. She'll be able to make sense of it and not have any drugs dulling her mind." Holly stood. So did Morrigan.

"Ah, that's a big, fat no. We cannot drag anyone else in on this. The more people who know, the more danger it puts the Keeper in. I cannot stress that fact enough. No more will be brought into this. I'm dead serious here. No means no."

"You mean me. You mean, I'm in danger. Right?" Tamsin asked.

Morrigan turned to her. Damn, hard to think logically when she gazed into her lovely face. Her mother had never prepared her for facing off with a Keeper with such beauty it made her blood rush. No, indeed, not a single lesson that prepared her to feel like pulling her into her arms and kissing her. "Yes, of course, I mean you. Keeping you safe is now and always will be my number-one priority. Bar none."

A ghost of a smile flitted across Tamsin's lips. "You probably better stay real close then."

Holly cleared her throat. "You two want me to leave?"

"Ha-ha." Morrigan shook her head.

Holly walked to the door. "I think I will head out anyway. Give you some alone time."

She ignored the innuendo. "Do *not* tell your grandmother." The door clicked shut. She turned and looked at Tamsin. "She'll tell her grandmother, won't she?"

Tamsin smiled. "She totally will."

❖

"About fucking time you got here." Freddi ached everywhere, her broken fingers an impressive shade of purple. The wonderful hours with the mushrooms had worn off, and pain slapped back into her. Damn it anyway. So ready to be done with this crap.

"You look like shit." Ian chewed gum that smelled of peppermint and stared at her with dark eyes set too close together in his face. With a long, narrow nose, he reminded her of a hawk. In her opinion, not quite as smart as one though. Another reason why it irritated her that Aldo stuck her with him. Not fair, and she didn't want Ian or anybody else to close the deal.

"You roll your car and come out looking like a movie star, then we'll talk. Otherwise, shut the fuck up."

"You know you're a bitch, right?" His jeans-clad legs spread slightly apart, hands in his pockets, he appeared as though he had not a care in the world. "Class-A bitch, no less."

"Proud of it."

Ian laughed and grabbed her bag from the bed. "Always liked that about you. Sexy as hell when someone owns it. Now come on, get in the car, buckle up, and let's get out of here. This place is a shit hole."

She followed him to the parking lot, happy that he carried her bag. The pressure of a strap on her shoulder would leave her grimacing. She slid into the passenger seat, buckled her seat belt, and winced as she bumped her fingers on the door handle. "No kidding. I've seen their hospital, experienced their excuse for a police force, and got stuck in what they consider a nice hotel. You can't get me out of here quick enough. I started to wonder if you would ever get here."

He put the blinker on and pulled out into traffic. "There's a Starbucks down the road." He nodded toward the big sign advertising one of the ubiquitous coffee stores, ignoring her dig at his tardiness. Either that or it went right over his head. She suspected the latter.

"At least a bit of civilization. Let's make a stop and then hit the interstate." Good coffee did sound nice. She hadn't slept well as she'd waited for him. Her fingers throbbed every time they touched the bed or the pillow or the sheets. Frustration at being stuck when she wanted to get to the Keeper and end this thing made closing her eyes impossible.

For at least half an hour after they pulled out of the drive-through, they rode in silence. The latte tasted wonderful, the combination of milk and espresso, no sugary syrups required, relaxing. She'd not realized how much she needed this little bit of fine living.

Ian broke the silence. "You find it odd that Aldo wants to go along?"

Freddi glanced over at Ian. His hands were at ten and two on the steering wheel and his eyes intent on the road. His venti latte sat in the cup holder between them, the scent of vanilla filling the car. What kind of soldier drank vanilla in his coffee? Dismissing his questionable taste in hot beverages, she focused instead on gauging the true intent behind his question. "Not really. He loves to be in the middle of it."

He began to tap the steering wheel. "It's like he doesn't think we're capable."

There it was. A wound to Ian's manly pride. For her, what Aldo thought about her skills didn't matter at all. She understood people like him, and their opinion held no weight with her. "He thinks he's the only one capable and that if he's part of the Keeper's destruction and gains control of the *Book of Darkness*, Abba will reward him."

"I've never seen him do anything of substance." Ian shook his head but kept his eyes on the road. "He's full of hot air most of the time. Guy gets on my nerves."

When Aldo had first insisted Ian pick her up, her resentment had almost made her physically sick. As she listened to him now, much of the anger eased away. More on the ball with Ian than she'd given him credit for. A refreshing surprise. "That makes two of us."

"So." He glanced at her. "How should we get rid of him?"

She brought her latte to her lips to hide her smile. Definitely hadn't given Ian enough credit.

The Prophecy

His true self revealed,
he possesses the heart of a lion.
Of earth and water, wind and fire,
a warrior is born.
With mighty power, and eagle's sight,
a path will be revealed.
The power of three will raise the cleansing fire.
So it is written in the stars.

CHAPTER FOURTEEN

Tamsin hadn't slept well after Holly left. She and Morrigan moved through the rest of the day, walking on eggshells. At first, it was as if they needed to ignore everything that had happened in the morning. It all changed once they'd fed the animals that evening and sat in the living room staring at each other. The dam broke, and they'd talked and talked and talked. A lot of great ideas flowed with Morrigan settled into the brain-storming session. It took a while to convince Morrigan that they had time, but she'd finally gotten her on board. A major score.

In the midst of her first real challenge, she should be focused entirely on the job she'd been raised to do. Not that she didn't intend to protect the *Book of Darkness* at all costs. She could never let the Black Faction have it. The world would be besieged by evil, and as the saying went, not on her watch. Still, despite everything she'd been taught and the duty she felt all the way to her soul, she couldn't shake the belief that the day had arrived to make a stand. A time to not only protect the grimoire, but to stop the Black Faction once and for all.

The words of the Prophecy backed her up, so far, her belief shored up by the appearance of both Morrigan and Holly. No way could either of them see it any differently. Well, she knew Holly fell on her side. Morrigan, beautiful, sexy Morrigan inched closer. She wasn't quite all the way there, but she held tight to hope.

Tamsin made herself a cup of tea and sighed as she took a sip. It wasn't just the tea. Her thoughts turned to her warrior guest, and the mere thought of her made her heart flutter. It had been forever since she'd felt this kind of attraction. The more she thought about it, the more she wondered if she'd ever felt anything this strong. The answer that popped into her mind: nope.

She glanced toward the hallway. Down it, behind the closed door of the guest room, Morrigan slept. She imagined her long legs and sculpted arms beneath the blue-and-white quilt with the embroidered blocks of various flowers her grandmother had made some fifty-odd years ago. Her breathing quickened. *Stop it.* She closed her eyes and took a deep breath.

"You have any coffee? I mean, your tea is fine, but I really like something with more of a kick."

Tamsin dropped her mug, and hot tea splashed everywhere. "Ouch!" Her eyes flew open. Morrigan stood in the doorway, hair wild and wearing sweats and a short-sleeved T-shirt that put the ink flowing over her arms on full display. Her fingers began to tingle, and it wasn't from hot, splashed tea.

"Sorry. Didn't mean to scare you." She moved to the roll of paper towels and pulled several off.

"You don't have to do that." Yet something about watching Morrigan clean the tea off the floor made her heart pound. What the hell was going on here? She wasn't sixteen anymore.

Her laugh light, she wiped up the mess. "I can do more than slay dragons to protect the Keeper."

That simple comment came down on Tamsin like a bucket of cold water, put her in her place. Despite the earlier kisses that, holy crap, set her on fire, the fact remained, she was the Keeper, and that role had to be front and center. Morrigan wasn't wrong to believe that she needed to be kept safe. At least until she puzzled out the Prophecy and brought this thing to an end.

She got up and helped Morrigan finish cleaning up the tea. As she dumped the broken pieces of her shattered tea mug in the trash, the back door creaked open. Out of the corner of her eye she noticed the way Morrigan tensed and her hand drifted to the pocket of her sweats. Only then did she notice the small bulge. Just about the size of a small handgun. A new wrinkle. A witch who didn't depend only on her magic. Intriguing.

"It's okay," she reassured Morrigan. "I made a call before you got up. The plot thickens, so to speak."

The back door opened wide, and a man with dark hair cut close to the head and the shadow of stubble on his chin stepped into the kitchen. She smiled at him. "Hey, Triple. Thanks for coming over. You made good time."

"Good morning, sunshine. Always happy to answer a call from you." He smiled, and it warmed his blue eyes.

"Oh hell no." Morrigan shook her head though her hand drifted away from her pocket. One good sign anyway. "You did not."

Tamsin hurried to make introductions before Morrigan's trigger finger got itchy. "Morrigan, this is Triple. Triple, this is Morrigan."

Triple held out his hand. "Nice to meet you, Morrigan. Tamsin told me a bit about you. Impressive."

At first Tamsin thought Morrigan would ignore the greeting. The fury in her eyes shone like the sun at midday. Then she took his hand and gave it a brief shake, some of the anger seeming to ease away. She turned to stare at Tamsin. "We don't need anyone else brought into this, and what the hell kind of name is Triple?" Well, she didn't sound too grumpy.

Triple laughed. "My legal name is Michael John Greg. You know, three first names, hence the nickname Triple. If I remember correctly, you're the one who started it." He shifted his gaze to Tamsin.

She smiled and nodded. "I believe I did. Seemed to fit and it stuck. Everyone calls him Triple these days."

"Nice of your parents to give you a moniker like that." Morrigan's voice still held a note of irritation. She clearly needed the requested coffee, and Tamsin set about getting it brewed posthaste.

Triple's smile grew, and he ran a hand over his buzz cut. "Oh, no, can't blame the folks for the name. My parents gave me a very normal name. Jennifer Amanda Greenfield. Pretty, wasn't it?"

Morrigan's eyes narrowed as she studied Triple a little more closely. "Oh."

"You see, I picked Michael John Greg after my grandfather, father, and one of my brothers. They were appalled when I transitioned and haven't really talked to me since, so it felt appropriate to bring them right along with me on my journey."

"I like his style, don't you?" Tamsin asked. She'd been drawn to Triple from the day they met, and earlier this morning as she'd been brewing her tea, it hit her how he figured into the Prophecy. She'd wasted no time getting him on the phone and then over to the farm.

"I hate to admit it, but I do." Morrigan shook her head. "Tamsin, you make this more difficult by the moment. Fighting against your grand ideas is killing me."

"Somebody want to fill me in?" Triple poured himself a cup of coffee from the pot that had just finished brewing.

Morrigan crossed her arms over her chest, and her eyes narrowed. "First, I'll take one of those too, and then, I believe Tamsin owes us both an explanation."

Triple handed her a mug. "Yeah, girlfriend. What exactly is so important you needed my butt here at this unholy hour of the morning?"

"It's seven. Nothing unholy about that." Tamsin pulled out a chair and sat.

"Speak for yourself. Better yet, just start speaking."

Morrigan sat at the table across from her. "I'll second that."

❖

Morrigan took a sip of the piping-hot coffee and carefully set the mug on the table. It helped a little. "Well?"

Tamsin tipped her head from side to side as though she were on a carnival ride. Interesting. A way to gather her thoughts? Or a way to put off answering? Cute as she might be, she had a fair amount of explaining to do. Bad enough they'd had to bring Holly into this. Now this guy? There better be a damned good explanation.

"So, I got up, made some tea, and started thinking about the Prophecy again. You know, going through it word by word, looking for the importance of each one."

"We talked about this yesterday and how it brought in Holly." Morrigan didn't see how it would push her to call this guy and allow him into the inner circle. Enough with all the non-magic people. This coming battle required the skills of their craft.

Tamsin held up her hand. "It did point right to her, but I realized as I scrutinized each word individually, how we were missing a much bigger picture. We jumped right over a critical clue. The one that applied to him." She pointed to Triple.

"You've lost me on all of this. What Prophecy? What words?" He set his mug on the table. "How about you start at the beginning so I'm not completely in the dark."

She agreed with Triple. None of this made a bit of sense to her, and she knew a lot more of the background. Even the part about Holly required a pretty good leap. With Holly's own bit of magic, Morrigan could roll with her participation. Not that Tamsin had given her a choice. Thus far, Tamsin had been embracing whatever action spoke to her, and Morrigan had been on a dead run to keep up. This thing with Triple followed the established pattern, and she hated it. Talk about out of control.

She glanced at Triple. Good vibes that let her know he possessed a true soul, yes. Magic, not even a tiny whiff, and the reality of this situation called for a lot of magic. Regulars had no place in this battle. For the life of her, she couldn't see how he played a part in the Prophecy, but Tamsin appeared hell-bent on making him fit into this situation.

"No, Tamsin," she warned her softly. "Don't do this."

Tamsin held her gaze. "Ye of little faith. Morrigan, you read the words with me. Think them through. I mean, really think them through." She began to recite. "His true self revealed…" Her gaze held Morrigan's as she repeated the words they'd read together not long ago, and she paused for a moment before finishing the passage. "…the power of three will raise the cleansing fire. So it is written in the stars."

For a few seconds, she let the words settle. She tried to see it from Tamsin's point of view. At first, she didn't. She closed her eyes and rolled through the words one more time. Then it hit her. Her eyes flew open. "The power of three."

"His true self." Tamsin inclined her head toward Triple.

"Holy shit."

"Right?"

Triple tapped his fingers on the table. "Somebody want to loop me in?"

Tamsin had gotten so caught up in pulling Morrigan in that she'd almost forgotten about Triple. "Well," she said and sat at the table across from him. "I haven't been completely honest with you about who I am. I have a few things to share."

Darkness floated over Triple's face, and his hands went to the table as if he was prepared for flight. Morrigan thought she understood why. Being trans required great strength, and often, for one to share their whole truth with another drew upon deep trust. Tamsin had just announced to him that she'd held back in their friendship. He'd shared his truth, while she'd continued to conceal hers from him. That announcement could end the conversation here, and she sort of hoped it did because it provided a quick solution to Morrigan's hesitation to bring yet another in.

"Then tell me. Put honesty on this table." Triple tapped the table with his hands. "All of it."

Tamsin glanced at her. Asking permission? The genie had already been let out of the bottle. Clear that her hoped-for solution had flown out the window, she nodded. Tamsin nodded back.

"I'm a witch." Tamsin went for the quick and simple explanation first.

Triple tilted his head and studied her. The silence lengthened. Finally, he said, "I think I always knew that in the back of my mind. You have a different vibe." He turned his gaze on Morrigan. "You a witch too?"

"I am. A little different from Tamsin, but I'll let her fill in the finer points of that distinction."

Tamsin spent the next ten minutes giving Triple the down-and-dirty version of the Keeper and the issue they currently faced—a rapidly approaching war with the Black Faction. When she took a breath, Triple said, "I can understand why you wouldn't share that with anyone. It sounds a little more than crazy and probably a lot crazier that I believe you."

Pretty understanding, and Morrigan wasn't sure she'd have the same grace if put in his shoes.

Tamsin kept going. "It's more than my role as the Keeper. In the past, when we've come under attack, we move. We simply disappear and find another safe place. For hundreds and hundreds of years, the Keepers have moved to every possible location around the globe. I came here some years ago, and with gratitude, I've made a wonderful life."

"And you've been my friend for most of that time. You've seen me through some of the most difficult times in my journey and some of the best."

Tamsin nodded yet again. "I believe that's part of what brought me here."

Now Morrigan felt lost. Often the warriors sent to protect the Keepers determined their new locations. As a matter of course, Morrigan had already established a location for Tamsin far from this place. She'd been setting it up since she took over the job from her mother. Not to mention that her mother might have brought Tamsin here, though they never talked specifics. The Keeper's identity was always kept close to the vest, as the old saying went, and several of them were at the ready to protect the Keeper at a moment's notice.

"You're saying my mother, or whoever relocated you to this farm, thought the Prophecy would come to fruition here?" Morrigan had a lot of trouble buying into that concept. No way her mother would have taken it upon herself to make that kind of call.

Triple furrowed his brow and looked from face to face. "Wait, your mother? You guys are all over the map here, and you're losing me."

"My mother was a protector, just like me. I took over once we lost her. She could have brought the Keeper here. Brought Tamsin here."

Tamsin leaned forward across the table. "It *was* your mother, and I knew only that Molly's daughter would come for me someday. It always happens. No matter what we do, no matter how powerful our magic, the Black Faction finds us. Their drive to get their hands on the *Book of Darkness* has no bounds. It's Morrigan's family and others like her that keep us and our secrets safe."

Triple still looked confused. "Okay, so say that's all true. What's different this time?"

"Nothing as far as I'm concerned." Morrigan might as well be honest. Maybe she could recruit him to her side. Turn the tide here before it became too late. If it wasn't already.

"Everything is different this time." Tamsin gave her a pointed look. "You're part of it." She held up her hand when Morrigan opened her mouth to argue. "You are, and you know it in your heart. More than that, the Prophecy points to you as well." She nodded toward Triple. "You heard the words. His true self revealed."

The words hung in the air for a moment. "My transition." A light started to come into his eyes. "The heart of a lion."

Tamsin slapped her hand on the table. "Yes! See, Morrigan, I told you we needed him. He's part of it, and it's all coming together. We don't run. We make a stand. We stop them."

Triple smiled. "Has any Keeper before you ever stayed and taken a stand?"

She answered before Tamsin could. "Yes."

"What happened?"

This time she looked to Tamsin. Let her answer this one.

"She was slaughtered."

Morrigan figured that was it. The rug had just been pulled out from under Tamsin's feet.

But Triple slapped the table. "Count me in, mofos! Let's take these bastards down."

❖

Somewhere outside of Cheyenne a gut punch hit Freddi. Her hands flew to her midsection. "No!"

"What's up, man?" Ian glanced over at her, a rare moment when he took his eyes off the road. For at least two hundred miles, they'd been silent, and it had been a great two hundred miles.

The source of the punch wasn't a mystery. "Power. The bitch is harnessing power. We don't have the time to go pick up that prick, Aldo. She's already ahead of us and gaining more distance by the minute."

"Freddi, dude, I feel ya, but here's the thing. We don't have a choice. Abba gave the order direct. She'll crush us both if we defy her, and I, for one, don't want to go there."

"You're probably right." She hated that he had a valid point.

"Damn straight, I'm right. I've spent the last eighteen months with those two, and trust me. They're fucked up. I tell ya, I think they're sleeping together."

She snapped her gaze to his face. "What?"

"Oh, yeah. I saw him sneaking out of her room one night, real late, with just a towel wrapped around him. What would that say to you?" He shivered as if the thought made him uncomfortable.

"That's sick." She might be a lot of things, but into a sibling, never. Beyond being creepy, it made for bad magic. On the other hand, it might just be the Achilles heel she'd been searching for. She'd tuck that little bit of information into a back pocket just in case.

"Not surprising though, is it?" She heard the smile in his words.

"No." She turned her gaze back to the landscape whizzing by the window at eighty miles per hour. Thankfully she had no problem killing people when they got in her way or refused to see the world as she did. Aldo had crossed the lines she'd drawn in the sand one too many times. What Ian shared with her only added to Aldo's sins. All the more reason to end this charade and his waste of space.

Silence dropped down on them again, and she embraced it. Though she would never admit it, the quiet time in the car helped with healing. She could feel the changes occurring within her body, the aches and pains subsiding, the throbbing in her fingers almost gone. Good. The sooner she returned to full strength, the better.

She shifted her focus once more to eliminating the complications holding her back. She glanced over at Ian again, intent on the road. Did his thoughts align with hers? How to make Aldo's death slow and painful. As much as she wanted to get to the Keeper and secure that grimoire, the thought of putting Aldo through hell first held its own special appeal. Besides, his edict had given them no choice but to detour toward him.

"I'm really quite skilled with fire." She broke the silence.

He answered as though they'd been chatting all along. "I know."

"You know?"

A bit of a smile turned up the corners of his mouth. "I'm sure Aldo didn't tell you that I asked to be the one to come to you."

He had her undivided attention now. "Why?"

Now he turned and glanced at her. The spark in his eyes couldn't be hidden. "You're a bit of a legend."

"You didn't hear that from Aldo." Pain in the ass would be the first words he'd use to describe her. Bitch would come second.

Ian laughed. "No way. I only talk to the guy when I have to. No, dude, it's everyone else who talks about you. I can't believe you don't know what people think. You rock. More than that, you're the future, and I want to be there with you when you take it. Abba and Aldo are old news."

"What are you talking about?" She'd been very careful and kept her agenda to herself. She'd shared her intentions with no one.

"You never noticed me. Not when we were young and training at the camps. Not when we were called by Abba into service. I noticed you from the very first day, and I've watched you ever since. I'm not the only one. I'm just the best one."

A chill slid down her spine. How could she have failed to notice a stalker? How had she so underestimated Ian? "That's fucked up, you know."

"Maybe. Or maybe it took the right moment for you to see me and to understand that I'm the backup you didn't realize you needed."

"I don't need anyone." Truth.

He turned again and glanced at the splinted fingers. "Really?"

At that moment, a pain shot through her as if to remind her that she'd rolled a car and wasn't exactly at the top of her game. Healing, yes. One hundred percent? Not quite. "Maybe some assistance wouldn't be a bad thing."

"I'll take it. Now, let's brainstorm on how we get the drop on Aldo."

"I say we think bigger." A new idea started to take hold, and she liked it.

"Bigger?"

"Yes, a lot bigger."

"Do tell."

She put a hand on his shoulder. "We drop Aldo, and then we drop Abba."

"Fucking A."

CHAPTER FIFTEEN

A s much as she wanted to clap, Tamsin kept her hands on the table. It would be rude to celebrate a victory that Morrigan didn't share. That Triple jumped on board was enough to buoy her. Every molecule of air pressed against her, and it felt right. Further proof that she traveled the right path. Those confirmations kept coming.

She wished Morrigan didn't radiate continued skepticism. Confidence roiled inside her, and she wanted Morrigan to be there with her. In her head, she'd gone over the Prophecy at least a thousand times, and everything pointed to this scenario as her destiny. How could it be anything else? The connection between her and Morrigan. The ink. Holly. Triple. It all tracked right to those ancient words.

She turned the tea kettle on and waited for the water to boil. The coffee the other two drank didn't resonate with her. Once in a while, okay, not when she needed to be at full strength. "The team is complete. Now, we just need to get Holly back here."

Morrigan's expression darkened. "Did you forget to mention that she plans to bring her grandmother? Where does she fit into the Prophecy? I didn't read anything about a grandmother in there. I'm quite sure you didn't either."

She'd already mentally worked that out. "Holly and her grandmother are a package deal. Together they are stronger than alone, and we need that level of strength." Sounded good when she said it out loud.

"No, not buying it. What we need to do is haul ass out of here." Morrigan drifted back to her original stance.

Tamsin wasn't about to lose ground. Not at this point. They'd come too far. "You know you can say that a million times, and it won't change my mind." The truth as she saw it. She planned to dig her heels into said ground.

Morrigan shook her head. "I'm getting the sense of it, yes, and back atcha. Doesn't mean I'll stop trying either."

She could deal with truth and all the cards laid out on the table. "Understood. Now first things first. Let's make a formal plan."

Morrigan sighed, and it sounded of resignation. "You better call Holly."

"I think we're gonna need more coffee. That's my vote." Triple got up and headed to the coffeemaker. "So," he said as he filled the carafe with water. "Tell me what happens if this Black Faction gets their hands on the *Book of Darkness*. I'm getting the sense it'll be more than just bad."

Morrigan beat her to an answer. "You know this world you live in where you have the freedom to live your true life and most of the time good triumphs over evil?"

"Good typically does kick evil's ass. Or I'd like to believe it does, even though I've had to endure more than my share of bad behavior just because of how I'm living my true life."

Tamsin jumped in. "Take the number of bad days you've had and multiply them by a couple thousand, and that's how it'll go down if they get their hands on the grimoire. It will be ugly beyond comprehension."

"Grimoire?" The coffee brewed, he took a full mug back to the table and sat down.

"The *Book of Darkness* is a grimoire or, in simple terms, a book of spells. Only in this particular instance, it was created by compiling every piece of black magic into one book. If a witch with enough power gets their hands on it, they will be able to push out all the goodness in the world and replace it with darkness, as well as gain an ability to harness absolute power."

Triple squinted. "That seems far-fetched. That's an awful lot of bad ju-ju in one place."

Tamsin didn't employ magic in front of regulars. Though people often said her soaps and lotions were magic, she made them the old-fashioned way. Plain hard work. That she had a talent for making excellent natural products only spoke to the skills she'd spent years developing. Her true magic she kept close because most didn't want to know about witches and, more important, because she would do anything to avoid leaving a trail that could lead the Black Faction to her.

Best intentions aside, it happened anyway, and she supposed, no matter what precautions she employed, it always would. A dreadful cat-and-mouse game that had been going on for centuries, which made for all the more reason to bring it to an end. First, though, all the players needed to be on board. She stood, closed her eyes, and held out her hands. Her magic took Triple's chair into the air with him still sitting in it and, while she couldn't see him, undoubtedly trying not to spill the coffee he held. Her hands at head level, she allowed it to hover a good five feet off the ground.

Without opening her eyes or lowering her hands, she asked, "Does this seem far-fetched?"

"Point taken. Can you put me down now? I'd rather not wear this cup of coffee, if you know what I mean."

❖

Morrigan caught herself right before she burst out laughing. Tamsin's most decided bent toward the dramatic amused her. Most effective too. Triple's questioning of the power behind the *Book of Darkness* evaporated at the display of magic. Tamsin made a perfect choice when she ditched words and explanations. Sometimes, seeing spurred unconditional believing, and if he was to be part of this, he had to believe. No questions.

The thump of the chair legs against the floor signaled the end of the lesson. Mission accomplished, judging by the look on Triple's face. "Okay, okay. Maybe you aren't full of shit. What next?" He set the coffee cup on the table and stood, stepping away from the chair, as if afraid Tamsin would raise him off the floor again.

Tamsin held up her phone. "I'm calling Holly."

Time to take care of her bit of business, given she wasn't about to change Tamsin's mind on leaving, or anything for that matter. "I need to make some calls too." She started to step outside as she pulled her phone out of her pocket. Because she hadn't wanted to share Tamsin's reluctance to go the normal course, she hadn't reported in since she'd arrived. It wouldn't go over well at all. Postponing the news about the stay-and-fight plan had reached its end. The text messages could be ignored only so long before someone up the chain called her on it. Tick tock. Tick tock.

"Don't." Tamsin raced to her and put a hand on her arm. It tingled where her fingers touched her skin.

The pressure of Tamsin's touch made her pause and glance down at her phone, the number on her screen glowing red. Push to connect. That's all she had to do. "I've got to. They have to know."

"No, they don't. You realize as well as I do, they'll send in someone to stop us. They won't approve of my plan, and it's important we do this my way. Please, please don't make the call." Her fingers were warm against Morrigan's skin.

Tamsin wasn't wrong about what would happen once she reported in. The cavalry would arrive quickly. "They could help us." The upside, in her opinion.

"They won't."

Again, not exactly wrong. The downside. "I don't know." How many rogue missions had a positive end result? She couldn't think of even one.

"Please."

Triple got in on the pressure campaign. "I'm with Tamsin. You guys sucked me in, and now I want to see this play out. I'm really interested in finding out how I fit into this save-the-world-from-evil thing. Not that I needed validation for the decisions I've made about my life, but hey. It doesn't hurt either to find out my decision to transition helped keep the world safe. That would be sweet. You know?"

"See." Tamsin looked pointedly at Morrigan. "Triple gets it. Say you'll give me a little more time. If it doesn't come together by the end of the week, then make your calls and let them send in their reinforcements. Just a little time first, that's all I'm asking."

The end of the week? Tamsin had to be freaking kidding. She opened her mouth to shut her down. Nothing came out. Those eyes boring into her sent tremors through every nerve. Damn it anyway. When this woman looked at her like she could see her soul, it made her want to do anything and everything to make her happy. Not cool. At least not under these circumstances. In another place and time, it might be very cool indeed.

"Okay. I'll wait until the end of the week. I can't guarantee they won't call me and push for progress." She couldn't believe she'd just said that.

A ghost of a smile flitted across Tamsin's face, and she shrugged. "Easy enough to solve. Don't answer your phone."

"You make it all sound so easy."

"It is that easy." Tamsin's expression remained earnest.

"Hey, all." Holly breezed into the kitchen, an older woman, Morrigan assumed had to be her grandmother, right behind her. "What's shakin'?"

"How did you get here so fast?" Tamsin had called her what? Ten minutes ago? Maybe Morrigan underestimated the woman's magical abilities.

Holly waved a hand in the air. "We were already on the way when I got Tamsin's call. No grass growing under my feet, you know."

Tamsin left Morrigan at the back door and went over to hug the older woman. "Thank you for helping." Then she turned back to Morrigan. "Grace, this is Morrigan. She's a White Faction witch sent to protect me. Morrigan, this is Grace Two Wolf, healer extraordinaire and straight-up amazing woman."

Grace took Tamsin's face between her hands. "You darling girl. Thank you, and from what Holly has shared with me, this is the kind of fight I've been preparing for all my life. I've seen enough darkness and evil in my lifetime that I'm more than ready to take a stand and kick some ass. I am here for you."

Morrigan turned away from the back door and took a couple steps back into the kitchen. The second Grace had entered the room, the air changed. Not hard to understand Tamsin's draw to her. Every bit of energy rolling off her screamed of bright light and power. Grudgingly she admitted to herself that she might just hold the kind of magic they would need in the battle ahead, even if the woman appeared to be well into her seventh decade. Age wasn't a factor with Grace. This kind of power didn't bend to the passing of years. In fact, in her experience, it only grew stronger.

Morrigan reached out and took her hand. "So happy to meet you, and thank you for joining the fight. We need all the help we can get." She had to stop saying that stuff. It would give Tamsin the wrong idea.

Grace took a seat at the table and looked over at Triple. "Son, nice to see you again."

Triple smiled, and the warmth he directed at Grace told Morrigan everything she needed to know. "Always a delight to see you, and I'm ready to kick ass too. Ladies, the plan?"

❖

Aldo waited outside the main entrance of the hotel in Grand Junction as Ian pulled the car under the portico. Further proof of his incompetence when it came to the mission. He hadn't been close to either Denver or the Red Rocks. Freddi's hand had long since stopped throbbing, which allowed her to turn her thoughts to their plan. More her plan because, while Ian would prove to be useful, it all revolved around her. To consider sharing the power that would come once she had her hands on the *Book of Darkness* didn't factor into any of her objectives. Only one could sit on that throne, so to speak.

While it would be fun to watch Aldo explode if she refused to relinquish the front seat to him, she immediately got out and moved to the back. Better to put some space between them. She didn't want his toxic energy messing with hers. No dilution of her carefully cultivated aura. She'd spent too much time getting to this point in her life to have it diminished in any way, especially by someone as objectionable as him.

"About damn time you got here. What took you so long?" Tall and lean, with perfect hair, Aldo dropped into the passenger seat. Surprised her that he didn't wait for one of them to open the door for him. His highness must be in more of a hurry than she'd thought.

Freddi didn't give Ian time to respond. "Speed limits." Probably better not to fuck with him. Naw, always better to do it. More fun in any event. He hated when anybody challenged him in any way, regardless of how big or small.

He slipped on his expensive sunglasses and waved toward the window. Ian clearly understood that to mean move, and he put the car in gear. "Always a smart-ass. I don't know what Abba sees in you." He didn't look at her, though his comment clearly directed to her.

"She sees what's there. A competent master." Another little dig. Abba got her, at least on some level.

"I prefer to stick with smart-ass." It would kill him to give even an inch.

"The two are not incompatible."

Aldo said too loudly, "Just drive the fucking car."

Ian glanced back at her. "Which direction?"

The pull had grown weaker as they'd moved south. She wanted to get another charge to make sure they were headed toward the Keeper. "Leave this place and find a mountain or a hill or something that puts me closer to the sky."

"What are you trying to do? I thought you assured Abba you had some great plan and knew where to find the Keeper. Another one of your lies designed to keep yourself in good graces with Abba, I suppose. I keep telling her you're full of shit." Aldo threw a disgusted look her way.

She resisted slapping him with her good hand. The venom in his voice summed up their relationship. He didn't bother to even try to hide his dislike. *Well, back at you, buddy.* She kept her voice even. "I'll be able to narrow down her location. I don't want to make our trip any longer than it's already been." Dig number three. She could do this all day.

Aldo didn't bother to respond. He just waved a hand at Ian like the lord and master he wanted to be, though never would. Despite his own opinion of himself, he lacked the skills to be able to divine what lay in store for him. Ian drove away from the hotel.

An hour later, she directed him to stop. A decent hill lay just off the freeway, and with the day starting to wane, she liked the way the late-afternoon sun struck the rise. Perfect for what she had in mind.

"This is an unnecessary waste of time." Her guess? Aldo didn't like not being the one to make all the calls. If he understood what would happen in the next few minutes, he'd be even less impressed. In this case, he didn't need to know. The name of her game: surprise.

"It won't take long," Freddi promised, and one she'd make good on soon. At least a dozen times, she'd rolled the idea over in her mind, satisfied it would work to perfection. She tapped on Aldo's window. "Come and give me a hand. Quicker that way."

He scowled but got out. "Fine. I can tell you'll avoid our real mission until you do whatever it is you want to do. You've always been such a pain in the ass."

The child in her wanted to scream, "Takes one to know one." The mature adult in her kept her mouth shut. Just get it over with, and they could, indeed, be on their way. A little lighter and a lot faster. Ian's eyes sparkled in a way that let her know he'd caught on to her plan, even though she'd not shared it with him. A good partner in that sense. He picked up on the vibes and, most important, kept his mouth shut.

At the top, the hill leveled out to a broad grassy area, and she spotted enough rocks to make the requisite circle. Grumbling, Aldo helped her with the stones. No doubt, his idea of getting it done quickly so they could all leave. All the better. Freddi also worked to give the impression that she wanted to make this quick. Her palms itched with the desire to get her hands on the *Book of Darkness*. Her heart sang for the power that would soon be hers.

With the magic circle completed, she stood and surveyed the setting. Already the wind swirled as if in anticipation of what would occur inside the rocks. Perfect. That the universe had tuned in demonstrated the righteousness of her course. Not that she really required validation. She knew exactly how much was owed to her.

Her entire life, she'd been under the thumb of Abba and Aldo, and now her time for freedom had arrived. No longer would she bow to either of them, and all who once served them would kneel at her feet. She could hardly wait.

"Help me for a moment," she said to Aldo.

"What?" He stepped into the circle.

"I just need your boost while I do this."

"Whatever, but make it fast. We need to get back on the road and not deal with your stupid shit."

She'd make it fast all right. Raising her hands to the sky, she began. "Oh, Goddess, we fly to power. That which works against us bring into the darkness evermore. Mother of all that has been, all that is, and all that shall be, bring forth the fire and let the ash be driven before the wind. By your divine blessing, so it shall be."

Before Aldo could react, Freddi stepped outside of the circle, putting distance between her and the stones. A whoosh filled the air.

"You bitch!" Aldo dropped to his knees as flames flashed high into the sky, all contained inside the circle. In a matter of seconds, the conflagration obliterated Aldo, and his screams died as they were carried away on the breeze. The flash fire faded as quickly as it had roared to life, and only a pile of ash remained once the air cleared.

She stepped forward and kicked the rocks out of formation, then turned to Ian with a big smile. "One down."

His smile was equally as bright. "One to go."

CHAPTER SIXTEEN

The day dragged, at least for Tamsin. Not that she could complain. Before she left, Grace had walked a full circle of the property imparting protection. The first day Tamsin spent here, she'd placed a guardian spell on the entire farm, buildings, land, and livestock. To have Grace layer on yet more fortification gave her a level of comfort she hadn't realized she needed, not that she'd admit it to Morrigan. She'd take that admission from Tamsin and run with it.

After Grace completed her work, she declared that nothing more could happen until sunset. Tamsin wasn't sure she agreed with that prediction. Now that all the players were in place, she believed they were more than ready to stand and fight. Grace rained on that particular parade. No, more like she turned a hurricane on it with her firm stand-down declaration. As much as she'd wanted to argue, she didn't. While Tamsin might be an incredibly powerful witch, she remained a transplant to this land. That wasn't true of Grace. Her family had been on these lands since the beginning. How could she argue with someone whose roots ran that deep?

A simple answer: she didn't. If Grace said they needed to wait to go further until the sun set, then that's exactly what they'd do, even if it sucked. Each time she'd pushed Morrigan to stay and fight, she'd been prepared to do that. Fight. To make her case in a manner hard to argue with. Way different when it came to Grace. This hurry-up-and-wait thing hadn't been on her radar at all. No idea how to oppose her, and the respect she had for her caused Tamsin to do as instructed and stand down. Grace and Holly left, vowing to return by sunset, and she had to find a way to be content with that.

Triple had taken the opportunity to run home and see to a bit of his own business. She couldn't impose on him to hang around waiting for whatever his role would turn out to be. How she'd wanted to ask him to stay here. But she didn't and, instead, opted to keep her mouth shut. His promise to return in a few hours had to be enough. A man of his word, he'd be back before the sun set. He'd never let her down before. No reason to believe he would tonight.

That left her alone in the house with Morrigan, which sent a flurry of flutters through her stomach. Why did she smile every time she thought about Morrigan? She hadn't been this intrigued by another woman since she'd been seventeen and met Eleanor Hampton. Her arrival had turned the senior year of high school into quite an event, and to this day, it still made her smile. When it ended, as first love tended to do, she'd experienced deep heartbreak. Her heart eventually healed, as everyone predicted it would, and now she held the good memories close. She often thought of Eleanor and wondered how her life turned out. Had she moved away? Gotten married? Had a child or two? Someday she might look her up, though a good thousand miles stood between her and their old high school.

Maybe it explained why this draw to Morrigan made her breath catch. It reminded her of Eleanor and how she'd felt way back when. Excited and eager for their time together, mixed with the anticipation of learning more about desire and love. Since her early intense crush, she'd experienced only the kind of desire that resulted in a one-and-done relationship. Quick and satisfying, without any emotional investment. No getting to know someone beyond a few hours of fun. The strategy had been working for a long time, except now the universe seemed to whisper in her ear: buckle up.

She managed to move through the normal motions of the day on a sort of autopilot, tending animals and filling the latest orders.

Morrigan's expression as she'd helped package and label boxes of soap said she didn't believe it made sense to bother with something soon to be left behind. The words remained unsaid even as she nudged Morrigan into becoming her assistant.

By the time Holly's car pulled back up to the house, they'd completed all the outgoing orders and were sitting on the porch watching the sun begin its descent over the mountains. "Hey," she said as Holly and Grace approached them, a big bag slung over Grace's shoulder.

"Has our young man returned?" Grace grabbed the railing with one hand while continuing to hold the strap of the bag in the other. Holly offered to carry it for her, the offer firmly declined.

Tamsin did expect to see Triple any moment. Sunset had been the agreed-upon time, and the energies in the world around them appeared to have them all in sync. Another sign that she wasn't wrong about how to handle this situation. The energy that filled her made her almost giddy. Perhaps it came from the generations of women before her, including her own mother and grandmother, who'd been forced to flee, never having the chance to put down real roots. No more.

"He's on his way."

"Did he call?" Morrigan looked confused. Not that she blamed her. Tamsin's phone hadn't made a peep all day.

"No." She shook her head and smiled. "I just know he's on his way. You know, witch and all."

❖

Why did that look on Tamsin's face make Morrigan want to kiss her long and passionately? Her superiors would be hard-pressed to understand how she'd gotten into this predicament. Never been her style to lose it over a woman so quickly. Nobody would argue that she'd had her share of relationships, only that typically, she hung out with a woman for a few months and called it good. That's how she rolled, because her duties in life didn't give her a whole bunch of other options. She might even live with a woman for a bit, like Ginny, and then it would end. She'd walk away and get on with it, never looking back. Some might see it as cold. She viewed it as necessary. She glanced over at Tamsin and flinched at the thought of walking away.

When she'd first come here, the mission had been clear. Get the Keeper and move her to safety before the Black Faction Witch Finders could arrive. Protect the Keeper and the *Book of Darkness* at all costs. The only count she hadn't failed on was getting to the Keeper. Moving her to safety: fail. Falling for the Keeper: major fail. The Black Faction arrival: imminent.

The White Faction leadership would pull her in a nanosecond if they had even a hint of what she felt for Tamsin and what soon would happen here. All her life she'd trained for this job, and now, instead of falling back on her lessons, she put everything in jeopardy to make this woman happy. Could it be because she knew it to be the right thing to do? Or because her attraction overrode good sense? She gazed at Tamsin's face, and her heart did a little thump. She'd go with the former and ignore the little voice screaming, liar.

"There he is." The rumble of a powerful motorcycle engine coming down the long driveway reached her even though he couldn't be seen yet. She knew the sound of a good bike when she heard it.

"Good." Grace opened the door and headed into the house without looking behind her. Did she instinctively know Triple rode the bike toward the garage, or did she trust Morrigan?

As soon as Triple came up the steps after parking his bike, the rest of them followed Grace inside. They found her in the kitchen at the table, holding her bag in both hands. What in the world did she hold so tight?

"Sit," Grace directed them.

The tone in her voice commanded obedience. Her words didn't compel Morrigan to sit, but something about the older woman made her want to comply. Respect for one's elder, certainly. Respect for her power and knowledge, without a doubt.

"I have asked for guidance from the old ones, and they have given it." She pulled the bag closer to her body.

"What did they tell you?" Tamsin had her hands folded on the table as she leaned toward Grace.

The draw wasn't limited to Tamsin. Morrigan leaned in as well. Did Triple—the wildcard in this group, the one regular—feel the same way? Yet not quite so regular when they got right down to it. He possessed a strength of character that gave him his own brand of magic. Something of a pattern began to show itself to her, and it made her feel a little less guilty about not reporting this situation to her superiors.

Grace tapped the top of her bag. "The old ones showed me the stones."

"The Prophecy speaks of the stones." Tamsin's eyes were bright.

Grace nodded and smiled. "It is written in the stars."

"There are an awful lot of rocks around this place." She might not be from around here, but she'd taken a good look at everything as she'd driven in. Coming into Spokane from the west, she'd seen plenty of basalt rock formations, and the mountains that surrounded the area, well, hello, rocks. How in the world would they narrow it down to the right stones?

Grace smiled. "Patience, my friends. When it is time, all will be revealed."

Morrigan would like to say that those words filled her with confidence. If anything, it would be a healthy dose of dismay. Ambiguity wasn't helpful under the circumstances. They were already on borrowed time, and every moment they wasted on unclear action or direction put them in danger. Put Tamsin in danger.

Tamsin nodded while Morrigan stood and rested her hands on the table. "That's not working for me. We need more." Someone had to be the voice of reason, and in this group, it clearly fell to her.

Grace's calm expression didn't change. "It is what it is."

Not buying it. "As my mother would have said, hell no."

"We wait." Grace stared at her not blinking, not backing down, despite that the younger, stronger, and crankier woman towered over her.

"We don't." Morrigan caved and looked away from Grace's intense eyes as she glanced out the window, where the sun began its descent and a fog rolled in like an ominous warning that screamed: beware. She took it to heart, gathered her conviction, and looked back at Grace. The universe wasn't in sync with the suggestion either.

Grace finally released her hold on the bag and folded her hands on the table as she continued to stare, unblinking, at Morrigan. Nice try. If she thought it would intimidate her, she'd be mistaken. No one who grew up training under her mother could be intimidated by pretty much anybody. She squared her shoulders.

Tamsin must have felt the approaching battle. "A little time won't hurt. It's all coming together. I can feel it. You two need to relax."

Ganging up on her didn't work either. "No, it's not, and we're damned well not sitting around doing nothing. I've gone along with all this hurry-up-and-wait shit, and I'm telling you I'm done. Inaction isn't cutting it." Her voice rose, echoing the frustration that filled her. Why they couldn't see and feel the urgency whizzed by her.

Her gaze once more slid to Grace, who smiled as she tapped her mystery bag.

❖

Freddi had to tamp down the giddiness. Not necessary for Ian to get even a hint of how happy Aldo's demise made her. He said all the right words, yet she'd been around long enough to learn truth could be tenuous at best. The only person she'd ever fully trusted in life had been herself. Everyone else had let her down in some way or another, especially her older sister. The haughty bitch had never missed an opportunity to let Freddi know she didn't measure up. Not as a daughter, a sister, or a witch.

She shifted her gaze to Ian, who focused on the road, his eyes hidden by dark glasses, and his long, black hair pulled back in a ponytail. His looks were a key piece of his power and would have helped him gain favor with Aldo. That creep did love his handsome young men. Or, rather, that creep *had loved* his handsome young men. She smiled.

"What's so funny?"

Interesting that he caught her glee even though he hadn't turned his head. "Gloating a little bit." There were moments when honesty didn't hurt.

"Gotta tell you, Boss, that was impressive. You've got some mad skills, and it was fun to watch you use them. He never saw it coming. Arrogant sonofabitch."

"Skills alone wouldn't have been enough. I used straight-up witchcraft. My family goes back for more generations than you can count, and we've earned every ounce of magic I possess." She neglected to mention the theft from other witches. Wasn't necessary to share everything with him. Let him think she'd been born with it all. Besides, the way she saw it, what she stole belonged to her just as much as what she'd inherited.

"Whatever it is, I'm jealous. Any pointers you can throw my way, do it, man. I'd like to be a tenth of what you are."

She just bet he did. This time, she suppressed the smile because, as he'd discover down the road, she fully planned to throw magic his direction. Not in the way he hoped, but it would be coming nonetheless.

As she curled her fingers around the obsidian stone she'd ripped from around Aldo's neck, no pain flowed through her. Large and smooth, it vibrated against her fingers. Energy streamed into her, strong and warm, and powerful enough to nearly complete the healing process. If Ian weren't here, she'd be more than capable of driving herself. The mending had progressed even faster than she'd imagined. Good. When they confronted the Keeper, she'd need to be at a hundred and fifty percent. Not too far left to go.

"So." Ian glanced her way. "What did you see when you dispatched our fearless leader?"

"You mean not-so-fearless and definitely not our leader."

"Yup, that guy." Ian laughed.

She studied him and decided she could do him. Boy-toy handsome, he'd probably be an enthusiastic lover. A combination of magic and the rush from an orgasm could be exactly the medicine the witch doctor ordered.

The only question? How much to tell him? She liked to keep her cards close to the vest. As much as the Black Faction believed her to be one of their most dedicated and loyal warriors, they were as clueless as Ian. Mom's number-one lesson: look out for yourself. She'd been doing that since her first day, and she didn't intend to stop now.

She leaned her head back and closed her eyes. For just a moment when Aldo had ignited, the face almost materialized for her. So damned close and yet so far away. The urge to reach into the flames and grab hold had been intense. Now she wondered if holding back might have been a major mistake. The ache in her jaw reminded her to unclench her teeth, breathe through the frustration, and think. "I have a solid sense of direction."

"Already got that. You've been giving me a roadmap since I picked you up."

"I had a vague idea of where we were to go when you picked me up. Now, it's more like a pin on a map. Never heard of the place before, but it's right. I know it. I think Aldo's barbeque gave us the edge we needed."

"Go north isn't exactly a pin on a map."

Perhaps a little sharper than she'd given Ian credit for. "I'm still thinking through the signs. I've grabbed a lot of power from both black and white factions. I need more to pinpoint."

"More than Aldo?" He snapped a look at her.

Definitely more than Aldo, even though she'd thought it would be enough to steal his considerable abilities. That it hadn't quite been enough had her thinking of another course—a potential windfall. "More than Aldo," she murmured almost to herself.

Ian laughed and pounded a hand on the steering wheel. "God damn, you are the boss." Now, she snapped her gaze to him, and he laughed harder. "What?"

He got the laughter under control. "Abba next."

"Yes."

Now he glanced at her and said, "Except, taking Abba out isn't your whole plan. You want to drain her dry. I can see it in your face." He started laughing again

She joined in his laughter. Good boy. "If you want to be on the top, you have to take it all."

"I only got one question."

"Go for it."

"Before or after we kill the Keeper?"

CHAPTER SEVENTEEN

Regardless of how confident Tamsin felt about how to deal with the Black Faction threat, Morrigan's expression worried her. They were losing her, and that wasn't good. Once everyone assembled here, the rightness of their decision rushed over her. Confirmation at a level that went right to her soul. Not so, it appeared, for Morrigan.

"Walk with me." She held out her hand to Morrigan, who shook her head. "Please."

Blowing out a breath, Morrigan shrugged. "Fine. It won't change anything."

"Humor me for a few minutes. I am the Keeper, after all."

"That's the card you want to play?"

"Whatever it takes."

Grace winked at her. She sure did like that woman. She winked back and motioned for Morrigan to follow her out the back door. Instead of taking the path to the workshop, she headed toward the trees. The stepping-stones ended at the edge of the grass. She stopped there and once again held out her hand to Morrigan. She expected resistance, but instead, this time she took her hand, warmth spreading through her when their fingers clasped together.

"You're not changing my mind." Morrigan stared into the distance.

Tamsin only wanted her to feel what she did. "Let's just walk for a moment. There's music in the earth and songs on the wind, if only we take the time to listen."

"We don't need music." Morrigan's words were soft.

Tamsin smiled and started walking once more. She followed a deer path through the trees, and soon, the trees gave way to soft wild grasses and the sound of water lapping against the rocks on the shoreline. Near the water's edge she turned to Morrigan, released her hand, and ran her fingers across her cheek. "We can't run anymore."

Morrigan moved away from her touch, and it hurt a little. Actually, a lot. Blue eyes held Tamsin's. "We have to be real, and the reality is, we can't afford not to run. This isn't a game where failure results in nothing more than a lesson. The consequences would be catastrophic. Tell me you're willing to risk that."

Tears welled in her eyes, which was the last thing she wanted to happen. To stay strong in the face of Morrigan's resistance couldn't be more important. "Generation after generation of my foremothers were forced from their homes and the lives they built. The dark forces pushed them away from people and places they loved. I believe deep inside of me that the Prophecy is showing us that it's meant for me. I'm the one to see it through and protect the world once and for all from the evil within the *Book of Darkness*." She tapped her hand against her chest.

"You're killing me." Morrigan's gaze softened.

Tamsin cradled Morrigan's face in her hands. This time she didn't move away from her touch. "The last thing I want to do is kill you."

Morrigan put her hands over Tamsin's. "What is this thing?"

The question had nothing to do with the Prophecy. She shook her head slightly. No explanation came to her, only a cascade of emotions and sensations, none of them unpleasant. "I don't know. I've never felt like this before."

"I haven't either, and now isn't the time for something of this caliber."

She moved closer. "Born of fire."

"Forged in flames," Morrigan whispered.

Tamsin leaned near and kissed her, lightly at first. Morrigan returned the gentle kiss. Tamsin pressed closer, her tongue teasing

Morrigan's parted lips. Hard to breathe. Harder to pull away. Morrigan's hands came up to cup the back of Tamsin's head. Definitely not pulling away anymore.

Heat rose in Tamsin. More than heat, a rush of power. She kissed Morrigan harder. The power grew. Morrigan abruptly broke the kiss, jumped back, and stared.

"What the fuck just happened?"

She'd liked to give Morrigan a reasonable answer, if she had one. The only truth she could offer, her attraction to Morrigan overwhelmed her, and through mere instinct, she acted upon it. Each time she'd touched her, every ounce of magic she'd been born with, as well as developed, went into overdrive. It became too much, and she'd had to kiss her, creating the supercharged rush of magic. Yet another sign that she'd chosen the appropriate path.

"The universe confirming our jobs." That sounded pretty good, right?

"So not a kiss." Morrigan's eyes narrowed, the passion that had filled them a moment before sliding away, replaced by caution.

No need to come up with a lie. "Oh, most definitely a kiss, and I don't know about you, but I'm absolutely wanting to do that again. This." She waved back and forth between them. "Is more about joining together in bringing the white light to its height. About combining all that is good and kind to drive out evil."

"To protect the *Book of Darkness*."

She'd been thinking about that subject nonstop since Morrigan showed up, and she decided she finally had the answer. "To destroy it."

❖

What in the hell? Not one word thus far had been about destroying the grimoire. It hadn't factored into anything. Tamsin had been going on and on about stopping the Black Faction, and while Morrigan resisted her push, some of the arguments held enough merit that she could get on board with them. No one could argue against the need to end the trouble the Black Faction had been bringing into the world for too long. They could argue the timing.

The need to protect the *Book of Darkness* was imprinted deep in her DNA. Not once had anyone charted a course for its destruction. While she could stand and fight, destroying the grimoire must not happen. Really, it *couldn't*. An ancient spell of protection made destruction an impossibility. More than one witch had lost her life trying to turn it into dust.

At the back of her mind, a whisper lingered nonetheless. What if everything she'd been taught had missed something? Had been incomplete? She couldn't ignore the possibility, just like she couldn't ignore Tamsin. She could kiss her for hours and not want to stop. She'd never met anyone quite like her, and in a short amount of time, she'd wiggled her way into her heart. Morrigan wouldn't admit it out loud, but she could listen to Tamsin for a lifetime, which made her quest to save her even more important. It also cracked the door open for Tamsin's ideas to try to slip in.

Morrigan continued to try to make her case. "You know as well as I do that every single attempt to destroy the grimoire has ended badly, and we can't afford for anything to happen to you. Staying here is not worth your life."

Her eyes grew soft. "You care about me."

She could lie. She didn't. "Yes. You know it's more than that, though."

A shadow crossed Tamsin's face. "My successor."

Good. At least Tamsin hadn't forgotten the bigger picture. "Exactly, and that's another reason why I still believe we should get you to safety and abandon the stay-and-fight plan you're so intent on."

"A part of me agrees with you. It's a distinct risk because I have no daughter, and that's never happened in the history of the Keepers. I probably should have done something about that before now." A frown pulled down the corners of her mouth.

She didn't want to think about Tamsin married off to a man and creating a small family. She focused instead on their current situation. "If we go now, we have a chance to put some serious ground between us and the Witch Finder." Maybe Tamsin could finally see the wisdom in relocating.

Before she got the words completely out, Tamsin shook her head. "No. That's not what we're going to do."

"Oh, come on." Yeah, that sounded whiny. Didn't care. "What will it take to get you to see reason?"

"That's what you're not understanding. Everything I'm doing is based on reason."

Not any kind she could make sense of. "It's interpretation of an ancient prophecy that you're trying to make fit your desires."

"You can really say that after all the pieces have come together?"

"Coincidence." She didn't buy into coincidence.

Tamsin took her face between her hands. "Fate." She kissed her hard, and darkness fell.

❖

"I need a boost." Freddi took the tape and splints off her fingers. For a few seconds she flexed and straightened them. The mended bones were pain free. Most excellent. She smiled.

"What do you have in mind?" Ian glanced over at her.

Full function of her hand gave her a good idea. "First, you do me."

Even though he kept his eyes on the road, she could see the smile that crossed his face. "Can do." No hesitation.

She patted his shoulder. "Some fun first. Then we kill a white witch and steal her power."

"Only one?" Now he did turn and glance at her. "The more power, the better."

"I like the way you think."

"I have a great mentor."

More than great—the best. She didn't bother to correct him. "There." She pointed to a hotel just off the freeway, its bright sign advertising available rooms. Not quite her standard accommodations but not her biggest concern at the present time. "Let's take our break there."

Ian went into the little lobby and made the room arrangements while she waited in the car. Keycard in hand, he got back into the car, drove around the building, and parked in front of the bright-red door with the number 106 on it. "This is us," he said as he got out.

The moment the door to their room clicked shut, he spun into her, pressing his lips against hers, thrusting his tongue between her lips. She pushed away. "Not so fast, little boy."

"Little boy?" He grabbed his crotch. "You won't be calling me that when you see what I'm packing in here."

Why did men tie up their worth in the size of their dicks? Not one of their more redeeming features, in her book. They served a purpose, and a very entertaining one at that, just not the most important one. "We'll do this my way or not at all." Freddi stretched out on the bed, her back against the pillows, her arms behind her head. "Nice and slow, take off your clothes."

A glimmer came into his eyes, and if he'd been insulted by her clear demand of control, he didn't show it. After a little salute, he started to unbutton his shirt. "As you wish."

An hour later, she stepped into the shower. Like many of the hotels these days, the bathroom had only a walk-in unit. No tub. Okay with her. The cool water cascading over her body dissipated the heat Ian had stoked without diminishing any of the energy. He'd done exactly as she'd commanded, starting with his effective striptease. Much to her delight, he turned out to be quite skilled with his tongue. Once naked, she saw that he hadn't been wrong about what lay underneath the pants. Little boy did not describe him at all.

Step one to energy upsurge complete. Most people might want a warm shower after sex, but not Freddi. The cool water helped her think, and right now she needed to focus on finding the witch with the most magic in order to finish charging her batteries. No sense wasting time or effort if it didn't result in the maximum benefit.

Besides, going up against Abba wouldn't be an easy task. Freddi might be ambitious, or overly ambitious, according to some folks, her family included, but that didn't mean she barreled ahead without a perfect plan. Failure wasn't on her agenda.

As the water ran over her head, she closed her eyes and whispered a small spell. When she opened them again, she smiled and turned off the water. Towel wrapped around her, she stepped back into the other room. "Time to rise and shine, princess. We have to get back on the road."

Ian groaned and threw an arm over his eyes. "Can't you give a guy half an hour to recover? I need some beauty sleep."

"No time." She tossed his pants onto his head.

He rolled over and his feet hit the carpeted floor. "You're the boss."

At least he got it and didn't offer much in the way of resistance. "I am. Now move it. Daylight is burning."

He patted the bed. "You sure you don't want to give it one more go? Ten minutes and we'll leave here smiling."

"If you want to shower, I'd take that ten minutes to clean up and dress." Her mind was already somewhere else. He was a good fuck. Once.

"All right, all right. I'll clean up. I think the boss likes me shiny and sweet." His laughter followed him into the bathroom. He didn't shut the door.

He managed to shower, dress, and have them back on the road in under fifteen minutes. She could appreciate a guy that wash-and-wear. Could be she'd keep him around once she finished this quest. If he proved his loyalty, that is. No place for anyone in her new regime who didn't subscribe to her rule one hundred percent.

"Which way," he asked as he backed out of the parking spot.

While he'd been cleaning up, she'd been scrolling through records on a secure site only a few, like her, had access to. She'd found what she'd been looking for before he had his pants zipped up. "Jackson Hole, Wyoming."

"Seriously?"

"Have you noticed anything about me so far that would suggest I'm not serious?"

"Good point."

"Just drive."

"Why?"

"You'll see."

CHAPTER EIGHTEEN

The kiss hadn't been a ploy to get Morrigan on her side. Tamsin simply followed her instincts, and her desires, and damn it, she wasn't sorry. If it also helped keep Morrigan in sync with her, well, how could that be wrong?

It all sounded good in her head, and it felt even better. At least until Morrigan dropped, as her mother would have said, like a hot rock. At least she'd been able to catch her before she landed hard on the ground. She'd folded with her to the earth to cushion her fall. Bad enough she blacked out. Didn't need to add a concussion to the mix. Now she sat cradling Morrigan's head in her lap.

Curls lay damp against Morrigan's forehead, and Tamsin brushed them back. Her cool skin, a good sign. Whatever triggered the loss of consciousness, at least it wasn't fueled by fire. That it had been preceded by her kissing Morrigan didn't shine a very good light on her spontaneous acts of passion. First time she'd ever kissed a woman into oblivion. Couldn't say she wanted to do that again either. It scared her because Morrigan lay so still, her chest barely rising and falling.

As she stroked Morrigan's forehead, she wondered if her fear might be misplaced. As her fingers touched her skin, they tingled. Nothing normal about that and not something she'd ever encountered before, at least not until she'd met Morrigan. She pressed her lips against her forehead, and power rushed through her. "Grab the magic, beautiful," she whispered.

Morrigan's lashes fluttered, and suddenly, blue eyes stared up at her. "Well, that was fucking weird."

Tamsin couldn't help it. She laughed. "Try it from my side."

She blinked several times. "What did you do to me?"

It didn't escape Tamsin's notice that Morrigan hadn't tried to sit up and move her head from her lap. Okay by her. If the world wasn't in jeopardy, she could sit here a month or two. "I kissed you."

"Ah, yeah, you did. Do women usually faint when you kiss them?"

"You're the first."

"Lucky me."

She brushed her fingers across Morrigan's forehead. "Lucky you." After a kiss on her head, she asked, "What happened?"

Now Morrigan did sit up and shifted until she looked at Tamsin. Her eyes were bright and full of life, not dull or confused like she might expect after a blackout. "It's something about you and me."

That part she understood. "I feel it too."

"Beyond the attraction. I mean, neither one of us can deny the draw. It's more than that though. Like in the air and in the ground. Lightning that strikes all around us each time we touch. When a kiss sends me to another realm, we're talking about something I've never encountered before."

That, she wasn't expecting. That they were more powerful together didn't come as a shock. From the first moment they'd met, the difference made itself known, but that it would send Morrigan's spirit somewhere into the universe? A little shocking. "Tell me." It had to be important, or it wouldn't have happened. Random magic didn't just occur, especially to witches with their pedigree. They needed to figure out the underlying purpose so they could harness it and use it.

Morrigan blinked a couple of times and brushed away strands of stray hair from her face. "A woman is coming for you."

"Not a big revelation. I might not have seen her face in my vision, but I heard her voice. Definitely female. Besides, I'm expecting at least one Witch Finder, and since most are women, it's almost a given."

"Witch Finder, yeah, but she's different. Like the vision you experienced, I couldn't quite see her face, but I can tell you, her magic is strong and very dark."

"Black Faction, black magic. They go together." Another given in her book.

Morrigan put her hands on Tamsin's face, her gaze intense. "Listen to me. She's more than a run-of-the-mill Black Faction Witch Finder. Something's different, more frightening about her. We have to be ready, or I'm afraid she'll kick our collective asses."

"We will be ready." Tamsin had been waiting for this fight her whole life. Rather than fear, Morrigan's vision filled her with resolve. "We have help, we have white magic on our side, and we have all the pieces of the Prophecy falling into place. We can do this. We can take on this Witch Finder and beat her."

A shadow crossed Morrigan's face. "Maybe. I'm calling in help."

"We have help." They were already locked and loaded.

"White Faction kind of help."

"We have everyone and everything necessary right here."

"We need more."

"Trust me, Morrigan. I'm right about this. We don't need more."

Conflict showed in her face, and Tamsin readied for the coming fight. She could do this all day if she had to. Morrigan blew out a breath. "Damn you."

❖

Sometimes good strategy meant giving in. What she'd seen after the blackout kiss scared the crap out of her yet filled her with energy. A mental list of names of those with the necessary skill set to help formed in her head, and as soon as they got back to the house, she planned to call each one of them.

"No, no, no." Tamsin stood staring with her hands on her hips. Slim and haughty and beautiful. Maybe intimidating, too. Well, maybe to someone else. Wasn't working with Morrigan. The ability to stand up to this Keeper defined job one, and she'd figured that out fairly quickly.

"No what?" Not quite sure what Tamsin protested about now.

With her index finger to her temple, Tamsin raised her eyebrows. "I can almost hear your thoughts. You're planning to call in more warriors, and you're making a mental list about who to call. I'm saying no. Nobody else is needed for this to work. We have the platoon already assembled, and it's complete."

Yup, give it up. This beautiful, amazing woman wasn't about to be moved off what she believed to be right, and maybe time to consider a buy-in. Tamsin was the Keeper, after all, and that position didn't fall to someone too weak to carry the burden. Stubborn too. She'd been steadfast in her desire to stand and fight from the first minute Morrigan arrived. Kudos for being consistent. As much as she wanted to do this the old way, could Tamsin be right in her belief that real change might be past due? She stared into Tamsin's eyes and made a decision, one she could very easily come to regret.

"Okay. We do it your way." At least as far as not calling in White Faction reinforcements.

Tamsin didn't look convinced. "No more bucking all my ideas?"

"Can't guarantee I won't balk now and again, but I'm giving you the benefit of the doubt for the time being and will follow your lead."

Tamsin searched her face before she kissed her hard. This time, no stars, just a rush of warmth. "I'm starting to love you."

Before she could react to those five words, Tamsin had turned and started to jog toward the house. "Help me, Goddess," she muttered under her breath as she ran to catch up. Why did she feel like the crazy train had just departed from the station?

"Oh, the Goddess is in our corner," Tamsin threw back over a shoulder.

And the Goddess obviously gave Tamsin incredible hearing. "You're so confident."

"I am. Everything in its time and it's ours."

She didn't know about that. Time would either prove her right or…she didn't want to think about the *or*. "I hope you're right." The best she could do.

A sly smile lit up Tamsin's face. "I'm always right." Morrigan's heart did a little flip.

"Lacking in confidence, are we?"

"Mama raised me to believe in myself."

"Job well done."

That pleasing feeling lasted until they came into sight of the driveway. "Oh hell, no." Could this get even worse? Judging by the addition of two more vehicles there, the answer was yes. It absolutely could get worse.

"Well, isn't that interesting?" Tamsin's voice held more happiness than confusion.

Neither happy nor confused described Morrigan's state of mind. Pissed would be much closer to accurate. This should have been a mission that went according to a well-established and successful script. Scoop up the Keeper and move her to a new, safe location. Nothing had gone to script. Absolfuckingnothing.

She stopped, leaned over, and put her hands on her knees. With her eyes closed, she sent out a little plea. "Help me, Mother. I don't know what to do." The answer came immediately. *Trust.*

Fuck.

❖

Good boy. He got them to Jackson Hole before sunset, just as she'd told him to do. The route she'd programmed into the navigator brought them right into the national park. Once he parked, she grabbed her trusty bag from the back seat. "Follow me and be quiet."

Still behaving in a manner she approved of, he kept his lips zipped. He did give her a little salute that she could have done without, and she ignored him. Not necessary to let him know that anything he did annoyed her. She rose above it.

A winding path took them toward the river, and as they neared, the sound of voices floated through the air. The sun began to set, and a canopy of stars twinkled overhead, beautiful and almost romantic. Not a bad setting for what she had in mind.

Ian managed to stay quiet, though the energy that poured off him revealed the effort it took to keep his mouth shut. That he did went a long way toward his potential for longevity. Freddi didn't require the presence of anyone else to make this happen. She also didn't mind having a fuck-buddy. Surprising that as time passed, her initial resentment at being stuck with him faded. As long as he followed directions, anyway. Any bit of pushback and it would be a whole different story. Enough about Ian. She returned her focus to what waited just beyond the trees. This latest pop of energy could—no, would—get her a vital missing link. Once she had the Keeper's face, game over would be hers. The final weapon in her arsenal, the key piece to destroying the Keeper and taking possession of the *Book of Darkness*, a few hundred miles away in the mountains known as Red Rock. But she wouldn't get ahead of herself. This first. Then Red Rock.

At the edge of the trees, she motioned for Ian to stop. "Listen." The murmur of several voices floated on the air. An ancient prayer offered up to the goddesses. When she was a child it had been one of the first the elders taught them. Black or White faction, it didn't matter when it came to the old magic. They all learned it. Of course, from there they diverged. Her mother's magic had been as powerful as it had been black. So many talked of being seduced by the darkness. She called bullshit on seduction. It had been about survival in the beginning. About fighting back against a patriarchal society that strove to subjugate women and punish those who refused to obey.

More than one in Freddi's family had been destroyed by fire, her hands bound, her screams entertainment for the men who were their judges, juries, and executioners. The very reason why, though many men joined them, a woman always led the Black Faction. Hell hath no fury, century after century after century.

"A coven." His words were a whisper on the cool, refreshing breeze.

"A battery." She smiled. "Wait here."

"You don't need me to help?"

A little of her recent goodwill toward Ian slipped. Another man thinking the petite witch couldn't do it on her own." She patted him on the arm. "Watch and learn."

There were five of them this time. One very old, three middle-aged, and one quite young. She liked the mix. More potential than she'd anticipated when she'd uncovered this particular gathering. The air around her grew heavy with magic, even heavier with promise. She stepped into the clearing. "Ladies," she announced at the same time she raised her hands to the sky.

Half an hour later they were back on the road. Her blood ran lava-hot. Better than expected. If she harbored any doubt about what would happen in the next two days, it had been wiped away. The universe had sent her a message so clear, she couldn't ignore it.

"That was pretty fucking wild. You are fucking amazing. How did you fucking do that?"

He did better with silence than by displaying his pathetic lack of vocabulary. For the moment, she'd let it slide. "Magic, baby. Pure magic."

"What did you see? Where are we headed next?"

She ignored the first question, the answer to that a need-to-know, and he didn't need to know. "Red Rock."

He pounded the steering wheel. "Fucking A."

CHAPTER NINETEEN

The energy from the disapproval rolling off Morrigan nearly knocked Tamsin to the ground. In a way, she understood. Additional cars in her driveway surprised her as much as she was sure it did Morrigan. When they'd left the house, their band of warriors had been complete. So, who were the newcomers, and who called them in? She had a nagging suspicion.

"Come on," she said over her shoulder. "Looks like we have company. Let's find out who's here to join the game."

"Not a game," Morrigan muttered. Tamsin ignored her.

Inside her house, Grace, Holly, and Triple had been joined by two older women, both Native American, though neither bore any resemblance to either Grace or Holly.

Grace smiled. "Ladies, I'd like to introduce you to my good friends. Ella, she's from the Shoshone Tribe, and Georgie, she's from the Kalispel Tribe." Her suspicion as to who called in the reinforcements confirmed. Grace.

"You brought them here without checking with us?" Tight anger in Morrigan's words. This could put her over the edge, and she'd been pretty darn close to it already. Tamsin better yank her back somehow, or she'd be tumbling over any second.

Grace didn't blink, and her words came out as gentle as Morrigan's were angry. "I did."

"Why? Why would you do something so foolish?" Her voice rose.

Tamsin could feel why without Grace needing to provide any additional explanation. The energy in the room had multiplied a dozen times over since they'd left earlier for the walk down to the water. Grace understood what they were up against, and she'd proceeded to stack the deck without waiting for permission. Rather the ask-for-forgiveness scenario. She liked her even more and wished her mom and grandmother were still alive to meet her. The three of them would have been her instant best friends.

"My precious girl, we are the daughters of this land, and it would only be foolish if I didn't call in the powerhouses who are guardians. You need all of us in this fight, for you are but one thread in the woven web of the universe. We are all bound together, and together we will defeat evil."

"Thank you," Tamsin said as she took Grace's hand and squeezed.

Morrigan sank to one of the kitchen chairs. Her sigh filled the room. "I can't win."

Tamsin walked over and kissed the top of her head, inhaling the sweet scent of her hair. "Winning is exactly what we're trying to achieve here."

She ignored the shocked looks from Holly and Triple. Both had known her long enough to realize she didn't indulge in PDA. Ever. A million or more questions were certain to be whirling in their heads, and after they saved the world, she'd get bombarded by most, if not all, of them. By then she'd have had enough time to come up with some good answers.

Triple looked between Tamsin and Morrigan. "While you two were out doing whatever you were doing, we've been brainstorming." The ghost of a smile flickered across his face, and it had nothing to do with their planning session. No doubt, she'd be getting grilled at some point about both the walk and the PDA. "Anyhow, we decided that you've accurately decoded this Prophecy thing." He pointed to Tamsin. "And you come with a lot of good background info on the enemy that's headed this way." He nodded toward Morrigan. "Now it's the elders' turn to step in. Or the grandmothers, as we've decided to call them."

Tamsin liked the idea immediately. It felt right, to her. Poor Morrigan, still kicking and screaming against ignoring the old ways, held up a hand, her eyes stormy and her lips pressed together.

"What do you mean by the elders stepping in?"

Holly spoke up first. "Grandmother and I believe the land will talk to us. You have to understand that the Spokanes, Kalispels, and Shoshones have been here living and respecting the land since the beginning. They understand it, they listen to it, and more important, they protect it. The parts you need to play up to this point are done, and our interpretation of the Prophecy now requires the elders to ask, to listen, and to follow. They will show us the way."

"Show us the way to what?"

Grace folded her hands together. "The stones. They will show us the stones."

It made sense to Tamsin. Another piece dropped into place. "What do you need us to do?" She glanced at Morrigan, sending her a silent message: trust.

It must have been received because Morrigan didn't argue. Instead, she held her gaze as the storm in them passed and her expression softened. "Yeah. What do you need from us?"

❖

As much as all this drove her up the proverbial wall, Morrigan also couldn't deny what she'd felt today—both the surge of power when she connected with Tamsin and when she'd walked into this room to face the three older women. Something about them, unseen and yet touchable at the same time, commanded respect without a word ever being spoken. They embodied a mixture of grace, wisdom, and power. She could get on board with that, even if her best-laid plans hadn't just gone to hell but had been hit by a nuclear bomb. Grace nodded as if she'd heard and understood every thought in her head. Scary intuitive described her with pinpoint accuracy.

Somehow Morrigan didn't believe her capitulation came as a surprise to the emerging leader of their group. If she were a betting woman, she'd put down a hefty wager that when Grace talked, people listened and did as they were told. "We will have a ceremony once darkness has completely fallen. We will join together and ask our questions. If we are worthy, and I hope we are, the land and our ancestors will listen and answer."

"And if we're not?" She didn't want to be contrary. Instead, Morrigan preferred to go into any event armed with as much information as possible. Look at all the sides to any situation. Cut down on the surprises.

Tamsin rested her hand on Morrigan's shoulder. It was nice, calming. "We will be worthy. We are worthy."

"Damn straight," Triple added. "There's enough combined karma in this room to float a tanker. Maybe an aircraft carrier too."

At this point, Morrigan gave up. So far, going against the grain had gotten her precisely nowhere. Besides, something about Grace instilled both a sense of peace and of trust. Combine that with the indicators that Tamsin's argument about the Prophecy appeared to be falling into place, and she didn't have much to support her own jump-and-run plan. Other than a few hundred years of experience, that is. Still, as much as she wanted to do things her way, looking at different points of view might have some merit. To be more precise, looking at what Tamsin and Grace brought to the conflict.

"The moon will be full tonight." Grace folded her hands on the table.

Morrigan understood the importance of her statement. The moon held magic, and tapping into it could only play to their advantage. "You want to do whatever you plan to do once the moon is up."

Grace nodded. "Yes. Though it needs to be more than simply up in the sky. It needs to be center sky."

Position also played an important part in ceremonies from many different cultures. "Middle of the night, right?"

The three older women nodded in unison.

Morrigan slapped a hand on the table. "All right then. Maybe everybody needs to get some rest and we reconvene here at midnight? That work for you, Grace?"

Even in the light, the sparkle in Grace's eyes was easy to see. "Yes. Midnight, ladies." She turned her head and winked at Triple. "You too, young man."

Triple gave her a little salute. "Wouldn't miss it for the world."

Everyone stood. Grace, Ella, and Georgie talked softly among themselves as they walked out to the driveway and their respective vehicles. Holly hurried behind them, and Triple followed her. In less than a minute, three cars and one motorcycle disappeared from view. Morrigan stood, hands in her pockets, alone with Tamsin.

"That was pretty weird." Or, as she really thought of it, out of control.

"Not weird at all. I'm calling it pretty perfect."

"You think?"

"I believe it with my whole heart. All is as it should be. As destiny wants it to be."

"I'm still worried. The stakes are sky-high."

Tamsin turned to her. "I agree, and I don't do any of this lightly."

Morrigan studied her face and believed her. At first, she'd thought her reckless and a most irresponsible Keeper. The more time she spent with her, the less that sentiment resonated with her. Tamsin took her role as the Keeper with the gravity it demanded. Her desire to stand and fight wasn't born of folly and selfishness. Every vibe coming off her screamed of a heartfelt belief they'd prevail and end the battle that had waged for countless generations. Morrigan hoped to hell she was right.

❖

As they neared the ever-important destination, Freddi flexed her fingers and smiled. Energy flowed through her, and the bones in her hands, a mess so recently, were now as strong as ever. Perhaps even stronger. God, she loved magic. More accurately, Goddess, she loved magic.

"How do you want to do this?" Ian pulled into a gas station and stopped at an available pump. "I better pay in cash just in case anybody is looking for us. Those digital transactions have too many tails." He left her to walk inside and pre-pay.

Impressive. Indicative of a good mind for details. Each time she wondered about him being a companion beyond the immediate, he did or said something that curried good favor. She murmured a small spell to make certain the security cameras on the canopies over the pumps didn't capture their images.

He sauntered back out a few minutes later. "We're good to go." He took the nozzle out of the holder and put it into the tank.

"Perfect. After you top off the tank, let's find a quiet place to strategize." Not that she really needed input from him. She wanted to talk her strategy through. Always helped to hear it out loud.

Ian got back behind the wheel and pulled away from the gas station. Down the road, a scenic pullout offered a good place to stop. She'd been mulling things over since the river witches. Her hoped-for result occurred, and she'd seen the face she'd been searching for. But that wasn't all she'd extracted with the power of the circle of five. The weapon she'd need to stop Abba had also been revealed to her. She wasn't sure which one filled her with more excitement. For years she had wanted to get her hands on the *Book of Darkness*. It belonged to her, as did the power the pages of the grimoire promised. Along the way, stealing the throne from Abba had become equally as important. She wanted it all, and there wasn't any other way to explain it. No one else deserved it.

Her mother would accuse her of being greedy. She never really understood her and, in her opinion, never tried to. Freddi hadn't been thrilled with being a mere Witch Finder. Plenty of them in the Black Faction. Despite her yearning for more, she'd learned the lessons taught to her well and excelled in every single discipline. No one should consider it a fault that she'd wanted something greater, more divine. Any other mother would have been pleased by her ambition instead of constantly comparing her to a saintly sister.

All water under the bridge now. Mom, long gone, would never see the glory soon to be hers. Saintly sister didn't factor in either. They hadn't talked to each other since their mother died, and one day, hopefully sooner rather than later, she'd be gone too, unlike Freddi, who would never really die. Centuries from now, they'd be revering her name. She smiled.

"What?" Ian asked.

The smile faded. "Just thinking things through." Not a lie.

The car in Park, he turned to look at her. "Tell me the plan. What you need me to do. I've got your back, whenever and wherever."

The question rolling through her mind centered on how to get Abba alone. She required only a few minutes face-to-face with her, and while that sounded simple, she always had witches around her. She'd built the fortress that represented the best of the Black Faction and maintained it for decades. She'd been able to capture the top spot and keep it for all these years because of her beauty, power, and whip-smart intellect. At least for another hour or so. Then Freddi planned to make some long overdue adjustments, including a change of venue for the location of headquarters. No remote mountains for her. She'd been hiding long enough.

She caressed Ian's neck, his skin warm under her fingertips. "I need five minutes alone with Abba."

A sly smile crossed his face at the same time he leaned into her touch. "Easy peasy."

"I need perfection." She focused on keeping her touch light and seductive. Hard to do when she really wanted to squeeze.

"Baby," he drawled. "Perfection is my strong suit."

They had different ideas of what constituted perfection. "Ian, I'm not kidding. We have zero room for mistakes." Now she did squeeze. Not hard, but enough for him to understand she meant business.

He reached back and put a hand over hers. He turned a smile on her that showed off his pearly whites. "You underestimate me. I spent a lot of time here, and let's just say, at one point, Abba and I got *real* close."

Apparently, she did underestimate him. He didn't need to know. "You're kidding?"

"I like to spread my charms around, if you feel me." He laughed as he took her hand and placed it on his crotch.

"Perfect. Let's get this ball rolling." She pulled her hand away from the tempting hardness between his legs. No time for that kind of distraction.

"Five minutes?" He winked. "I'll make it quick and satisfying."

"Drive." She didn't do quick, didn't see the point.

"Killjoy." He put the car in gear and pulled back out onto the highway.

Night rolled in deep and dark before they made it to the impressive landscape that defined the red rocks of Utah. That he pulled off well before the long driveway that snaked up to the front of the fortress where Abba ruled the Black Faction came as a bit of a surprise. Through the years, she'd been here plenty, yet she knew nothing about this road. He navigated it well enough to tell her he knew it intimately. Not his first rodeo, as the saying went.

"Abba doesn't like to advertise her fuck buddies."

"Explain." The term fuck buddy didn't accurately describe those Abba took to bed. In fact, from her observations, Abba didn't have anyone around her that would come close to qualifying as a buddy. The only one close to her had always been her brother. No one else. She defined the term tight circle.

"There's a secret entrance into her bedchamber. Her special friends come in at night, screw her brains out, and then she sends them on their way. Wham, bam, thank you, ma'am. There's no spooning, if you catch my drift."

"How have I never heard even a peep about this before? I've been part of the elite circle for years."

"Easy enough to explain that one. Nobody remembers. Once she tires of you, she casts a spell that wipes your memories. The lady has some impressive skills." That explained a lot and, when she thought about it, was very Abba.

"She's not done with you?" An obvious question and one that demanded an answer. Her hands curled into fists as she waited for him to clarify. Couldn't help but wonder if she'd been traveling with a spy all along. Did he intend to deliver her to Abba as a traitor to gain favor? A possibility she'd be foolish to ignore.

He made a noise. "Oh, she's been done with me for a long time. Used me up quick and tossed me out like a bag of smelly garbage. You probably wonder why I was so quick to jump on the wagon with you? Well, you know what's she like, and it's insulting as hell. It's all about her and what you can do for her. I take exception to being treated like a piece of meat."

How well she did know Abba. Not all that different from Aldo really. Only more powerful and better looking. If she had to sleep with one of them, it would definitely be her. "Yes. I know exactly what you're talking about. Tell me more about the memory spell."

He rolled his head for a second, a slight scent of cologne wafting through the car as he did. "Here's the thing. I've pretended her spell took. For whatever reason, it didn't, and I remember every little detail, including how to get in and out of her private chambers undetected. To her, I'm unimportant, and she sees only what she wants to. She's never taken the time to figure out if her spell worked on me. I let her think it did because I figured at some point the knowledge of what happened in those rooms would come in handy. Guess I was right about that."

Deception didn't flow from him, and her earlier concern lessened. Not a spy. More like a pissed-off ex-lover. She could work with that. "I could kiss you."

He winked, and his smile grew bright. "Later, after we have something to celebrate in a big way. You can kiss me anywhere you want."

She put her hand on his inner leg, feeling the heat of his crotch. "Bank on it." She stared out the windshield at the sky. "We have to wait until dark."

"It's already dark."

"I'd feel better if it were darker."

He leaned forward and studied the sky through the windshield. "It would be better, as long as we don't run into her latest boy toy."

She raised an eyebrow. "You don't think you can dispatch one of her playthings?"

Now he laughed and leaned his head back against the headrest. "Oh, I can dispatch all right. Just say the word."

She smiled back. "Word."

CHAPTER TWENTY

Six hours. Six long hours before Grace directed them to meet with everyone down at the edge of the water. Tingling in the tips of Tamsin's fingers alerted her to the magic that gathered in the air. It grew in intensity, drawing strength from each of them. As it should be. Shared magic would solidify their triumph.

Or maybe that tingling in her signaled something else. She glanced over to Morrigan, who stood at the edge of the deck gazing out into the distance. The thousand-yard stare. How she'd love to know the thoughts going through her head. Just looking at her made Tamsin's heart beat faster. Fascinating only feather-touched how Tamsin thought of her.

"This wouldn't be possible without you." She spoke what her heart whispered.

Morrigan turned slowly and locked gazes with her. It made her catch her breath. "It's all so freaking weird."

"In a good way." Definitely in her case. She hoped Morrigan felt the same.

"Yes and no."

Not quite the comeback she hoped for. "Start with the no." Afraid of what the yes would be because it might not coincide with her thoughts on the good.

"No. It's not good because both you and the *Book of Darkness* are in real jeopardy. If the grimoire falls into the hands of anyone from the Dark Faction, they'll use it to push out everything good and kind about the world. And…" Morrigan looked away.

"And?" Tamsin stepped around so that they gazed at each other again.

"And if something happens to you and I can't protect you, we lose too. You have no successor."

Again, not what she'd been hoping to hear. "Things change."

Morrigan shook her head. "Not that."

"How do you know? It's never been allowed to play out differently. We've always just assumed it had to go mother to daughter." She'd even asked her mother about this possibility, and like Morrigan, she'd brushed Tamsin's question aside, choosing instead to focus on what had been done for generations.

Morrigan put both hands on the railing and returned her gaze to the landscape beyond. "It's been written in the magic of the stars since the beginning, and it's always worked."

"The Prophecy." No matter how she looked at things, her thoughts came around every single time to the Prophecy and how it played out now. Possibly set her free. Set them all free. Had anyone before her ever really taken the time to look at its potential?

"You're trying to make it fit because you don't want to leave here."

In many ways, it would be wrong to discount Morrigan's view. In her mind, Tamsin worked hard to make it fit her circumstance. The reality was quite different, as she didn't have to work hard to make it fit, because it just did, easily, and more than anything she wished Morrigan could see it too.

"There's a lot of truth in that comment, and I'll grant you that." To make that concession didn't require much of a stretch. "You're also not giving enough weight to the fact that it's not all the truth. Can you really deny how the players have come together? It's never happened that way before, and that it is occurring now fills me with great confidence beyond my own desire to live my life here. I'm not trying to make it fit as much as it just does, period. I'm simply grabbing it and running with it."

Morrigan stood straight and sighed. "While I think it's a little more complicated than that, it's moot anyway because your mind is made up."

Not wrong on that count either. Her belief in the rightness of what they were trying to do was unshakable. "It is."

Morrigan's shoulders dropped. "I've given up trying to fight you."

Tamsin smiled. A small victory that she'd take with gratitude, though she suspected some fight still remained within Morrigan's heart. "What's the yes piece?"

Now Morrigan turned slowly and then closed the distance between them. "Weird in a good way because I find myself faced with a witch who makes my blood boil."

"As in mad?" Her breath caught in her throat.

She shook her head slowly, her gaze intent on Tamsin's face. "As in on fire for you."

She held her gaze, and the fire roared through her too. "Right back atcha."

❖

Morrigan couldn't help it. Blame it on stress or zero training in a scenario like this. Anything except her own lack of restraint. She didn't want to ignore the attraction a minute more. Who knew how long they had left. Tamsin might believe the will of the goddesses rested on their side, but she wasn't as sure. Within a day or two, everything they'd ever worked to achieve could be undone. The world could descend into darkness in a matter of minutes. They could all be dead.

Century after century, wars had been waged over the *Book of Darkness*, and each time, goodness and light prevailed. The approaching threat came darker and more determined than any before. An ache in her bones warned Morrigan the battle ahead would likely be the last one. How she wished she could embrace the absolute confidence of final victory that Tamsin embodied. Nothing she said seemed to shake her vision for a different future.

So, she threw caution away and went with what the hell. The hours ticking away could very well be her last, and damned if she wanted to live them wondering what might have been. Not once had she ever felt a draw like this, and she had to see where it could go. She took Tamsin's face between her hands and kissed her. Lightly at first, tasting a sweetness that sent a buzz throughout her. Inhaling her scent, a mixture of flowers and spice, light and pleasing.

Tamsin whispered against her lips. "Mm-mm. Now that's what I'm talking about."

She kissed her harder, her tongue seeking and meeting magic. "I want more," she murmured. "So much more."

Breaking away, Tamsin took her hand and pulled her toward the house. Her cheeks were flushed, and her eyes sparkled. "Ask and thou shall receive."

She didn't resist and followed her, hand in hand, through the door, down the hall, and into the bedroom she hadn't yet stepped a foot into. A quick glance around and she smiled. It looked like Tamsin. Muted colors of green, gold, and tan. Nature at its most soothing and magnificent. A queen-sized bed covered with an impressive handmade quilt and two pillows. She almost chuckled. How she hated those beds piled high with decorative pillows that had to be moved on and off, on and off. No mountain here required removal. They were only beautiful and functional. *Be still, my heart.*

Tamsin stopped at the edge of the bed and put both hands on Morrigan's shoulders. A tiny push and she fell back, landing on the quilt. Little force was required to gain compliance, the push as gentle as the smile on her face. Morrigan propped up on her elbows at the same time Tamsin took a couple steps backward, a look on her face as she pulled her shirt over her head and tossed it aside that made Morrigan shiver. No bra. Another shiver. Tamsin stepped out of her jeans. No underwear. Dear God. Her heart pounded hard enough she had to hear it.

"We have something special between us. You feel it too, don't you?" Tamsin moved toward her, shoulders back, head high.

No reason to lie. Besides, she wanted only the truth between them. "I do."

"We were meant to be here. Now. Together."

"It feels right." Oh, did it deliver all the feels.

"It is right." Tamsin leaned over and put her hands on Morrigan's knees, spreading her legs apart. She stepped between them, stared down at her, a naked goddess.

"I give up resisting you." A woman would be insane to pull away.

Tamsin's smile grew. "I am irresistible." She dropped down on top of Morrigan.

"You're killing me."

"Last thing I want to do is kill you." Tamsin's kiss was deep and probing. Her hands slid down Morrigan's arms. "You're wearing too many clothes."

"I can remedy that." Geez, she sounded breathy. Not at all like herself.

"Let me help." And she did.

The light had faded by the time they showered and dressed again. Something incredible had happened, and it filled her heart. All the way into her bones it flowed. More powerful. More focused. Falling in love.

She glanced at Tamsin, who, fully dressed, ran a comb through her wet hair. The aura she'd sensed in her since the moment they met suddenly became visible, the light white and strong.

"You're glowing."

Tamsin turned and smiled. "Hate to break it to you, but so are you. I told you we were something special together. You want to tell me I'm wrong?"

"No can do."

The comb set aside, Tamsin walked to her and put a hand on her cheek. Her eyes met Morrigan's. "I've never met anyone like you."

"Same here."

"It's like we're meant to be together. I feel…"

Nothing ventured. "Love."

Slowly Tamsin nodded. "Yes, love."

Resistance came naturally to her. "I don't do love."

Tamsin's smile held something else behind it. Sadness? Maybe. "I've never felt it in the cards for me either. The whole must-produce-an-heir thing always made me a little crazy. Daughter of a daughter of a daughter. Sort of lends itself to the whole hetero thing."

"Not my thing."

"Mine either."

"But this feels right." Tamsin's hand moved to her heart.

"One hundred percent."

"Does it make anything else feel right?"

And, there it was. Some mind-blowing sex, a singular connection that shifted everything she'd believed in her whole life, and a centuries-old prophecy that just might come true right here, right now. Tamsin had her. Denials be damned.

She sighed and put her hand over Tamsin's. "I believe it all. We fight."

Tamsin kissed her hard. "We win."

❖

After this night played out, Freddi would screw Ian's brains out. He not only got them inside the fortress, but he also took her right to the inner sanctum. Exactly where she needed to be to make this go down the way it must. By the looks of it, Abba had commissioned the construction decades ago and hadn't touched it since. Narrow and well-built, with a rough concrete floor, it burrowed into the hillside bordering the compound that made up Abba's fortress. Obviously constructed to withstand harsh winters and hot summers, it also boasted enough light to make passage quick and easy. Made her wonder what other secrets the sneaky old bitch might have.

"Go back." She whispered as she peered through the tiny peephole offering her a narrow look into Abba's private chamber. Because she'd been inside before, as an invited guest, a panoramic view wasn't necessary. On her previous visits, no less than five or six other witches attended. No one ever seemed to be alone with their fearless, though seemingly ageless, leader. That never-aging part would change in less than a minute.

"Go back?" His words were as soft as hers as he stood close behind her. His breath whispered across the fine hairs on her neck. "You need me." He leaned in closer and kissed her ear.

She turned and pushed him away. He stumbled though managed to stay on his feet. "No. I must do this alone."

"After all this, you're pushing me out? That's messed up." The whine in his words came through even though he kept to a whisper.

She didn't owe Ian an explanation. "It has to be this way. Please. Go back and wait for me." That she managed not to scream at him testified to her great control.

The argument she'd been certain would follow, didn't, and she sent silent thanks to the goddesses. Her shoulders relaxed, and she imagined she could hear his retreating footsteps. He moved as silently out of the tunnel as they'd done coming into it. The location might be secret, but, he'd been quick to point out, soundproof it wasn't.

It would take him a couple of minutes to reach the entrance, and she continued to wait for a good five. Her fingers curled and straightened, curled and straightened. The air inside the tunnel was stale and musky, so she worked not to cough. Chilly too and she shivered. With her eye once more to the peephole, she scanned the room, empty when they'd first arrived. It wasn't any longer.

If Abba sensed her presence, her behavior gave no clue. In a wingback chair with her feet curled beneath her, she read a hardback book. The long silver hair that framed her face didn't make her look old. Nothing about Abba gave away her age. Her unlined face and bright blue eyes were those of a woman in her early thirties. That she'd been at the helm of the Black Faction for more than three decades made a mockery of any attempt to reconcile her age with her command. Did anyone except Aldo know exactly how old she was?

Abba never lifted her head or took her eyes from the pages of the hardback. She never turned a single page. Her long, slender fingers cupped the book without moving. Oh, she knew she wasn't alone.

Finally, she lifted her head and turned her gaze to the spot where the hidden door would swing open once Freddi pushed the lever. "You might as well come on in instead of standing in the cold spying on me." Her words were silky smooth and calm. No anger or fear. The always-in-control Abba.

Freddi smiled, pushed the lever, and stepped through the open door. The hinges didn't creak. "Hello, Abba. No spying. Only waiting for your invitation. Didn't want to intrude, you know." Warmth wafted over her from a fire roaring in the fireplace big enough to walk into without the need to duck. The rug covering the tile floor muffled her footsteps.

"Little Warrior. Why am I not surprised to see you here?" No longer needing the prop, Abba tossed the book aside and stood. At barely over five feet tall, she wore black leggings that made her legs look long. A gem-toned blue blouse flowed around her like a cloud. Beautiful as always, beneath the ethereal beauty existed the heart of a predator, and those who underestimated her fell beneath her sharpened claws.

"You've been expecting me." Not a big mystery. She'd been around Abba enough to witness her powers at work. For a tiny woman, she possessed a long and powerful punch.

"Since the moment Aldo dropped out of sight. Only one name came to mind with balls big enough to try something with my brother." She looked pointedly at Freddi.

Nice to have her skill set acknowledged. She gave a little bow, disrespectful as it might be. "Well, Aldo had a higher purpose, and I helped him find it." It had been the sweetest moment so far in her quest, but she didn't say that part out loud.

"That is?" Abba intertwined her fingers and watched her with a serene expression. The phrase "still waters run deep" rolled through

Freddi's mind as she watched. No turning her back on the queen. The current queen, she corrected herself.

She shrugged. "That *was* to charge my battery, so to speak." Might as well put it in the correct tense. Abba was entitled to know the score when it came to her little brother.

"I'm your next charge." Abba hadn't moved. Her relaxed body language told the tale: she didn't see Freddi as a threat. Such arrogance deserved the kind of reward Freddi intended to deliver.

"Not exactly. Your purpose is even higher than Aldo's."

"That would be?" Again, calm as though they talked about nothing more important than the day's weather. Blue skies and sunshine, birds singing and fresh air. Abba still believed she maintained control. Her mistake.

"I'm taking your magic." Now, she smiled. Couldn't help it. The glee could only be contained for so long.

Abba laughed, her first real display of emotion. "That's priceless. Foolish witches just like you have come here before thinking they had a chance to stand against me. Look at you, like you're even a tenth of my power."

She wasn't wrong in that assessment. That fact alone had more to do with her continued control of the Black Faction than anything else. Only the most gifted witch could take it and keep it. Her argument failed anyway, because she didn't plan to go magic-to-magic with her. Aldo, she had been able to handle on a level playing field, mano a mano. Not stupid enough to try that with Abba. She had no intention of failing, unlike those other "foolish witches" who came before. Abba had never encountered someone like her before, and her continued underestimation would be her undoing.

She let her hand drift to the small of her back. "True enough, Abba. You are far stronger than me, and I know it. Still not a problem. How many times have you told me I'm a creative Witch Finder who can do anything I set my mind to?"

"I still believe that." Abba began to flex her fingers. "You have, however, a blind spot when it comes to your true abilities. You're missing something."

Oh, this would be rich. "Missing something? Like what?"

"A compass."

"A compass." Really? That's what she hits her with? If she'd had any doubts about her timing to end Abba's reign, they'd just evaporated.

"Like your sister. She might not always see things our way, but she has a compass to guide her. You, Witch Finder, have gotten too much into your own deluded fantasies."

Boring and a mistake to make a comparison to her sister. "I have a compass all right, and it's brought me here." Freddi shot her right in the middle of her forehead.

CHAPTER TWENTY-ONE

Tamsin wondered if she'd ever be able to move again. Despite taking a shower and dressing, the draw had been too great. Clothes were tossed aside and heaven revisited. Relaxed and happy didn't even begin to describe her feelings now. Hair stuck to the sweat on the back of her neck, and her breathing had just now returned to normal. She closed her eyes and allowed the contentment to settle over her entire body. Her heart too.

"That was…" She couldn't come up with the words to adequately describe her condition.

"Amazing." Morrigan lay next to her, naked and gorgeous again. More accurately, still.

"Absolutely." The something more she'd felt from the first touch hadn't diminished at all. From the moment she'd first seen Morrigan it had been there. Their coming together, both times, hadn't been some random act. It had been foretold. The Prophecy.

"I'd like to argue with you, even say this was just a hookup—" Tamsin slapped her on the leg, and she laughed. "But even I can't pull that off. This was more and it was fantastic."

Tamsin turned on her side and propped her head in her hand. "We will stop them, you know."

"God, I hope you're right."

"Beautiful girl, when will you let go of doubt? You read the Prophecy. You've seen all the individual elements coming together to form a complete picture. You met those three amazing women today. Everything is lining up as it's meant to be. You even said earlier, you're in, and I'm going to hold you to that."

"I've let go of a lot." Morrigan put her arms behind her head and stared up at the ceiling. "I'm gearing up for the battle I can't seem to get away from."

"And I realize I'm challenging everything you've trained for your whole life."

"We're quite the pair." She turned her head to stare into Tamsin's eyes, and warmth filled her.

"We're unstoppable." If she'd felt that way before, her conviction now hit rock solid. They were meant for this. All of it and together. That pesky word love flitted through her mind like the sounds of an unrelenting wind.

Morrigan pushed up to a sitting position and patted her on the hip. "Not if we don't get our asses out of the bed. Again." She laughed.

Tamsin scooted over and kissed her, loving the warm, soft pressure of their lips meeting. "That's the spirit. Race you to the shower." She jumped off the bed and sprinted to the bathroom.

All she could say was thank goodness for a quick-recovery hot-water tank because they gave it a hefty workout. Not sorry in any way. Worth every dime it cost her to put in that thing.

By the time they were dressed and back to the kitchen, her energy level had skyrocketed. While she'd expected to feel renewed, she'd never imagined she could feel like this. It went buzzing right past awesome. She handed Morrigan a glass of iced tea, no sugar. She didn't need to ask. Definitely not a sweet-tea woman. One more check mark in the keeper category, although she'd hold that thought to herself for the moment. Pretty sure she already scared Morrigan, and she'd likely run away screaming if Tamsin threw things like love or forever out there in the open too much. Ease it all in.

"Thanks." Morrigan took a sip of her iced tea. "We still have time before we meet everyone."

"We could…" She nodded toward the bedroom, and a trill of excitement raced through her.

Morrigan shook her head. "As tempting as that might be, no. We have to be bright and alert and clearheaded for whatever Grace has for us tonight."

Disappointed, she challenged Morrigan. "Are you saying I wear you out?"

"Oh, God, yes. You drain me."

"In a good way?" While pretty sure that's what she meant, she wanted confirmation just the same. Her rock-solid confidence wavered ever so slightly in a few areas.

Morrigan held her gaze for a long beat. "Yeah, in a good way."

Progress and, oh my, would she take it. "All right then. I'll give you a pass. For now."

"If we live through this, we can revisit." Morrigan winked, and Tamsin's breath caught.

"Oh, we *will* live through this." She meant it too. Not only were they destined to win, but after they did, she and Morrigan were going to take this thing between them and run with it. Her goals for a dream forever included more than just keeping the farm.

Morrigan put her hands together and rested them against her lips for a moment. Her expression grew serious. "I really wish I had your absolute confidence. I do believe we're strong and powerful together and that the rest of them add a boost to what you and I bring to the battle."

"I'm with you there, although I hear more than what you're actually saying. What's still bothering you? What are you afraid of?"

If pushed, Tamsin would admit she feared Morrigan wasn't feeling the same emotions she did. Or, that what had happened between them wasn't as special to Morrigan as it was to her. Those things scared her. The approaching Witch Finder, not as much. Yes, she had a respectful appreciation of the power that went along with those who were tasked with destroying a Keeper. Respect aside, she felt confident in her ability to face them down and win. It would be a special kind of fool who lacked healthy respect.

Morrigan glanced down before bringing her gaze back up to Tamsin's. "They're stronger and more powerful. They've trained for confrontations like this for years. Are we really ready to take them on? Can we be successful if we do?"

The answer, in her mind, came easily. "Absolutely. We can beat them."

Morrigan listened, and she could tell she rolled the reassurance over in her mind. "Who knows how many they're bringing."

She had this one. Rock solid in her belief. "She comes alone."

Now Morrigan stared at her with narrowed eyes. Oops. Maybe she should have shared that tidbit before now. "What aren't you telling me?"

"There was a moment." She looked toward the bedroom again. "In there. I saw her face. I felt her. Like a flash of lightning. Bright and strong and deadly."

"You should have shared that earlier."

"Probably, but I'm sharing now."

"Okay. You're right. Doesn't matter at this point. We go forward. How do you know she's coming alone? What else aren't you telling me?"

"I saw that piece of it too." She closed her eyes and replayed the brief vision.

"I feel a *but* in there."

Tamsin opened her eyes. "But she's more powerful than any other Black Faction witch." That piece of information came more as a feeling than something shown to her. Her sense about the approaching witch warned her to be extra cautious. To not underestimate either her craft or her drive.

"How so?"

One other tidbit shown to her really highlighted why they had to be wary of this Witch Finder. "She just stole the power of Abba."

❖

"Lord, help us." Bad didn't even begin to describe a scenario where someone stole the magic of a Black Faction witch with skills so far beyond anyone else, the theft defied explanation. Morrigan and every other warrior in the White Faction were well-schooled in Abba's history and the strength of her hereditary powers. Like many of them, Morrigan included, she came from a long, long line of witches with skills and cunning minds that spared them from the fires and nooses of those who came to destroy that which they didn't understand. Born into the magic, Abba had stood alone at the top of the Black Faction for decades, striking down any wannabes who attempted to challenge her seat at the head of the table. Abba didn't subscribe to the concept of mercy. She employed a one-and-done strategy to any and all challengers.

"We'll be ready for her." Tamsin's confidence reflected the opposite of Morrigan's pessimism. Made her wonder how they could be compatible in bed and on such opposite spectrums everywhere else. Maybe not, as she thought about it. A certain kind of symmetry that made sense.

"If this witch is strong enough to take down Abba and steal her power, we don't have a chance in hell of stopping her." Morrigan's place as the voice of reason seemed to be defining itself more and more. Someone had to take the view opposing the rose-colored-glasses approach, and, to be honest, she'd been born to that particular role. Somehow, she had to get Tamsin to see reason.

"The Prophecy."

Stop already. As delightful as she found Tamsin, she'd become a stuck record in that respect. They had to keep their attention on the here and now, and not some words written on a piece of paper hundreds of years ago. Tamsin stared at her, and that beautiful long hair with those fascinating streaks of white threatened to derail her focus. Sticking her hands in her pockets, she rallied, took a deep breath, the sweet scent of hibiscus soap from their shower filling her, and looked her straight in the eyes. "Fuck the Prophecy. We cannot allow her to get her hands on the *Book of Darkness*. Can you even begin to imagine what evil she'd let loose on the world? She's a freaking nightmare with zero morals. A lot of innocent people will die if we don't stop her. Not to mention that the White Faction will be destroyed. The worst of what people believe of witchcraft will become truth. No, no, no, it can't happen."

Tamsin's expression didn't change as she listened to Morrigan's tirade. The same calm, easy vibe rolled off her. "It won't. We've got this."

Chills hit Morrigan as though she'd just stepped out into a sub-zero day. All her previous acquiescence toward Tamsin's desire to stand and fight evaporated. She fell back onto the tried and true. "We have to leave and leave now." Pressure like a hand on her back made her want to run fast, Tamsin in tow.

"No." Tamsin's voice retained its calm, easy tenor. Little seemed to rattle her.

She wasn't feeling it regardless of how steady Tamsin remained. Her hands shook as if she'd downed a pot of coffee on an empty stomach, and she shoved them into her pockets. "Stop with the bullshit." All the good vibes they'd built together over the last few hours grew muted, overtaken by the real fear of what came their way. If it didn't make her look like a three-year-old, she'd stomp her feet. Things had just turned very dark, and inaction was absolutely not an option. Tamsin seemed to read her mind.

"We're not doing nothing."

She respectfully disagreed. "Hanging out and waiting for a Witch Finder to come kill you, take the *Book of Darkness*, and send the world into chaos is not just doing nothing. It's freaking insane."

Tamsin sat and folded her hands on the table. An air of calm determination floated around her. "Witch Finders have been coming at us forever. If we don't stop them, they'll continue to come for us. It doesn't change our plans."

"How can it not?" What a mess she'd gotten herself into. As the saying went, she had one job.

"It prepares us."

A few deep breaths helped her regroup and gave her a few seconds to gather her thoughts. Tamsin wasn't seeing things clearly. They had to deal with reality, not dreams. "It prepares us to flee."

"Morrigan, trust me, please. I know what I'm doing." More denial. Beauty could carry her only so far.

"Do you really? The thing is, I don't believe you do." She toned it down to at least attempt to be nice. If she'd voiced what she really thought, she'd have told her that she'd lost her fucking mind.

Tamsin didn't budge. "I know I've been saying this over and over since we met, but it's because it's true. It is time for this to come to an end, and you know what? I wouldn't have been able to see her face if the goddesses weren't preparing me for her arrival. I believe that with my whole heart."

Oh, yeah, play that card, and it made everything okay? Nice try. Two could play that game. "I believe the message they sent directs you to take the *Book of Darkness* to someplace safe." Rational thinking had to rule here, and that remained her strong suit. At least it did generally speaking. Somehow things had become skewed since she got here, and she had to square herself and not be swayed by a woman who touched her heart.

"Nope. I still disagree. I believe they were telling me to face her down."

Why? Why? Why? It wasn't fair. Every other Keeper had been compliant, realistic, and thus their safety had been assured. Here she stood sparring with one who made her want to scream and at the same time want to throw her onto a bed and make love to her. In what world was any of this okay? It didn't seem to matter what argument Morrigan used to try to persuade her to take the preferred course. She consistently balked.

"I can't convince you to change your mind, can I?"

Tamsin pressed her lips together and shook her head. "Never."

"You make me want to throttle you."

"Is that all you want to do with me?"

"I want to hate you right now."

"But you don't hate me at all." The twinkle came back into her eyes.

The world headed toward hell, with her right behind it. "No. Damn you, anyway."

❖

Talk about a rush of epic proportions. The moment that bullet pierced Abba's brain, a bolt of lightning struck Freddi's body. In a million years she'd never be able to describe the feeling, and to think, once she got her hands on the *Book of Darkness*, that feeling would be multiplied about a thousandfold. Her desire to get to the Keeper had just skyrocketed.

Abba sprawled on the sky-blue handmade rug, her blood turning it crimson, a slight metallic scent filling the air. It would take a master to clean it enough to restore its original hue. She'd burn it. Anything that reminded her of the high and mighty duo of Abba and Aldo deserved to be turned to ash.

The disposition of expensive furnishings didn't interest her. Give them away, burn them, let them sit unused and moldy for the rest of eternity—none of it mattered. She looked around the room she'd stood in many times, the obedient soldier, at Abba's beck and call. No. She would never return to this place once she walked away. A lot of memories. None of them good.

On one knee next to the body, she reached down. "You won't need this anymore." The gold chain popped as she yanked it. The emerald, deep and dark, pulsed against her palm. From the first moment she'd seen it glittering against the white skin of Abba's throat, she'd known that one day it would hang around her neck. She didn't expect that it would be the key to Abba's power, yet in this moment, as it flowed from the stone and into her body, the truth about it became known to her. "You sneaky bitch," she murmured.

Her head tipped back, she closed her eyes and wrapped her fingers around the emerald. The sensation outdid even the most body-shaking orgasm. It would be easy to sprawl on the floor and revel in the amazing sensations, let them wash over her again and again. Sadly, no time for pleasure. Hundreds of miles away, tasks awaited her attention. First and foremost, a Keeper to destroy and a grimoire to master.

She stood and fastened the gold chain of the emerald necklace around her own neck, pleased that the clasp hadn't broken when she pulled it from Abba's body. As it had done while it lay against her palm, power flowed into her, sliding down her spine, into her arms and legs, into her soul. "Thank you ever so much." She looked down at Abba's still body and smiled. See. She could show gratitude. Then she spit on her before turning away.

Just as she'd made her way into Abba's inner chamber undetected, she made her way out. Anybody's guess how long they'd have before one of her loyal followers discovered her body. While she could use her skill with fire to finish this job, it would sound the alarm too early. This called for stealth in order to give Freddi enough time to get out of the area. She knew now exactly where they were headed and who they were looking for. She flexed her fingers as she scurried through the tunnels toward the door where Ian waited. The tingling in them grew stronger the closer she came to the end.

"It's done?" Ian held the outer door open for her.

"It is. Let's go." She stepped out into the darkness and hurried toward the car.

"Where?" He hurried behind.

"Eastern Washington."

"All the way across the country?" At the open car, the interior light reflected on his confused face.

Oh, dear Lord. Each time she leaned toward giving him the benefit of the doubt, he said something stupid. "No, as in eastern Washington state."

"Oh. Why didn't you say that?"

Goddess, give me strength. "Just drive."

"Whatever you say, Boss." He slid behind the wheel of the car and closed the door. Blessed darkness dropped down on them both.

As soon as he had them heading toward Salt Lake City, she tuned him out. A good twelve hours of driving time ahead of them, she would use the time to think through her plan. Then she'd need to spend a few hours scoping out the landscape once they arrived. No charge-in-with-swords-waving type operation. The Keeper would be expecting that, and thus the goal would be to take her off guard. Easy enough to do with the powers she'd managed to secure. As much as she'd like to finish this the moment they reached Spokane, taking time to do it right would ensure easy and clean success.

She smiled and looked out the window as the colorful landscape whizzed by. She'd miss it here. The Red Rocks were like no place else, and just the energy pulsing out of the earth helped plug her into the vibes of the universe. No wonder so many people of the non-witch variety flocked there. The strength of the energy could and would touch everyone even if they didn't realize it. Too bad she'd never return.

For those born into the magic, the vibe here manifested as nothing short of amazing. Abba drew from it every day, and while she'd never said anything, Freddi always believed it had a lot to do with why she never left. Abba had feared walking away from the epicenter. Freddi didn't share that worry. Everything she'd been born with, and everything she'd taken as her due, meant that no matter where she stood, she could not be diminished. She reached up and touched the emerald. The Keeper had no idea about the strength of the storm that came her way.

CHAPTER TWENTY-TWO

Tamsin needed to throw a bone Morrigan's way. Despite her confidence in the upcoming battle, her dedication to the protection of the *Book of Darkness* had been hardwired into her psyche. Her role in its protection defined her entire life. Strong magic ran in her bones, and never would she compromise her duty toward the grimoire. She hoped Morrigan understood that but could tell she still harbored doubts about her.

The spells cast upon the *Book of Darkness* were powerful and had kept it safe for hundreds and hundreds of years. Didn't mean it couldn't use a bit more. The really amazing part came with the boost she'd gathered when they'd made love. Not shocking given she'd felt the difference the first time they touched. She knew it to be something special, further proving her point. Each step along the way verified her interpretation of the Prophecy. She'd made great inroads with Morrigan, although each time her resistance flared up, they took steps backward. An intelligent and magically gifted woman, she should be able to see things as clearly as Tamsin.

Events would unfold as they must, and that didn't hinge on whether others believed her about the Prophecy. Even with her strong belief in her actions, she wanted to give back to the woman destined to play a key role in the coming battle. She hadn't seen it as clearly as other pieces of the puzzle. She felt it deep in her bones. Morrigan remained important, perhaps even more important, than anyone else, including herself. She could never say that bit to her because someone with Morrigan's training would have been taught that the only person who really mattered was, and always would be, the Keeper. Funny how centuries' worth of the same lesson made it an absolute when it might not actually be.

"I want to share something with you."

Morrigan raised an eyebrow. "Share away."

"Come." She turned and walked out of the house, down the walkway, and toward the workshop. A cool wind blew across her skin. Clear and fresh, carrying the scent of grassy pastures, livestock, and pine trees. No whispers of the evil heading their way. Her first thought, someone masked the voices, and it would take a powerful witch to be able to do that. Someone of Abba's strength.

Oh, the Black Faction thought they shielded their power structure well and that the White Faction had no idea of who led them or where she stayed. They were wrong. White Faction intel excelled, and Tamsin knew all about Abba and her asshole brother, Aldo. She'd also seen his work, demonstrating his lack of character. If he'd been simply a regular, he'd have been a reprehensible human. With magic at his disposal, he was even worse.

That Abba wouldn't be the one to come here for Tamsin didn't concern her. She didn't leave her stronghold, ever. She sent her Witch Finders to do the dirty work. Besides, to date, they'd failed in their quest for the big win and destroyed a lot of decent witches along the way. They wanted the Keeper, and they wanted the grimoire. They failed over and over. So Abba sat in her castle dispatching her people to do her bidding and never, ever got her own hands dirty.

Yet, right now, it would take someone with the level of Abba's magic to control the wind and the earth and the sky. The thing about it was, why exactly would Abba lend her power to a Witch Finder? She hadn't done it before, so why now? The question made her very wary.

Disturbed even more by the answer flitting through her mind, Tamsin hurried into the workshop. Time ticked away faster than she initially believed. A good thing they were convening with everyone soon. This ship had to set sail and catch a mighty strong wind.

Before Morrigan stood next to her, she'd cast the spell to open the safe and held the *Book of Darkness* in her hands. It vibrated. Or did it tremble? Damn.

"What in the world?" Morrigan's eyes were wide. "Why would you bring it out now? You don't have to prove anything to me, and it's safer in there with the Witch Finder coming." She nodded toward the magical safe.

"More layers." She grabbed Morrigan's hand and held it to her heart. No time to explain. "North to south, east to west, light of the Goddess, encircle us now, body and soul. Bind us in harmony, and grant us power in protection until the light of the moon shall no longer shine. So shall it be."

The swirl of light that encircled them lasted for only a few seconds, and then it vanished. What it left behind was invisible but felt just the same. The *Book of Darkness* stilled once more in her hands. It approved.

"What did you do?" Not anger in her voice. Awe. Good. It signaled to Tamsin she could feel it too, and that's what she'd been aiming for.

Tamsin looked into her eyes. The go-big-or-go-home moment had just arrived. "I gave you every ounce of trust I have. You are part of this now."

"Part of what exactly?" Morrigan's eyes narrowed as she studied her face.

She looked down at the *Book of Darkness* and then returned her gaze to Morrigan's face. "Touch the grimoire." Demonstration had a way of surpassing the need for any explanation, and this promised to be one hell of a demonstration.

Morrigan held up her hands as though she'd been asked to touch flesh-eating acid. Couldn't blame her. It went against everything they had both been taught and, under any other circumstances, was dangerous. "I thought only the Keeper could touch the *Book of Darkness*? I don't need to go up in flames, especially right now."

Sometimes, rules needed to be broken. Not only needed to be broken, they had to be. "Until now."

"No way." She kept her hands away, understandable uncertainty darkening her face.

"I trust you with my life and the lives of everyone the Black Faction could hurt if they were to gain control of the grimoire. Witches and normal alike." Her confidence in the spell she'd placed on the grimoire couldn't be more solid. She knew it would work. Knew of the importance of this warrior coming into the inner circle. It had to be.

"No fucking way." Morrigan dropped her hands and studied both Tamsin and what she held. For a moment, Tamsin thought she'd lost her, and then slowly, she reached out, touched the Book of Darkness, and screamed.

❖

Images raced through Morrigan's head the second her fingers came into contact with the cover of the *Book of Darkness*. Fire, battles, death, and the faces of one Keeper after another until finally Tamsin's face flashed before her. She dropped to her knees with a bang, the force of her fall sending waves of pain up into her thighs.

"Are you all right?" Tamsin knelt beside her, tears in her eyes. "I'm so, so sorry. I wasn't expecting that. Are you hurt? What can I do?"

As soon as she caught her breath, she found the energy to ask, "Define all right." Freaking weird, and she wasn't sure about anything at the moment. Her heart raced and she blinked, a pain needling behind her eyes as her knees throbbed.

Tamsin studied her face and seemed to be okay with what she saw there. Her tears dried up, and she put a hand on her shoulder. "Do you understand now?"

She opened her mouth to ask yet another question and then stopped. It hit her in that instant that, yeah, she did understand. "Yes." It all sort of flowed into her like a stream of consciousness. Enlightenment of the highest order. And it rocked.

Tamsin's hand moved to her cheek, a tiny smile on her face. "We're in this together. We've always been in it together. We just didn't know it in our souls until now."

She stood up and blew out a breath. The rapid beating of her heart calmed, and the pain in her head faded. The knees were going to take a while longer to recover. The fight, at least the fight with Tamsin, flowed out of her. "Maybe."

Tamsin also stood and gave a little laugh. "Really?"

She smiled back. "Okay, maybe—" she held up a hand "—just maybe, there's some credence to the Prophecy and what's happening here. Maybe your view about what's coming has merit, and we need to take a stand against the Witch Finder."

"That had to about kill you." A light came into Tamsin's eyes. Pretty sure it signaled triumph.

"A little bit." She could acquiesce only so far.

Her expression turned serious "We're the destiny. You and me." She took Morrigan's hand and held it to her heart. She swore she could feel it beat beneath her palm.

The words she'd read flowed through her mind, and now she touched something no witch beyond a Keeper had ever held in their hands. All the signs pointed to Tamsin's truth. "We might be."

Tamsin leaned in and kissed her lightly. "We are. You're no longer only a warrior sent to protect me. You are now as much a Keeper as I am."

"That can't be. Your spell gave me only the ability to touch the *Book of Darkness* and to see its secrets. That's all it is." Keepers were born to the duty, mother to daughter, on and on and on throughout the generations. One couldn't make a Keeper regardless of the strength of their magic. On that score, Tamsin was wrong.

The expression on her face remained one of supreme confidence, and her words backed it up. "Only a Keeper can touch the book and live."

"You drive me crazy." She'd never met someone with a stubborn streak this strong. She couldn't deny that it held as much appeal as it did irritation. Or that it made her even more attractive to Morrigan. If she'd wanted easy, she could have had that with a dozen other women. Intelligence and challenge were an irresistible combination. A tornado that sucked her right into the vortex.

"Did anyone ever tell you the Keeper would be a breeze to deal with?"

Reading her mind again. In fact, as her thoughts rolled back through a lifetime of lessons, not once did anyone ever mention that the Keepers were quiet and compliant. She'd assumed they acquiesced with the jump-and-run situations because, in the past, the relocations had been successful. She'd never thought to ask if the Keepers had been quick to agree to the plans of the warriors sent to whisk them away. Part of the training that consisted of an on-the-job learning moment? Mom could be sneaky like that. Damn her anyway.

"Somehow, I think you take resistance to a proven plan to new levels." She could be stubborn too.

Tamsin's smile grew. "You might have a good point, and I won't bother to argue it. You get me, and I like that about you. Now, I need you to give me your hand."

At this point, what the hell? She held out her hand. "Another spell?"

"Not exactly. A final binder. We'll make this really solid." Tamsin took a small knife from the work counter and, in a quick move, made a small cut on Morrigan's palm. Then she did the same to her own. As blood flowed, she held their crimson-tinged palms together.

"Pretty sure the health authorities would have a big problem with this." Heat roared between their flesh as their palms met and blood mixed with blood.

"They're jealous because they don't have our powers."

The warmth flowed from her hand to flood throughout her. Not the kind of happy feeling from their lovemaking. No, more an inferno that reached all the way into the marrow of her bones and every cell in her brain. Intoxicating, and it sucked the breath out of her.

Tamsin watched her intently. "You understand?"

She nodded. No turning back now. The Keeper had made her call, and Morrigan threw all in whether she believed it to be the right path or not. The spell had been cast and their bond sealed in blood. Mom had never prepared her for this, and maybe, just as well. She became bound to Tamsin and the *Book of Darkness*. She had only one path forward from here.

Tamsin let go of her hand and took the *Book of Darkness* back to the safe. A few whispered words and once more it disappeared behind the painting. "Shall we get ready to meet everyone?"

"I have to make a call first. I've put it off too long. I'm surprised no one has contacted me yet." Ignoring the hierarchy would have certain ramifications. She'd deal with those when they came, and they would.

Tamsin made a face. "Can't you delay a little longer? We don't need them."

Them, of course, being additional White Faction warriors, and while she might go along with Tamsin's plans, she had a more difficult time resisting help. Power in numbers was another tried-and-true strategy. "They can help. I'm not the only one trained to protect you."

"I'm telling you, we don't need them." Tamsin leaned against the counter and shook her head. "No, just no."

Morrigan ran her hands through her hair and rubbed her fingers against her scalp. As exciting as she found Tamsin, she could also be exasperating. "I'm making the call, and you'll have to deal with it. I cannot simply ignore them indefinitely. It doesn't work that way. If I don't check in, they'll think something has gone wrong and find us one way or the other. Do you want them showing up without the full story?"

Tamsin sighed. "Fine. Make your call, but tell them you're handling me fine and don't need any more help. I'm doing as you instruct."

"You want me to lie?"

"I would never ask you to lie. Maybe just a little stretch of the truth."

Morrigan's phone rang. She held it up for Tamsin to see. "Told you."

❖

"I need a drink." Freddi pointed to an upcoming freeway exit, where plenty of lighted signs promised food, gas, and spirits. To hop out of the car and walk around for a little while appealed to her. They'd been driving for hours, and the car had become claustrophobic.

"You told me to drive straight through." He sounded like a little kid who wanted to argue when being disciplined.

"Yes, I did. And now, I'm telling you to get me a fucking glass of wine."

"Aye, aye, Captain." The click-click of the blinker filled the car. At least he could follow directions.

When he started to pull into the parking lot of a restaurant near the exit, she pointed forward. "There." The sign of a Hilton. Even better.

"Hotel? I thought you wanted a glass of wine. This is a freaking wine bar." That little-kid whine again. Oh, yes, she had to get out of the car right now.

"I want a bottle of wine, AND I want a shower." She'd be better able to roll with his annoying little-boy tendencies after a good drink and the time to freshen up.

As soon as they were checked into a room at the Hilton, she sent him out for a bottle of wine—not a cheap one—while she took advantage of the time and stepped into a steaming hot shower. Her goal had been more complicated than a drink and time to freshen up.

The quick shower to recoup her energy made a huge difference, and while she'd wanted to linger beneath the warm water, she didn't. The errand she'd sent Ian on would take him a good amount of time. She'd made sure of that by requesting a specific bottle of wine. He'd find it, eventually.

The buzzing in her body had started about fifty miles back. Something had changed while they were driving north, something important, and the push to find out what had become all-consuming. To do that, she needed time alone, some coffee grounds, and a bottle of vodka. A driver out on a difficult errand, combined with a hotel room equipped with a coffee machine and a mini-bar, provided her everything she needed.

After she dressed, she spread out a silk scarf that had been folded up inside her bag and sprinkled the coffee grounds on it. She took a sip of the vodka, not bad, and then poured a liberal amount on her hands. Nice and wet, the smell of alcohol filling her nose, she placed her hands on top of the scattered grounds. Her head jerked back, and her eyes closed.

"I call upon Circe, Goddess of vengeance and sorcery. Dark maiden and powerful hunter. Wisdom of the underworld. Mother of transformation. Hear me now, for I seek your aid. Circe, by your power, I call upon you to grant me vision. May she who is both mother and maiden bless me with sight. Come, Circe. Aim thy wand and show me the way."

Images sped through her mind. Beautiful faces. Pine trees. The clear rushing water of a river. Massive basalt rock formations. A swinging bridge over white-capped water. A large wooden sign with bright white lettering: Bowl and Pitcher.

Freddi's hands dropped away from the scarf and the coffee grounds as she dropped to the floor. Her head down, she took half a dozen deep breaths, the air filling her lungs and clearing her mind. "Thank you, Circe," she said quietly.

She'd known they were headed to Spokane on the northeast side of Washington state, but the greater Spokane area was large and spread out. She'd needed additional clarity, and the Goddess had just given her a far more accurate look at her final destination. A perfect spot for a showdown. She'd always loved water. Not quite as much as fire, but it held its own certain appeal.

It took only a few minutes to wash away the coffee grounds and rinse the vodka out of her scarf. It quickly dried when she used the hairdryer on the bathroom wall. Folding it carefully, she put the gift from a favored lover many years ago in India back into her bag, where it would stay until she needed it again.

The click of the keycard access lock announced Ian's return. She glanced at her phone to see the time. He'd been marginally faster than she'd given him credit for. Either he'd succeeded quickly or failed and gave up the quest.

"I don't know what's so fucking special about this wine. It better be worth it 'cause it was a son of a bitch to find. Took me six stops in this one-horse town and probably twice as expensive as it would be in a decent city."

Still whiny and wrong in his characterization of the place, given the fair size of the town. A far cry from one-horse. "But you found it." She smiled at him, wondering if the smile brightened her eyes.

He made a face. "Of course, I did. I'm a damn genius."

Genuis would be an unreachable stretch for Ian. She'd point it out to him, only it would crush his fragile male ego, and Freddi needed him to hold onto that confidence, misplaced as it might be, until this came to an end. Once the battle reached its pre-determined conclusion, and the *Book of Darkness* rested in her hands, then she'd crush anyone and everyone who got in her way. Or those who simply annoyed her. A new world order, so to speak. It could go either way with Ian.

"It's special." She didn't feel she owed him any more of an explanation. She asked him to do something, he did it. Period, end of story. That defined the nature of their relationship.

"Better damn well be. Kinda expensive too."

What? Did he expect her to pull out her wallet? "Put it on your expense report."

He laughed and set the tall, skinny brown paper bag on the bureau top. "How about we just drink the shit, and it better be good." He took a glass from the tray next to the empty ice bucket and pulled off the protective plastic.

"It is. I promise." She tossed him the corkscrew she carried in her bag. Always be prepared with the essential tools.

He caught it and had the cork out of the bottle quickly. Setting it aside, he unwrapped the second glass. "I'm gonna wash these while the wine breathes. I don't trust that these glasses are clean. You feel me?"

"I feel you." Agreed with him too. She didn't give out trust easily or often, and it rolled all the way down to things like glasses in a hotel room. Trust no one held special meaning for her.

By the time they were halfway through the bottle, Ian acknowledged the value of the tasty wine and admitted it had been worth the effort to find it. Back to being her good boy. Now, leaning against the pillows propped up on the bed, he snored softly. Either a lightweight drinker or exhausted from the hours of driving. Whichever way worked for her because the less he knew, the better. Handy as he might be, only one person needed to know all the details, and that one person would be her. Do as she told him, and all remained good. So far, he'd been fulfilling his job description well enough to keep from being dispatched. He might make it for the long haul. Sometimes miracles happened.

With her wineglass topped off, she took it and her phone out onto the small balcony. She stared off toward the west, the direction they would travel soon enough. Once she entered Bowl and Pitcher into Google, the results were quick and pleasingly specific. Plenty of pictures and detailed directions from their current location. Riverside State Park, Spokane, Washington. She smiled and took a healthy drink of her wine. It went down smooth and pleasing. She held the glass up. "Ready or not, Keeper. I'm coming for you."

CHAPTER TWENTY-THREE

Tamsin wasn't at all excited by Morrigan's phone conversation. Granted, she heard only one side, but enough to get the gist. Morrigan's superiors were demanding an update on the relocation of the Keeper. She'd give her an A plus for smooth talk. At least from what she could hear, and surprisingly, she took full responsibility for their continued presence at the farm. No hint that Tamsin had twisted both her arms to get her to do it her way. This woman amazed her at every turn. Proved her right about the trust she placed in her.

"I will have more updates in the morning. I promise. The report will be to your satisfaction." She slid the phone back into her pocket and blew out a breath. Then she looked at Tamsin and shook her head.

"We have less than twenty-four hours, don't we?" She could see it in her eyes.

Morrigan didn't even try to sugarcoat it. "They're coming. We might have twenty-four hours, but we might not. I don't know how close they are."

A squad of White Faction warriors didn't bode well for her plan. She might be able to bring Morrigan along. A group of witches trained for one path and one path only? A different story altogether, and time wouldn't allow for much effort on that front. Things needed to ramp up in a hurry. That they were meeting with everyone in less than an hour helped.

"No way to deter them?

"They didn't call to get my opinion on whether I needed help. Let's just say they're none too pleased with my progress thus far. They expected you to be far away by now, and the fact that you're not didn't go over well at all. It's entirely possible." She stopped and looked away. "No, that's not accurate, and we don't have the bandwidth for half-truths or worse."

"What?" Unease rippled through her at the tone beneath Morrigan's words.

"It's likely that I'll be expelled."

Tamsin stared. "They can't do that to you. None of this is of your making."

"They can and they will. The details don't really matter. You're too important, and as far as they're concerned, I'm failing."

"I know enough about how things work for you to also know that they can't expel you for one strike." The absurdity of the possibility baffled her.

Part of her lessons growing up were about the skills, abilities, and rules for the witches who protected the Keepers. It wasn't a one-and-done type group. Not a three-strikes-you're-out group either. They allowed for an error, even a fatal error, as long as the warrior didn't make two. After the second one, the witch could, and most likely would, be expelled from the White Faction. Shunned, as it were. To her knowledge, it rarely happened, and the transgressions that precipitated them were great.

"You and the *Book of Darkness* matter more than me. I'm not saying that for sympathy. It's a fact, and you know it as well as I do. If I can't get you to safety, for whatever reason, I've failed."

"Again, I don't understand. This isn't on you. Just tell them the truth. It's me that's holding up this whole show."

She took Morrigan by the arms and stared into her eyes. Something flickered there, and it made Tamsin's heart beat faster.

Morrigan shook her head slightly. "The truth won't matter in this instance. Doesn't make a difference if the bog-down is because of you or me. We're still here, and that's on me."

That look in her eyes pulled at her. "No. I don't accept it. I will talk with whoever comes. I will explain the truth, and you absolutely will not be expelled just because I'm refusing to leave. Unacceptable and unfair. I won't let them do that to you." No way would she allow Morrigan's expulsion. The Keeper's word had to count for a lot.

Morrigan blinked and sank to a kitchen chair. She put her head in her hands. Quietly she said, "I haven't told you something kind of important."

❖

Talk about an oh-shit moment. This had it written all over it in giant black letters. In the back of her mind, Morrigan had always hoped she could tuck her ugly history away and never let it see daylight again. Massive wishful thinking. Or, more accurately, delusional thinking. Twenty years in the rearview mirror and it still wouldn't let her go. Mom hadn't been wrong when she'd told her that when a person played in the pig pen, they got covered in crap. She'd never been able to wash it completely away.

Tamsin knelt in front of her and took her hands. The warmth helped, and she'd miss that feeling when it came time to leave. Broke her heart a little bit too. All over again. She'd thought she'd made her amends years ago, cleaned her slate. In the intervening years, she'd taken extra care to do everything right and to not judge or demean others. To never cast the first stone. To do only good work. How to explain any of it to this amazing woman who'd found a place in her heart?

Thanks to Tamsin's persuasion, taking a stand against the coming Black Faction warrior felt like the right path as well. This beautiful, powerful witch had managed to convince her there were two right paths. She chose to follow Tamsin's option, and she could make peace with her decision. She hadn't expected that it would lead her to this moment filled with truth and heartache. Her secret would destroy it all.

"You're safe with me. I promise." Tamsin squeezed her hands. Safe? Yes, she believed that. But safety had nothing to do with what her secret would do to them. "My truth will make you hate me, and that breaks my heart more than you can possibly know."

Tamsin shook her head and squeezed harder. "You're wrong. Nothing you could say would make me hate you. Nothing."

"Don't be so sure. My secret is dark and ugly, and there's no coming back from it once the words are out there." It wasn't an exaggeration. She couldn't take it back.

Tamsin kissed her. Her touch, slow and filled with emotion, brought tears to her eyes. It told her more than words ever could. "Tell me, love."

A tear escaped and rolled down Morrigan's cheek. Oh yeah. Some big, bad warrior she turned out to be. She could almost envision her mother's disappointment if she could see her right now, with her bent shoulders, hands shaking, and a hang-dog expression. Rule number one, warriors don't cry. She took a deep breath and straightened up. At this point, she had nothing to lose. Either she would tell Tamsin, or they would upon their arrival. "I was eighteen years old."

"You came into your powers."

Tamsin didn't have a clue about the shame about to pass her lips.

True-enough statement, because for most of them the age of eighteen meant their powers manifested at full strength. It separated the warriors from the healers. No mystery about which direction her powers would take. All the women in her line were warriors. Blood ran hot and strong in her ancestors, and she'd inherited it all. She folded her hands in her lap. Harder to see the shaking that way. "Yes, but that's not what made that year important in my life."

"Tell me what happened." Tamsin pulled up a chair and sat right next to her. The heat of her body wrapped around Morrigan like a blanket, and she closed her eyes as she breathed in the sweet scent of her.

She opened her eyes and dropped her gaze. "I fell in love." The start of the end.

"Didn't we all? Chloe Markim, in my case. Not a witch. A neighbor with long blond hair and the bluest eyes you've ever seen. Let me tell you, my family was not impressed. A regular had no place in my world, and trust me, they told me that a thousand times before we broke up. They had a different idea of who I should love, like male and magical, but there I was, falling in love with these young women. A lot of head-shaking in my family and muttering about how they hoped I'd grow out of my girl stage."

How she wished it had been that simple for her. She kept her gaze on her clasped hands. No way did she want to look into Tamsin's eyes. "If I'd fallen in love with a regular, that would have been a whole lot better than what actually happened."

"It can't be that bad." Tamsin kept a note of optimism in her voice. She'd noticed in their time together that Tamsin had a way of seeing the best in everything, while Morrigan tended more toward the other direction. Pessimism and caution had served her well.

"Oh yes, yes, it can." No exception here. Bad on every front.

"Tell me. My feelings about you won't change, I can promise you that. This thing we have is special, and I know you feel it too. Besides, everyone has secrets, and everyone is entitled to them."

Morrigan believed Tamsin, at least when it came to the depth of her feelings. Never before had she experienced emotion at this level. Everything about Tamsin screamed love and a future, except the part about maybe dying at the hands of the Black Faction. That sort of rained on the idea of a future together. That very real possibility weighed heavily on her. She would protect Tamsin to her dying breath, and that wasn't simply a corny saying. Straight-up fact. She'd do it willingly and without pause. She'd have done it for any Keeper. For Tamsin, she'd rise from the dead if she had to in order to keep her safe. That's what people did for those they...no, she wouldn't think it.

She finally looked up at Tamsin. A mistake. To have to confess a horrible moment in her life, a serious lapse in judgment, hurt way more than she could have imagined a couple of days ago. What she wouldn't give to let it stay a secret.

"You can't say your feeling won't change when you have no idea what I'll tell you."

Tamsin sat back in her chair and crossed her arms. "I absolutely can. Nothing you can tell me will change what we have growing between us."

"Don't be so sure."

Her eyes narrowed. "Quit stalling and spit it out. This beating around the bush isn't you. I like the straight-talking Morrigan better."

Ouch. She stared at Tamsin, whose eyes shone with openness and sincerity, and steadied herself for what would come. Tamsin believed what she said about remaining steadfast in her feelings, and Morrigan appreciated that quality about her. She'd expected the Keeper to be strong in her convictions, and Tamsin delivered on that belief one hundred percent. She hadn't expected the warmth and generosity of spirit that she also possessed.

She also hadn't expected to fall in love with her. Damn it, she'd thought it, and after she'd promised herself not to. Even unspoken, the thought made it real. It made the hurt more intense.

She licked her lips, took a breath, and blurted out the ugly truth. "I fell in love with a Black Faction witch."

❖

"Rise and shine." Freddi shook Ian's foot.

"Dude, I'm sleeping." He threw an arm over his eyes as he jerked his foot away from her hand.

"Look, big baby, how about you get your butt out of bed? I'm leaving in thirty, with or without you."

He sat up and pushed the hair out of his eyes. Bed head worked for him, not that she planned to get distracted at the moment. She'd rested herself for about an hour. Between the information gleaned from her spell, the wine, and a little sleep, her energy soared. Before too long, would she even need any rest? With the passing of each hour, power built in her body and soul.

True enough, she'd taken power from other witches for quite some time. A neat little trick her mother had taught her and one they kept as a nice family tradition. What good old Mama had neglected to mention might be the most important piece. The quality of the power taken made a huge difference. Regular witches were good for a quick charge. Great witches, like Abba, were unbelievable, indescribable. If she'd realized what Abba possessed, she'd have come for her sooner. Better late and all that. Made her want to hunt down each and every witch with even a hint of Abba's strength and take it from them. Combine that with the promises found inside the *Book of Darkness*, and nothing and no one would ever be able to stop her. She would stand alone as the greatest witch to ever walk the earth.

He dropped back against the pillows, his arm once more over his eyes. "You can't leave without me. I have the keys."

"You mean these keys?" She held them up so he could see them. The sooner she got back on the road, the sooner it would all be hers, and she didn't intend to hang around waiting on his lazy ass. "Get up!"

"God, you can be a bitch." He peeked out from beneath his arm.

"You like that about me."

He sat up and laughed as he swung his feet to the floor. "A good bitch is hard to beat." He scratched his butt as he walked to the bathroom. "Room for two in the shower."

She started to turn away and then changed her mind. Why not? Any bit of energy grabbed from another only enhanced the metamorphosis happening to her. Hot water and a good fuck— couldn't go wrong there.

Wasn't an unwise decision either. Having delivered a worthy performance, Ian strutted as he dried off and dressed. Lack of confidence wasn't his problem, though it could end up becoming one for her. If their odd partnership were to survive, he would have to do exactly as she told him without question and without taking it upon himself to improvise. The latter had her somewhat worried. If he thought the fact that she fucked him gave him rights, he'd be very, very wrong.

Back in the car, he navigated away from the hotel and to the freeway on-ramp. "Okay, you said head north, and that's what I'm doing. Exactly where north would be helpful." He merged into heavy traffic that would lighten as they left the city.

She leaned forward and began to enter the location into the navigation. "Spokane, Washington."

"I thought you said we were going to northeast Washington? Now we're going to Spokane."

Through narrowed eyes she stared at him. "Ian, do you have a clue where Spokane is?"

He shrugged. "By Seattle, right?"

"No, dumbass. It's in northeast Washington state, just like I told you before."

He made a face. "Really? Who the hell goes there?"

"Apparently, the Keeper."

"No shit. No wonder nobody found her before now."

"Have you ever been there?" She'd already noticed that Ian liked to make it sound as though he knew more than he actually did. As some great world traveler with knowledge of just about everything. She doubted he'd ever left the continental US.

"No. Who would want to go there? It's not like it's Seattle, which actually has something to offer. I prefer civilization over the nature-is-everything types. I'm pretty sure you do too."

Freddi didn't discount any town or city, state, or even country. Each place, regardless of where, had its own charms. No, she'd never been to that part of Washington state either. Didn't mean she wouldn't like it. Didn't mean it wasn't a great hiding place for a Keeper. They'd been tracked down in some most unlikely locations over the years. Given the size of the greater Spokane area, according to her web search, it appeared as though she'd been hiding in plain sight for years.

"Just drive. It is what it is, and you'll have to deal with it. You have no freaking idea what it's like."

"Still sucks. Just saying."

She reached up and wrapped her fingers around Abba's emerald and Aldo's obsidian, both of which now lay against her throat on a single chain. Warmth spread into her hand, and she leaned her head back, eyes closed. A face appeared, long black hair streaked with strands of white, dark eyes that shone with intelligence and magic. *I'm coming for you.*

CHAPTER TWENTY-FOUR

Of all the things she might have guessed would come out of Morrigan's mouth, that had to be the absolute last. Tamsin didn't mean to let the shock show and knew that it did. No way on earth to hide it. "Oh." The only word that came to mind.

Morrigan's eyes glistened, and she bit her lower lip. Tamsin's response, or lack thereof, hurt her and the sadness in her words reflected that pain. "Not my finest hour."

Okay, regrouped, expression neutral, she tried again. "Tell me. I know there's a story behind this, and I want to hear it. You're not the kind of person to run headfirst into danger, especially not the Black Faction kind of trouble." Tamsin wasn't about to judge. She'd made her fair share of mistakes through the years. One of the reasons she possessed such confidence in how she wanted to proceed now. All the trial and error forced her to learn the difference between a solid plan and one based on shaky facts. She needed to extend latitude to Morrigan for mistakes made.

Morrigan drew in a deep breath and let it out slowly before she started to speak. "Real simple, at least in the beginning. Young love, and I don't think you'll have any problem guessing how blind that made me."

Did she ever. "Oh, I remember the early ones. Don't we all? Blindness in that kind of situation isn't unique to you."

The shadow of a smile crossed Morrigan's face. "Early flush is pretty intoxicating."

"It is." She remembered falling in love like that, and it had been glorious and exciting and crushing.

"The blindness part is where I stumbled down a rabbit hole that's been with me ever since."

"It's hard to see the truth when you're in love, especially when you're a teenager. Everything is more intense."

Morrigan tapped on the tabletop, her gaze roaming around the room. Anywhere, it seemed, except on Tamsin. "Here's the thing. I can rationalize everything through the lens of a teenager except for the fact I saw the truth, and I made a choice."

"Oh." Geez. She did have a fairly good grasp of English and should be able to come up with a better response than that.

Morrigan finally looked at her and shrugged. "Yeah, oh. I knew what she was but ignored it. I believed love would make it all okay. That I could change her. Bring her with me into the White Faction."

"Again, you're not unique in that mindset. We all believe love can fix everything. Sometimes it can."

"More often it can't."

"What happened?" She needed to know the rest of the story. It tore Morrigan apart—she could see the self-loathing in her eyes and the tenseness in her body. That mistake, even years later, weighed heavy on this warrior.

"I snuck her into my room one night, and after I fell asleep, she went into my mother's bedroom and stole the bracelet of the elders. Handed down from mother to daughter for hundreds of years and, because of me and my stupidity, lost. To this day, I believe that the theft of that bracelet had a lot to do with my mother's death. The shame of my actions killed her."

"I don't believe that for a minute. It wasn't your fault, and I'd be shocked to find out your mother thought any differently."

"If I hadn't brought that witch into our home, the bracelet would have been around my mother's wrist when she went up against the

Black Faction witches. The added protection might have saved her life."

"*Might* being the operative word." In her mind, *might* often rivaled *should*. Lots of things might have been. Lots of things should have been. Didn't mean any of them would have been. They could be very destructive and demoralizing words.

"Would have saved her life."

No. She didn't necessarily buy into that one. "I believe in the magic the talismans can provide just as much as the next witch. I also know that they are not an end-all and be-all. We fight the battles to the best of our abilities with whatever we have in a given moment. Most of the time we succeed because we've been blessed and the Goddess has our backs. Even with all of that, our magic isn't infallible."

"Other times we do not succeed."

"And those losses are not because one young witch made a bad choice in a lover when just a kid. It takes a lot more than that, and I think you know it. You've been needlessly beating yourself up over this for how long? You have to let it go and move forward. We're headed toward the future, not the past."

"I can't let it go, and the piece you're missing is that it was my first strike. I'm now staring down the barrel at number two."

"They shouldn't have held you to that. You were a kid. We don't exactly make our best decisions when we're that young. You're not unique in that regard. When we have more time, I can give you a list of my poor decisions."

"True enough, except a major error gives it a lot more weight, and they were right in giving me the strike. I should have known better. I had been taught better, and I ignored everything. I let everyone down and got what I deserved."

"Nope. You followed your heart, and sometimes that's exactly the right thing to do. We can't always live in our heads. At times the heart deserves to rule. Not to mention, they had to believe in you because they sent you to me. Whatever mistake you made back then, you regained their trust, and let me make this crystal clear—you have mine."

Morrigan shook her head. "I can't afford not to be realistic. This is my second strike. They won't give me another chance, and I don't believe I deserve one."

"That's total bull. We haven't done anything wrong, zero, and I won't let them do this to you."

"You're not hearing me." Morrigan's eyes were full of pain.

Tamsin tamped down the urge to grab her by the arms. How could she make Morrigan see reason? "*You* haven't done anything wrong. A little different set of rules when it comes to me. I'm not allowing you to force me into something I don't intend to do. They can't hold you accountable for my exercise of free will."

"They do." Resignation rang heavy in Morrigan's words.

Conviction rang just as heavy in hers. "They're wrong."

❖

Morrigan didn't see any of it the same way as Tamsin. They were not wrong about her failure to follow protocol, and it had nothing to do with whether the Keeper agreed. A good warrior would take charge and do what needed to be done. Back to the throw-the-Keeper-over-her-shoulder-and-physically-removing-her-from-danger. Fail. The second strike wholly deserved.

So far, she'd done pretty much zip when it came to utilizing the training of a lifetime. Instead, she'd waltzed in here and promptly succumbed to the charms of yet another woman. This time, she wasn't young and impressionable, and Tamsin was as far away from a Black Faction witch as one could possibly get. Still didn't change a thing about what had happened. Or, rather, what didn't happen here. She'd been given a direct order, one she'd waited her whole life to be considered worthy enough to undertake. Instead of following it to the letter, she'd done the exact opposite and would now pay a heavy price. She looked at Tamsin. Worth it.

She wanted her to understand the whole picture. Things would not go the way Tamsin believed they should, and only fair she understood why. "They're not wrong. I deserve to be expelled."

"Oh, wait a damn minute. That is not true. Your orders have always been to make sure the Keeper is protected and to ensure that the *Book of Darkness* does not fall into the hands of the Black Faction."

True enough. "Yes." Simple really. Made it all the sadder how she'd crashed and burned.

Tamsin took her hand, another charming little trait she'd noticed about her. She'd miss it. "Stop thinking about how you deserve punishment. All kidding aside, I can almost hear your thoughts. You believe that by taking an alternate course, you've betrayed the warriors of the White Faction, and I'm telling you that's simply not true."

"How can you say that? It's absolutely how it's gone down."

"Easy to say because it's the truth. You haven't failed, and neither have I. We're both going against everything that was taught us, to the lessons that were drilled into our heads and our hearts year in and year out. Here's the thing. Just because we're doing it a different way doesn't make it wrong."

Different definitely made it wrong in the eyes of the White Faction, and Morrigan didn't have the same level of confidence in this alternate path. "I'm defying a direct order and putting you in real danger." That part hurt the most. She wanted Tamsin safe more than anything in the world, magical or regular.

"Screw orders. Sometimes you have to dig deep and find the courage to do what's right." Tamsin put a hand on Morrigan's chest. "Tell me you don't feel it right here. Tell me. I dare you."

She stared into Tamsin's eyes. Or was it her soul? All her resistance drained away. At this point, the die had been cast. The elders knew she'd defied orders and had probably already voted to expel her. The thing about it, she could live with their disappointment and decision to banish her. If successful in this fight, and Tamsin's absolute conviction swore they would be, then what happened to her afterward didn't matter. Tamsin would be safe, and so would the world. The Black Faction would be stopped at long last. Song over. Mic dropped.

She stared into Tamsin's eyes and nodded. "I can't deny any of it. I feel it."

Tamsin kissed her. "When this is all over, I plan to show you how much you mean to me. I don't give a good goddamn about your moment with the Black Faction witch. I know your heart. I feel your soul. You are as good as they come, and I want you in my life."

If I live through it. She kissed her back, savoring the sweetness of her, and kept her dark thoughts to herself.

❖

"What in the hell is that?" Freddi leaned forward and stared hard out the windshield. Colored lights flashed, and the cars ahead of them slowed to a stop.

"Accident."

"Really?" Like she couldn't see that herself?

"Everybody's stopped."

Another duh. He did like to state the obvious. "We really don't have time for this. We've got to get to Spokane." She tapped her fingers against her legs.

Ian touched the navigation screen. "Alternate route." He stared at the screen and then sighed. "Not too helpful. We'd have to backtrack quite a distance, and then it's all country roads for miles and miles before we could return to the freeway. Doesn't crank me up much to drive in the sticks. Crappy roads, no lights, single lane. No gas stations. All sucks, if you ask me."

She looked around, hoping to see something that might inspire her. With traffic at a complete standstill, even if they wanted to turn around, they couldn't. No way to escape the hell they'd just found themselves in.

"You're pretty amped up." Ian turned and looked at her. "Use your magic to make something happen here. Clear this shit out so we can get moving again."

Even her greatly enhanced powers had limits. Moving a freeway clogged with stopped vehicles, tangled cars, and emergency responders fell out of her range. Sort of. Perhaps with a bit of a nudge she could move things along. At least enough to get one lane open. It would be slow, but movement was movement. Definitely worth a shot.

"Give me a few minutes."

"Whatever you need, Boss. If we can get through here and avoid back roads, I'm all over it. Who in the hell wants to go wandering around roads in the middle of nowhere? Not my kind of country, if you know what I mean. The sooner we make it out of this state, the happier I'll be."

She did know. Like Ian, she'd come from a major metropolitan area. In her case, Atlanta, and rural travel wasn't her jam. Ian had grown up in Los Angeles, or at least that's what he told her. She believed it, even if he didn't have the stereotypical California look. More West Coast, urban way of talking that gave him away, and she suspected his comfort zone leaned toward six-lane freeway rather than two-lane back roads.

Freddi wrapped her fingers around the two stones at her neck and closed her eyes. Warmth began to spread from her fingers to her arms to her shoulders. Images whizzed through her mind. Random at first and she forced herself to focus. She smiled. Her initial thoughts about not being strong enough were wrong. The power in her had grown more than she imagined it could, and all she had to do was take the time to control it. Breathing slowly in and out, she visualized the accident cleared enough for traffic to once again begin to flow. See it. Feel it. Make it happen.

Silence dropped over her, and as it did, her spirit floated away from her body. Above the mass of cars and emergency vehicles, she moved with clarity and purpose. "Part the sea," she murmured. "Let us pass."

Below her, a rising murmur. A path began to appear in the tangle of broken vehicles and the highway littered with shattered glass and metal shards. Two ambulances, loaded and with lights flashing, disappeared into the encroaching darkness. The patrol cars blocking all the lanes moved out enough to open one of them, and uniformed officers signaled for cars to begin slowly driving past the accident scene.

"We're clearing out." Ian put the car in gear and waited for the movement to reach them.

Ian's words and the motion of the car brought her back to her body, and her hand dropped away from the stones. She blinked, and everything came back into focus. Ahead of them taillights were coming on. Movement, albeit slow, began. They would be able to continue their journey without having to navigate bleak, back-country roads.

"Good."

"Only cost us two hours."

Two hours? As she'd watched from above, Freddi could have sworn only minutes had passed. "We can make up the time."

He glanced over at her. "You do know we have more than one mountain pass to go through, right? I don't think making up the time is in the cards on this stretch of the trip."

It occurred to her that he liked to grab onto pessimism. She, on the other hand, worked more from optimism, primarily because she had unshakable faith in her own abilities. It had been with her since childhood and would be with her forever.

"Just drive, and make up time where you can." Did she really have to explain everything to him in minute detail? All of a sudden, she wondered about his critical-thinking skills. No question that would not be a check mark in the keeper column.

For the moment, she'd let it go. Too many other things to focus her energy on. Her head tilted back, she closed her eyes again. Some rest would do her good. This last exercise had taken a little bit out of her, and she wanted to be at a hundred and fifty percent when they made it to their final destination. Her body relaxed and she drifted into sleep. An hour later, a jolt brought her upright, and her eyes snapped open.

"This cannot be happening. Fuck. Fuck. Fuck." Ian smacked the steering wheel with the palm of his hand at the same time he pulled the car over to the shoulder.

She blinked, pushing away the effects of slumber, and worked to focus. "What is it? Why are you stopping? We don't have time to make another stop." He could pee later, or whatever he thought he needed to do. Pee in his pants for all she cared.

He brought the car to a stop and turned it off, then glanced at her with a scowl. "We have a damn flat tire."

CHAPTER TWENTY-FIVE

Tamsin waited with Morrigan by the water as the sun disappeared behind the mountains to their west and darkness dropped over them. The breathtaking colors buoyed her spirit. Not that Tamsin needed much in that respect. In her mind, everything over the last few days had dropped into place, the picture very nearly complete.

As confident as she liked to appear and sound, a tiny bit of doubt found a way to wiggle into her heart. At least over the last few hours. She swept her gaze over Morrigan, and it didn't take much of a leap to figure out why questions assailed her now. Never before had she felt anything this intense for another woman, and she didn't care one bit about her secret. Her so-called critical failure.

But she did care about Morrigan. She wanted to go to bed with her every night and wake up to her face every morning. So what if they'd only met recently? That didn't change how she felt. Tamsin knew the real deal when she found it. Just like she knew that this place was meant to be her forever home. It all landed right in the depths of her soul.

It also scared her a little. She'd finally found someone special, and her own decision to stay and fight the Black Faction could, probably would, jeopardize her hopes for a lifetime together. Her decision could get people killed, and it weighed heavy on her, no matter how she rationalized it.

She stared out at the water, the wind causing small ripples to spread across the surface. Trees swayed, and a single pinecone thudded to the ground at her feet, bouncing and rolling. Was it telling her to beware? Should she abandon this course and keep everyone safe? Give up on the idea that she could change history?

"Too late." Morrigan's voice was as soft as her hand holding tight to Tamsin's.

She turned and looked into her eyes. "What?"

"Lady, I can almost hear your thoughts. You know, kind of like you're always saying to me? Now that we're in the eleventh hour, you're giving in to doubts. Go ahead. Tell me I'm wrong."

She shook her head slowly. "You're not."

"Shocker."

"I've been so sure about all of this until now, and I can't help thinking that I'm dragging innocents into a war they have no business joining. You could be hurt, or worse. I've always known there's danger, but all of a sudden it's gotten way too real."

"Here's the thing. I'm a big girl, and I've made my choices. I could have done things differently, and I, alone, chose not to. I'll take my lumps."

That should make her feel better. Why didn't it? "But Holly, Triple, the grandmothers. They didn't ask for any of this. They have no real idea what they're up against, and I've dragged all of them right into the middle of a fight that's not theirs. That took some elephant-sized balls, and now I'm having some elephant-sized doubts."

Morrigan squeezed her hand. "I have three words for you."

"Turn and run?" That's what she'd been hearing from Morrigan all along, and now she gave her the opening she'd been looking for.

"Nope. Too fucking late for that one."

Not the response she expected.

"It's not. We could make a run for it." If they hurried, maybe it wasn't too late to get ahead of the Witch Finder.

"Oh, sister, it is way too late. She's on her way. I can feel her like a bad cold coming on, and she's bringing hell with her. We would be wise to accept any and all help offered, and once we do, we'll take her down. Got it?"

"I don't know." She didn't get why her confidence had fled in this eleventh hour. Up until now, she'd been solid and sure of herself.

Morrigan took her face in her hands. "I asked, got it?"

Tamsin stared into Morrigan's eyes. Her throat tightened. "Got it."

❖

Odd as it seemed, Morrigan took heart in Tamsin's moment of doubt. All along she'd been adamant about staying to fight, and, at least in Morrigan's mind, she leaned solidly toward selfishness by wanting to keep the life she'd built at the risk of anyone and everyone. This hesitation, even if it happened at the last minute, gave Morrigan more confidence that they would prevail. It let her know that Tamsin wasn't blind and deaf to the magnitude of the danger that roared toward them. It filled her with hope.

A welcome sound came with the murmur of voices coming closer and closer. After all the back-and-forth with Tamsin, she found herself more than ready for things to come to a head. That and she could feel the press of the coming battle. A Witch Finder, a very powerful one, drew ever closer, bringing oppression and darkness with her. It would take all their respective forms of magic combined to stop her and keep the *Book of Darkness* safe. No matter what else happened, its protection was paramount. They could not allow the evil within its pages to fall into the hands of those who would use it to harm innocents.

"Honey, we're home." Holly's bright voice preceded her appearance through the stand of trees. She emerged from the shadows, followed by Triple and the three grandmothers, as she'd started referring to them in her mind, a headlight looking like a beacon strapped to her head. "We're here, and ladies, we're ready to get this show going. Kick some evil ass."

"As are we." Morrigan's body buzzed. The approach they were about to embark upon didn't sync with any of the lessons she'd been taught, and, strangely, she didn't give a damn. Her heart leaned into the time-for-the-new-approach philosophy, and maybe learn something along the way. While she'd always had great respect for the indigenous peoples, she'd not studied their cultures in detail. She'd spent too much of her life learning the ways of magic of her foremothers in order to fulfill her destiny of protecting the Keeper. Shame on her. Well, never too late to do better.

Just like all of a sudden, this felt right. The sight of the three older women, each holding a flashlight, did her heart good. They came from generations of people who lived in harmony with nature and the spiritual world. They held their own form of magic, and that they came together now in a merger of mind, body, and spirit felt an awful lot like destiny. The universe wanted them all here as a cohesive unit to share the individual blessings they'd been given and protect the world from the forces of evil that wanted to rip it apart.

"What do you need us to do?" Triple stood with his feet slightly apart, his hands in his pockets, his light clipped to the bill of his cap. His appearance might convey casual, but his aura didn't. Energy pulsed from him, strong and deep. Good. They'd probably need it before this thing ended.

Grace gestured toward a spot not far from the water, where the wild grasses swayed in the breeze. The flashlight she waved whispered across the yellow wildflowers growing among the grass, and as the beam of light hit them, it was as though they blinked in welcome. "Please sit in a circle and join hands. We need the circle to remain unbroken. Whatever you hear or see, do not let go."

Dampness seeped into her jeans as she sat cross-legged on the ground—Tamsin across from her, with Triple on her left, and Holly on her right. The grandmothers stood in the center of the circle they formed, their hands joined and their voices low as they chanted. She couldn't make out the words. The magic they stirred was a different story. The air grew thick, and the sky grew even darker. Thunder barked in the distance, and the scent of pine wafted over them.

Her body began to buzz with a sudden, shocking intensity. It had obviously been the same for Holly and Triple because their hands began to tremble. She held on tighter. Grace told them not to break the circle, and she wasn't about to be the one to do it. She'd messed up enough in her life and didn't intend to do it again now. Magic flowed up her arms and toward her heart. She'd been around some powerful women in her time, but this flew right off the charts.

The wind kicked up, whipping her hair around her face, and the chanting of the grandmothers grew louder. She trembled head to toe and tightened her grip. Holly and Triple's hands shook harder. She didn't know how much longer she could hold on. Across the circle Tamsin's eyes were wide.

And then, silence.

❖

"Hurry the hell up." Freddi stood on the side of the road, tapping her foot, as she watched Ian change the tire. Even getting to this point had been a clusterfuck. It had taken forever for him to find the jack, and then to get it positioned under the car yet another ordeal. The man had zero chances for a career in the automotive industry. After watching this performance, it surprised her he'd been able to figure out how to start the car. Her confidence in him wavered greatly, most excellent skills in bed aside.

"Fast as I can, Boss." He seemed oblivious to her displeasure.

"Not fast enough." Maybe a slap up alongside the head would help.

He rocked back on his heels and waved toward the tire with three of the five bolts reattached. "You want to do this. Maybe you can speed it up." Maybe not as oblivious as she thought.

Freddi had opened her mouth to respond when her feet were swept out from under her. She tumbled backward and landed hard in the ditch, her head bouncing against the solid-packed earth. Stars flashed behind her eyes, and her breath rushed out, the taste of blood in her mouth as her teeth collided with her lips. Her so recently broken fingers sparked as though they hadn't healed at all. For a few moments she lay there unmoving. What just happened? Ian hadn't moved, and besides, he didn't have the guts, or sufficient magic, to take her down. That left only one other possibility, and it sent a sliver of fear down her spine.

"Boss, Boss. What the hell. Are you okay?" Ian leaned over her.

She took his outstretched hand and allowed him to help her to her feet. Dirt and weeds were stuck to her clothes and hair, which made her feel dirty inside and out. She'd kill for a quick shower and a change of clothes.

"Boss," he said again. "Are you hurt?"

She brushed at the dirt and weeds, trying to dislodge as much as she could. "I'm not hurt." Technically correct. The invisible shove had knocked the wind out of her and sent her flying, but that appeared to be the extent of the damage. Even her tingling fingers had returned to normal, the pain fading as quickly as it appeared.

"What happened?" Ian still held onto her hand. "I don't get it. One minute you're standing there giving me shit, and the next you're flying through the air like a foul ball. Dude, it was wild."

He should have been on her side of it. Now that she'd had a minute or two to think, she knew exactly what had happened, and it didn't please her. "It's her." Saying it left a bitter taste in her mouth. The magnitude of what it would take to do that to her didn't escape her.

For a second he stared, and then a spark came into his eyes. "The Keeper?"

She couldn't help the eye roll that despite the darkness would have been hard for him to miss. "Yes, the Keeper. Who else could do something like that?" Besides me, she didn't add. Would probably go right over his head anyway.

"I mean, yeah, I get that it has to be her. What I don't get is how she could have knocked you off your feet clear out here in the middle of nowhere. She can't know we're coming. Nobody knows where we're headed, right? I mean with Abba and Aldo gone, we're on our own. Coming in with full-on stealth mode."

She ran her fingers through her hair, pulling out a few more twigs to toss to the ground. A shiver raced through her. *A shower, please.* Not in the cards for the foreseeable future. She didn't bother to roll her eyes this time. "Of course, she knows we're coming. They don't become a Keeper because they're a run-of-the-mill witch. The bitch is letting me know she's waiting and ready."

"But how, Boss? I still don't get it."

Another of those moments when she wondered how he got this far in life. Or was he deliberately being dense? Either way, the stupidity of his questions hit her last good nerve. "She's the fucking Keeper, Ian. Do you think for one second that job falls to a weak family?"

"Well, ah, no."

"Well, ah, no is right. She's a fucking rock star, and only the most powerful can do the job of Keeper. The. Most. Powerful. Get it?"

"If she's that amazing and she knows we're coming, what real chance do we have to take her down?" He edged perilously close to insulting her. She flexed her fingers, and it took effort not to throw a punch. Not a punch of magical variety either. She wanted her knuckles to connect with his face.

"What makes you think I'm not at her level or beyond?" She straightened her shoulders and held his gaze. *Keep challenging me, you little shit, and I will throw a punch.*

He looked away before answering. "Well, nobody has ever taken down a Keeper."

"Until now." She said the words very slowly.

He swung his gaze back to her, and a smile lit up his face. "Man, I like your attitude. It would be sick if we were the ones to finally do it."

There would be no *we* and definitely *if* about it. This job would fall to her and her alone. No room for failure. She might let him continue to drive the car and warm her bed now and again. Take credit for destroying the Keeper and taking possession of the *Book of Darkness*? In his dreams. She didn't say that to him now. Not quite the time to burst his bubble. "It's not an attitude. It's a fact. She's mine, and so is that grimoire."

He nodded as if he were listening to a punk-rock song. "Righteous, Boss. I'm in for the long-haul, ride-or-die together. I'll finish up the tire, and then we'll make tracks. This time of night, I can make up the time we've lost on the straightaways. The passes might be a bitch, but I'll drive them as fast as I can without crashing. I can't wait to see you take her down. It'll be history, dude."

History would be the least of it. She intended to change the whole damn world.

CHAPTER TWENTY-SIX

Triple broke the silence first. "I don't know about you guys, but that was awesome. I've never felt anything like that before, and wow, what a rush. Those ladies have some serious mojo going on. Need to bottle that crap. We'd be millionaires."

He'd called it perfectly. Tamsin felt it throughout her body. Between them all, they'd harnessed energy like nothing she'd ever experienced before. That said a lot, considering her birth family. They had been known for centuries for the good, clear magic they possessed, the spells they could conjure, and the healing they could produce. Yes, indeed, she'd seen some amazing things in her time, and this surpassed them all. Every single one.

"We have what we need now, don't we?" She looked at Grace. If she said no, Tamsin would be shocked and sad.

No one answered her. Instead, the three women leaned toward each other and touched foreheads. It almost killed her to wait and even more so to stay quiet, the unspoken message she'd received from Grace. Fortunately, she didn't have to wait long and didn't embarrass herself by acting like an impatient child. After maybe a minute, they stood tall and turned to her and the others as they lined up next to each other, waiting.

Grace spoke, her hands folded in front of her, and a little frown on her face. Not encouraging. "It's a bit of a puzzle."

"What? I thought you said you'd be able to call on the wisdom of your ancestors to show us the way. I don't get it." Tamsin's heart dropped, and tears pricked at her eyes. Don't cry, don't cry, she repeated over and over in her head.

Grace inclined her head slightly. "Oh, child, you misunderstand me. They gave us what we need. It's still up to us, up to you, to take what they showed us and work with it. What I was shown is the place. You'll need to go to the Bowl and Pitcher."

A frown crossed Morrigan's face. "Bowl and Pitcher? What the hell is that?"

Tamsin knew it well. In fact, she loved it and went there often. "It's a place. A lovely part of Riverside State Park, right on the river with a swinging bridge and rock formations that resemble a bowl and pitcher, hence the name." She'd always felt energy there, and somehow it seemed like the perfect place. Magic lived in the stones, the waters, the trees. Yes, it made sense.

Morrigan still looked confused. "Okay. That clears up pretty much nothing."

"I'm with Morrigan. I don't get it. That place is all rocks and river and a crapload of trees. Why would anyone go there to try to get a book away from you? Wouldn't it make more sense if they came for you at the farm?" Triple stood, hands in his pockets and frowning. "Easier to defend at the farm too."

Grace shrugged. "The *why* isn't part of the message. No explanations for *how comes* and the *whys*. I only know what we were shown, and that is why you must take the grimoire to the Bowl and Pitcher. That is the message the universe delivered."

"What else?" Tamsin looked to Georgie. There had to be more to it, right?

She nodded and smiled. "The message that came to me was about the land. While my people lived mostly north of here, it still spoke to me. The land and our ancestors sustain us and always have, even in times of great conflict and peril. That's what I'm told now. Great peril is upon us, and the natural gifts will sustain us all once again."

Tamsin wasn't following that at all. Way too cryptic. Her magic, likewise, revered the natural environment. The land, the air, the water. It just didn't seem to click together with what lay ahead for them. "I really don't understand. Isn't there more you can explain to us?"

Georgie nodded again. "As Grace shared, you must make your way to the Bowl and Pitcher. It is there that the ancestors will help guide you and the land will protect you."

"How?" Her frustration at the vague information made her words sharper than she intended. She tried not to be ungrateful, only she'd hoped for more. Oh, hell, she'd expected more, and tears pricked at the back of her eyes. This wasn't helping at all.

This time Georgie shook her head. "That I cannot tell you. It will take the magic you all possess for the solution to be fully revealed."

Morrigan frowned as her gaze moved from face to face. "I don't find any of this particularly helpful, do you?" Her gaze met Tamsin's.

Her first thought aligned all the way with Morrigan's, not helpful at all. She paused, pondering. Maybe not as vague as she first thought, and she turned to number three. Just maybe there was more help here than she first thought. "Ella?"

Georgie had her flashlight pointed toward the ground and swung it back and forth in her hand. The light swept across the grass and the flowers. An attempt to distract?

"It is much more than simply the location," Ella said. "Understand that, like Georgie, my people lived far from here. We dwelled in the cliffs and the mountains. There we learned to respect and revere the wisdom of the stones."

"What?" Morrigan's frown deepened into a scowl. "This is getting more obscure instead of clear. We need directions, a map. This isn't even close."

Ella put a hand on Morrigan's shoulder. "The answer will be in the stones." She said it as though it made perfect sense. and suddenly, in a way, it did. At least for Tamsin.

"I need more." Morrigan pressed her lips together.

"It's all I have."

Morrigan threw up her hands. "Oh, come on. This is what we waited all day for?"

The frustration that was clear in Morrigan contrasted to the peace that washed over Tamsin. No clear answers, she'd give her that. At the same time, the pieces flowed together in a way that made her believe in the Prophecy even more. It would come together, and in a strange way, it started to drop into place for her. They would protect the *Book of Darkness*. They would stop the Black Faction. Tamsin's spirit buoyed.

She took Morrigan's hand. "Let's go get the *Book of Darkness* and make tracks to the Bowl and Pitcher."

Morrigan, shaking her head, pulled her hand free. "It's almost midnight. This is getting crazy, and we know precisely zip. This wasn't helpful at all. You think a Witch Finder will find us in the middle of the night?"

This time Tamsin took both of Morrigan's hands and stared into her eyes. "I know she will."

❖

Way back when she'd fallen for a Black Faction witch, Morrigan had felt like a fool. The same feeling washed over her now. She'd come out here believing that the three elder women would be able to harness their own particular brand of magic and put the spotlight on their next course of action. Instead, they'd provided only cryptic messages that didn't move them forward one step. What the hell kind of help did that give them? None, and that answer burned. They were at a point that required decisive action, not vague references to some park with big rocks.

Even more disappointing, she expected Tamsin to feel the same way, but instead, she seemed to be supercharged. Holly and Triple, after initial confusion, now sported looks of expectation, which told her they were on board with Tamsin. Why did it appear she remained the only one thinking they didn't know jack shit? Why did she always have to be the one standing on the outside? Just once she'd like to be on a united team.

"Morrigan." Holly touched her shoulder. "Don't stop believing. It will all be as it should be." The quietest one in the group, Holly surprisingly helped to reassure her. Sometimes the person who said little heard the most. She suspected Holly weighed it all carefully and reached her own conclusions. She respected that trait.

Respect aside, she still harbored reservations. "They didn't tell us anything that will help." She watched as the grandmothers walked away, chatting among themselves as though they'd just solved all world problems and didn't have a single concern. Everything they ever cared about could blow up before the next sunrise. The flashlights they carried jumped around as their arms swung, and soon enough they disappeared completely as they walked deeper into the trees and toward the farm. The breeze carried their voices away.

"Am I the only one who sees this going south?" She didn't like always being the naysayer. Still, somebody had to be the voice of reason, and again and again that job fell to her.

Tamsin, Holly, and Triple all stared at her. "Yeah," Triple said. "I think you are."

Figures. On the outside looking in. Again. "Shit."

Now Tamsin stepped up and put her arms around her. Her embrace brought her comfort, and she let her arms encircle her in return. Into her ear, Tamsin whispered, "Trust me. We've got this. I promise. Trust me." She kissed her on the cheek.

She sighed and leaned into Tamsin. Breathing in the sweet scent of her that was becoming familiar, she let the tension flow out of her. Useless to fight, and she simply didn't want to anymore. "I do." And that admission came hard.

She kissed her cheek and stepped back. "Then come on. We have a little journey to make, and please, nobody stumble on the way back. We need everyone for this and can't afford any wounded warriors tonight. No broken ankles or smashed knees."

With the help of the headlamps and flashlights, they made their way to the house without even so much as a single trip on a downed branch. Pretty good feat considering the downfall that littered the ground. Tamsin declared this uneventful journey another sign that the universe remained on their side. Morrigan wasn't as sure. Good headlamps and awareness played a far larger part in her opinion.

The little trip Tamsin declared necessary once they gathered together in the kitchen entailed retrieving the *Book of Darkness* and then piling into Triple's SUV. Buckled into the backseat, she fidgeted. Things were raw and messy to her and, apparently, only her. It went against her nature to have no plan and no preparation. Just jump in the car and drive to a place where the river ran strong and hard, surrounded by massive, immovable stones. What could possibly go wrong? She pressed her lips together hard to keep from screaming: EVERYTHING.

Sitting next to her, Tamsin put a hand on her arm and leaned close. "It will work out, love. It will."

The way the word love rolled off her tongue sent a rush through her. She could listen to that endearment for about a thousand years. If only she didn't have to worry about all of them dying at the hands of the Witch Finder. She turned her head to look out the window, darkness making the road hard to see, and enemies even harder. "I'd feel better if the grandmothers had come with us."

"Not safe for them." Tamsin spoke matter-of-factly, as if it were obvious, which, in her opinion, it seemed to be.

She didn't disagree. She also believed they could probably hold their own in almost any situation. They might be older, but she would never make the mistake of discounting their abilities. "They have a pretty interesting form of magic."

"Not the kind we'll need to defeat the Witch Finder."

True enough on the surface of it. She saw it a bit differently. "We can take any and all magic. It's not a new witch coming for us." She'd never considered bringing anyone else into the fray beyond those like herself who came from a long legacy of warrior witches. The grandmothers were an exception.

Tamsin patted the bag resting against her back. Inside was the *Book of Darkness*, retrieved one last time from the magical safe. Its energy pulsated within the SUV to the point of being stifling. Or maybe just to her. Nobody else seemed to be struggling to breathe. No, not a panic attack. Tougher than that. She hoped.

"I'm telling you, we've got this." Tamsin leaned against her shoulder.

She leaned back into her. The connection helped. "God, I hope so."

"Believe, Morrigan. Believe."

If only it were that simple.

❖

Freddi smiled when the big green sign announced the city of Coeur d'Alene, Idaho. The freeway snaked along the massive lake where multi-million-dollar homes dotted the shoreline, the reflections of their interior lights like diamonds on the water. Quiet on the water now, the boats that came out in the daylight would probably be as impressive as the homes where they were moored. Interesting and beautiful as it was, arriving in Coeur d'Alene meant they were closing in and were less than fifty miles from their destination. Maybe an hour or an hour and a half until the Keeper would be no more, and best of all, the world would kneel to her. She looked out the window and smiled.

Her smile turned to a frown as their speed dropped. "What the hell, Ian. Don't slow down. We're close."

Ian gave her a side-eye. "You want us to get pulled over by a stater or get to Washington? Can't have it both ways."

She curled her fingers into a fist. "Don't tell me what I can and can't have."

"Just saying."

Back to being a pain in her ass. Back to rethinking his position within the new order. A lot of other men, or women, out there could step into his role without bringing his mouth along with them. She could train someone up to his level of bedroom skills too. She'd have to see how things went once they were face-to-face with the Keeper. No sense rushing into a decision.

"All right. Point taken. Keep it at the speed limit, and don't draw unwanted attention. I do not want any additional delays. The clock is ticking, if you catch my drift."

Her phone buzzed in her hand, and she glanced down. Well now, wasn't that interesting? Word of Abba's early demise must be circulating, and given how silent her phone had been up until now, they'd been trying to figure out the who, what, and why. "Yes." She drew out the single word as Ian glanced her way.

"What did you do?" A familiar voice, though one she'd managed to avoid for a fair number of years now. Would have liked to have maintained that non-contact infinitum.

"Nice to hear from you, sister." Last time she talked with her older sister, Franci, she'd been in the south of France enjoying good food and even better wine. She'd been far less inclined to follow the warrior path than Freddi, and that had worked for her sister. With Franci out of the picture, for the first time ever, Freddi hadn't been constantly compared to her. An intoxicating freedom she enjoyed.

"I repeat, what did you do?" Quite the bite in her words. Where did Franci get off scolding her? She didn't have the right to question her about a single thing. Franci walked away from their birthright, their duty, not Freddi, so fuck her.

She kept her voice neutral. "Why would you think I did anything?"

"Oh, I don't know. Maybe the fact that you've talked of nothing else your entire life except getting your hands on the *Book of Darkness* and using it to rule the world. Always wrote it off as you talking big. Now, I'm not so sure. I'm hearing things that I don't like, and they all point to you."

"Well, I don't have it." She didn't add the *yet* piece.

"You're motivated and strong. Not strong enough, unless you steal power from others. You need to remember, I had the same lessons from Mother as you did. I know what you can do."

"Don't know what you mean. I'm simply following orders." Strictly speaking, she *was* following orders. That she expanded upon those orders to suit her own needs didn't have to be verbalized, especially to Franci. Or the fact that the order-givers were no longer with them. When she left the Black Faction corps, Franci gave up the right to know any of the business of the order, and since they had no sisterly bond despite sharing the same birth parents, she didn't share any of her personal business with her either.

"Bullshit. You killed Abba, and probably Aldo too, given no one's heard from him in days. I know you, Freddi. I know you did this, and they'll come for you. Bank on it." Oops, so apparently, she did know about the demise of the order-givers. Maybe not as disconnected as she thought.

She smiled, glad for a voice-only call. "Aldo was a jerk."

"Was?"

Shit. Might have tipped her hand there, and Franci always had been sharp. Her fishing expedition had worked. "Was, is, what does it matter? Asshole is asshole, dead or alive."

"I won't let you get away with this. You don't have the right to kill anybody, let alone Aldo." Her words were low and full of menace. She might have taken her leave from the Black Faction, didn't mean she'd lost any of her training. Franci could be lethal too, if she wanted to be. Wouldn't put it past her to lose it on her own sister.

Now she laughed. She had gotten over being threatened by Franci a long time ago, despite her skill set. "Oh, please, like you scare me. Why don't you go drink your fancy French wine and eat your dainty pastries. Besides, what the hell can you do from your cottage in France?"

"Who said I'm in France?" The connection went dead.

The Prophecy

Once dark, now filled with light,
she stands tall and true.
Her heart is pure, her vision clear,
she sees both wrong and right
and answers the call for goodness.
The path will be revealed.
Her hand extends to close the circle.
So it is written in the stars.

CHAPTER TWENTY-SEVEN

Tamsin closed her eyes as they neared the park. Before they'd left the farm, she'd slipped the *Book of Darkness* into a backpack, pulling the straps over her shoulders. It now pulsed against her back as if tapping on her shoulder to let her know they were in the fight together. During her tenure as the Keeper, it had been silent and uneventful, though she'd heard the stories of the grimoire seemingly coming to life in moments of great peril. Before tonight the stories had been something of legend. Over the last few minutes they had gotten very real, scarily real.

"Houston, we have a problem." Triple didn't slow at the entrance to the Bowl and Pitcher. Instead, he drove right on by.

Tamsin opened her eyes and turned her head. They didn't have time for a scenic drive, especially not at this time of night. Then she realized why he'd continued by the turnout that would take them where they needed to be. "Damn."

"You saw the California plates?" Triple kept glancing into the rearview mirror, his expression grim. He might not be one of magic, but his instincts were spot-on. He made a good call to drive by and especially to not even tap on the brakes.

Holly had turned in her seat and was peering out the back window. "Kind of hard to see in the dark. I'm pretty sure a man and a woman are standing at the car."

"Probably them." Not probably, absolutely, though Tamsin wanted to maintain everyone's sharp focus. Keep the energy high and on point.

"It's them." Morrigan didn't appear to share her thoughts. Not surprising. It had been her way all along.

No reason to deny the obvious. Besides, it would become clear soon enough. "It is. The woman is the Witch Finder. Don't know about the guy. I suspect he's a Black Faction helper."

"Now what?" Triple stopped in a small pull-out parking area at the corner of Aubrey White Parkway and Rifle Club Road. The Rifle Club sat just across the road on the banks of the river, tall fences on the ridge, a tidy parking lot at the end of the sloping driveway. Not that anyone used it this time of night or that anything at the club might help them. "And what's a Black Faction helper? I thought you said they were all witches."

"Give me a minute." Explanations of the finer workings of the Black Faction would have to wait until later. Tamsin got out of the car and started to walk across the road. Might as well use what was available to her, and at the moment, a bit of guidance would help. She'd really thought they'd have time at the Bowl and Pitcher before the Witch Finder arrived. She hadn't thought she'd beat them there, and frankly, it pissed her off. A few minutes to regroup and recharge would go a long way toward re-centering herself.

"No way." Morrigan jumped out of the SUV right after her. "You're not going anywhere alone."

She took Morrigan's hand. The comforting charge flowed through her, and right now, she could use it, and some of the anger melted away. "You're right. We're better together."

Morrigan's gaze held hers for a moment, and then she gave a tiny nod. "We are. Now tell me. What exactly are we doing?"

She'd been thinking about this question since they buzzed by the park. A return to basics would be their best bet. "We're about to ask for guidance."

"All right, but I'm confused. I thought that's what we got from the grandmothers. What other guidance are we seeking?"

"Part of the story. Not all of it. We need more." Hard to explain her thought process in a way that made sense, partly because she didn't fully understand it herself. More working off instinct than anything else. Morrigan might get it. She might not.

"We need to leave." Morrigan tugged at her hand.

She tugged back. "Might as well give it up because I'm not about to. I have to see this through."

"Can't fault me for trying." She stopped tugging and squeezed Tamsin's hand.

"No. I don't blame you even a tiny bit, and, in fact, I'd be disappointed if you didn't try. I've sort of come to expect that from you, and I kind of like it too." Her consistency steadied her. That counted for a great deal right now.

"All right then. We'll do this your way, tonight at least. Where to?"

She'd been looking around while trying to not trip on anything in the dark. "There." She pointed to a trail just off the road that appeared like it would take them down to the water. "I think that's the spot to call on the goddesses for help."

"If we don't kill ourselves walking down there in the dark, we could use their help."

Tamsin hugged her close. "They'll help us, but you know what? We have each other, and that's pretty powerful. We've got them too, and we can't discount what they bring." She waved in the direction of the parked SUV, where Triple and Holly waited. "It will be enough."

Morrigan said, "Let's do this."

Her sentiments exactly. She'd waited a lifetime for this encounter and believed herself to be ready. Or she would be as soon as she called upon the wisdom of the goddesses. It might look to Morrigan and the others as though she plunged ahead without worrying that the *Book of Darkness* might fall under the control of the Black Faction. It wasn't that way at all. She took every risk to heart, understood all of them, and the fear of failure on any of them made her hands tremble. Still, the pulsing of the grimoire tucked into her backpack kept her hopes high. In her mind, it told her the moment had arrived for action, the time they'd all been waiting for, century after century, keeper after keeper.

Yes, she wanted to stay here and live her life like others without the title and responsibilities of a Keeper, the selfish part of her that fueled the desire to fight. It went way beyond selfishness. The potential to live a normal life only served as a lure. The promise of safety for everyone remained the golden egg, and that's what drove her, even if she couldn't convince Morrigan of that basic truth.

That no one around her truly understood her motive wouldn't be enough to hold her back. She would see this through and, from all signs, with Morrigan at her side. She glanced up at her profile, and her heart did a little flip. This feeling she got every time she gazed into Morrigan's face amazed her. Love stories were full of such sentiment, but she'd never believed in it for herself. She'd resigned herself to the reality that more than likely, she'd marry a man of magic, and the next Keeper would be born, the legacy continuing on and on. She whispered to herself that she could do it differently, which gave her hope for a fuller life. Currently, she didn't need a man to fulfill a biological need. Doubts whispered in the back of her mind that she'd find the strength to break tradition. The likelihood she'd settle for tradition loomed large. It didn't matter that she'd never love him. Love wasn't a prerequisite to an heir.

Then a few days ago Morrigan had walked up her steps, and tradition had crashed and burned. All the maybe-she-could-do-it thoughts evaporated, and along with it her belief that she could carry on the legacy with a man. Now she understood how she didn't want to live without love. How she didn't want to live without Morrigan. All the more reason to bring this to an end. The Prophecy had to be written and waiting for her. It had to be for this night and this fight. It just had to be.

❖

A shift occurred, and it hit Morrigan like a slap to the back of the head. The energy that flowed from Tamsin and into her made her shudder. The force of it made her think that Tamsin's earlier doubts had washed away on the night wind. She squeezed her hand. Her own resolve hardened as well because, frankly, they were in this all the way up to their ears. Too late to turn back.

"Here." Tamsin stopped. The river water, clear and smooth, flowed by less than five feet away, the light of the moon reflecting on it. Beautiful and deceptive. Currents ran strong beneath that calm surface. A bit like the way she felt. Poised on the outside. Scared shitless on the inside.

"What do you need me to do?" Her magic didn't match Tamsin's, and so far, she'd not even cast a single spell. Tamsin had been front and center when calling on the power of the universe. If her fingers didn't tingle as though charged with electricity, she might think she had nothing to offer. That her magic had evaporated somewhere along the line. She still had it, and if pressed into service, she could step up.

Tamsin stood looking out over the water. "Sit with me here." She dropped to the riverbank and crossed her legs. The backpack stayed on her back. Not that she blamed her. It held precious cargo, and she wouldn't want to let it go either.

"Okay." She sat next to Tamsin and, following suit, crossed her legs. The moment she touched the ground, the tingling in her fingers spread throughout her. Definitely a good reason Tamsin picked this spot. The grandmothers would surely approve.

Tamsin reached into her pocket and pulled out a tea light. She set it on the sandy riverbank and glanced at her. "Ready?"

Morrigan wasn't sure how ready, but she nodded anyway, wondering at the same time if Tamsin always carried candles in her pockets. "Let's do this."

With a lighter, also pulled from her pocket, Tamsin lit the tiny tea light, the scent of lighter fluid wafting through the air. The flame flickered in the deepening darkness, swaying back and forth in a breeze gentle enough it didn't extinguish it. She reached over and took hold of Morrigan's hand, the spark strong the moment their palms touched.

SHERI LEWIS WOHL

"Divine Goddess, mother of all living things, of the sun and moon, and the shining stars. I come to you, a humble devotee. Goddess of great wisdom, queen of the sacred, the water, the moon, the night, you who are the truth and the light, bless us now and show us the way."

Given the energy in the air, she expected an immediate response. Or an explosion of light, the flame of the candle soaring toward the sky. Something big. Didn't happen. For at least a full minute, only silence and the gentle flickering of the flame surrounded them. Ready to call it a bust, she almost dropped Tamsin's hand when a form began to shimmer above the water. At first a short burst of light just above the waterline and then slowly rising and taking shape. The Goddess. Morrigan's breath caught in her throat.

"I don't believe it." Her words were so soft she doubted Tamsin would hear them, but then she squeezed Morrigan's hand. The pressure gentle, the energy flowed between them as hot as molten lava.

Tamsin dipped her head. "Thank you, Goddess."

In a flash, the Goddess disappeared, and once more only the whoosh of the river flowing by and the kiss of the soft wind blowing through the tall wild grass surrounded them. The energy that moments before had been palpable faded to nothing.

"I felt something but heard nothing." It had all happened so fast, but other than her own few words, everything had been eerily silent. "She didn't help us at all." Tears pricked at her eyes, and they had nothing to do with sadness. She dropped Tamsin's hand and stood up. If the Goddess abandoned them, what hope remained for them to mount a winning stand against the Black Faction? All options dwindled down to one. They had to abandon this journey and leave the area before the Witch Finder realized they were nearby.

"You're wrong." Tamsin pushed up from the ground, her features serene.

No, she wasn't. She'd been there, right next to her the whole time. "Silence. All we got was freaking silence. How will that help us? The Goddess has abandoned us, and you know what that means."

No way could Tamsin argue now. The universe had just sent them a strong message.

Tamsin glanced up at the shining moon and then brought her gaze back to Morrigan before she kissed her on the cheek. "Sometimes, my beautiful warrior, you have to listen with more than your ears. You heard nothing. I heard plenty. The Goddess spoke to my heart."

"And she said?"

"Trust."

If she could torch that word, she would. Trust had gotten them into this mess in the first place. "No."

Tamsin held her eyes. "Trust."

"Fuck."

❖

The narrow, winding road had taken them right to the park entrance. A locked pole gate prevented Freddi and Ian from driving deep into the park, but she didn't view that as a problem. The driveway blocked the entrance of a vehicle but didn't prevent them from making an easy walk into the interior. No six-foot chain-link fence with razor wire to scale. No wooden fence to block them. A simple duck under the pole and they strolled into the treed acreage that bordered the river on both sides.

"They'll see the car." Ian stated the obvious, and something she'd thought of too. The entrance had a half-circle drive that allowed them to pull off the main road without entering the park. It didn't provide any cover, making it easy to see their car, and with the lights illuminating the entrance, it would be even easier to spot them.

She had an idea. "Take it down the road to that waste-water-management place we passed, and leave it there. Walk back and join me down at the river." The large facility they'd passed as they drove toward the park had plenty of parking, and who would notice a car sitting in their lot? It did seem strange to have a waste-water plant right on the shores of the river, but apparently that's how they did things here. Creeped her out a bit but hey, she didn't have to live here and drink the water. He'd be able to make it back quickly, as it wasn't a long distance away.

"Walk back?" He frowned as he shifted from foot to foot.

"Please. You've been telling me for days how buff you are. The perfect man. It's not that far away, and if you're really as fit as you claim to be, it should be an easy jog back. Or did I get that all wrong?" Her assessment of him being the kind of guy who would take issue with his manhood being challenged wasn't off target.

"You got that right. Be back here in a few." His chest pumped up as he saluted before he jumped into the car and drove away. Too easy to play him. As the lights disappeared around the bend, she stepped into the shadows of the tall trees, and darkness enclosed her. The full moon cast light down on the pine trees, creating massive, ominous dark shapes. Fitting for the doom that would soon fall upon the Keeper. She smiled, stepped away from the tree she'd been leaning on, and ducked under the locked pole that prevented cars from driving into the park. A well-maintained driveway took her to the interior parking area, and from there, she could detect paths that snaked out in several different directions. Hard to tell in the darkness which one would take her where she needed to be.

On instinct, Freddi began to follow a path littered with fallen pine needles and good-sized pinecones, and dappled with moonlight. Halfway between the parking area and the river, she paused and closed her eyes. She breathed in the fresh air, listened to the sounds of nature, and felt the breeze on her skin. Yes, this was it, and she opened her eyes. The whoosh of rushing water filled the quiet night, and moonlight flowed down and over some rock formations located near a swinging bridge.

For a moment, she forgot all about the call from her sister. Everything here was so right. She was so right. Why should she worry about a damn thing? The ultimate power would soon be in her hands, and Goddess help anyone who got in her way. That included

Franci. She'd had to listen to that bitch her whole life. Franci always thought that her birth order made her superior to Freddi. Well, they'd see about that, wouldn't they? She laughed softly. Payback would be a delightful bitch.

"What's so funny, Boss?"

She turned and looked at Ian, who jogged easily down the path. Was it that easy, or was he putting on a show for her? Didn't care enough to find out. "Just thinking about how this night is about to end."

"Gonna be a shit show for the Keeper." He stopped in front of her and laughed, no hint of exertion from the run. Question asked and answered: easy.

"The White Faction will crumble." The thought almost brought her to climax right here. She smiled.

"Fucking A, Boss. Fucking A."

The wind began to pick up, and after a moment, it whipped her hair around her face. In her opinion, a very good sign. "Ah, the universe speaks."

He rubbed his hands together. "They're coming, aren't they? This show is finally getting on the road. About damn time."

"They are, and if you had any doubts..." She waved her hands at the weather picking up around them. "I hope you have abandoned them."

"I haven't had any doubts since about ten minutes after picking you up. You're the real thing, and like I said before, we're ride-or-die, you and me."

"You had doubts, did you?" That did surprise her. Who could possibly doubt her? She'd demonstrated her exceptional skill level consistently over the years.

He shrugged and looked away. "You have a bit of a reputation."

Now that didn't much surprise her. A lot of people were jealous of her skills and abilities, and that usually generated some kind of talk. Not always accurate talk either. "And that would be?" She would be lying to say she wasn't interested in the substance of the gossip.

"Ah, well, you know. A little bit lone wolf, a lot off script." He didn't look at her as he spoke.

She laughed. She liked it. Actually, it described her quite well. "I can live with that."

"Yeah." He smiled, and now he looked at her. Relief maybe? "Me too. It's boring to always do what you're told. More fun to take chances. Bigger payday too."

Enough with the talk of gossip. None of it would matter in a little bit. Her current off-script event would make it all moot. "We need to be ready. This way." She motioned toward the bridge.

"Right with you, Boss. Let's rock and roll. Get it? Rock?" He laughed.

Goddess help her.

CHAPTER TWENTY-EIGHT

The dismay on Morrigan's face wasn't hard to see, even in the deepening darkness, and Tamsin could understand why she felt as she did. The message from the Goddess had come only to her, and that had to be disconcerting to Morrigan. Tamsin hurried to reassure her. "I've got this. I swear to you. We're on the right path."

Morrigan shook her head. "We're walking into this blind. The Goddess gave you nothing, and we can't keep barreling head-first into danger."

"Not true. She gave me intuition, and that's what we need to triumph over the Witch Finder and stop the Black Faction forever."

"Please." First time she'd heard blatant sarcasm out of Morrigan.

She hurried to take her hand. "It's all we need. Together with the other pieces we've received, it's enough to get it done and keep everyone safe."

"I like solid plans. I like contingency plans. I like tried-and-true plans. We have none of that and haven't since we started this thing. The danger compounds every minute we linger here."

"I know you like the concrete, and that's your strength. I love that about you and how you push me to think things through. It's part of why we work well together. You have a brain full of training and strategy, and when the parameters of the battle are revealed, you'll be the one to know exactly what we have to do. None of this can happen without you and that big brain of yours."

"I like advance plans." Some resistance ebbed away.

Tamsin jumped on it. "Sometimes you just have to trust." She squeezed her hand. "Please."

Morrigan sighed. "I'm not you."

Now she smiled as she brought Morrigan's hand up to kiss it lightly. "And thank the Goddess for that. We need the strength of all four of us to end this. If we were all the same, it wouldn't work. You read the Prophecy. It describes each of us with our differences and our strengths."

Morrigan glanced back in the direction of the parked car. "They have no magic."

Tamsin swung her gaze up to where Holly and Triple waited. "That's not entirely true. They have their own kind of magic. No, they're not like you and me, but we can't discount what they bring to the mix. It's critical to our mission. They have their part."

"I'd feel better if we had backup of the White Faction variety. Warriors with both training and magic. They're coming. All we need to do is wait."

She agreed with Morrigan on that front. They'd put off the White Faction support as long as they could, and whether she liked it or not, they'd be there soon. Okay with her, because by the time they arrived, this would be over. "We have plenty between you and me. I am the Keeper, after all."

For the first time, Morrigan smiled, and Tamsin wanted to hug her. "Bragging now. I am the Keeper after all," she mimicked.

She shook her head, the smile still there. "Only stating a fact. I didn't ask to be a Keeper, and I didn't ask for the power that came along with it. It's mine just the same. Like all that came to you by virtue of your birth. We can't escape what we were born into."

"I'm not asking you to escape your birthright, only to keep it safe. It might be true that I inherited magic and learned to be strong and capable. The thing is, I'm not even close to a Keeper, and that's why more White Faction is better than less in this instance."

"Yet you come from a very long line of warriors. Your magic is as strong as your skills. I repeat, we've got this, and don't forget…"

She turned over her own palm and took Morrigan's hand to do the same, revealing the cuts on each.

❖

The blood pact made this situation real for Morrigan. She'd been tied to the *Book of Darkness* through Tamsin, and turning away from any of this became an impossible task. Tamsin knew just the right visual to drag her back into the fold. "I can't forget." She looked into Tamsin's eyes. "I'll never forget." One didn't touch magic of this magnitude and not have it seared into their memory.

"Good. I'm banking on it. Now I'm heading up to get Holly and Triple." Tamsin kissed her, the heat of her lips flowing all the way to her heart. "We can make our final plans." She leaned down to pick up the tea light.

"Leave it, please." Morrigan stepped back. She couldn't explain why, but she needed a little time alone. "Give me five. I want to stay here for a few minutes. I won't be long, I promise."

Tamsin straightened up without touching the candle. She peered at her and, seeming to find in Morrigan's face whatever she looked for, nodded. "Take whatever you need, and when you're ready, we'll be waiting for you."

After Tamsin disappeared up the hill, Morrigan glanced down at the tea light still flickering as the gentle breeze whispered over it. It surprised her the breeze hadn't put it out, and she took it as a sign. A good sign. Once more she sat on the ground, her legs crossed, the coolness of the earth seeping through her jeans and chilling her skin. She stared at the flickering flame, bringing her focus to a pinpoint. "Tell me," she whispered. "Help me."

No shadowy goddess appeared over the water this time, only the featherlike touch of fingertips on her cheek. A single tear rolled down her face. She knew that touch, had felt it a thousand times during her life. Comforting and loving, it brought her joy even in such a dark hour.

"Keep her safe." The three words were almost too soft to hear, but she did, and she reached out, wishing she could hold the ghostly hand.

Her hand dropped back to her lap as she continued to stare at the candle. "I will, Mama." The flame went out.

Morrigan wiped away the dampness on her cheeks with the back of her hand and stood. With the flashlight feature on her phone lighting the way, she managed to keep from stumbling as she climbed up from the riverbank to the road. On the other side, Tamsin, Holly, and Triple stood and waited next to the car. A motley crew, to be sure, yet her crew. Would she like to have a few of her fellow warriors tonight? Yes. Would she rally and fight with these three and feel supported one hundred percent? Absolutely.

At the edge of the road, she paused. Weariness dropped over her, heavy enough to bend her shoulders. All the time and energy trying to get Tamsin to roll with the old ways had caught up with her. She'd spent her entire life preparing to protect the Keeper the same way as it had been done for generations. It hit her in this moment how tired she'd become of life without a vision of change. Of the programming that dictated one path and only one path. Down the road, danger waited, coiled and ready to strike. If they lost, the world would descend into darkness. She shivered.

Then she stopped and stared at her crew for a long moment. The old way of thinking had to stop. She'd been focusing on the wrong thing—losing. She squared her shoulders and centered herself. No more worrying about failure. It wasn't an option she would choose ever again. They would stop the bitch coming their way. They would stop her and destroy the Black Faction. That change had been on the air for years, and it came down to two things: Tamsin and this night.

"All right, you guys," she said as she squared her shoulders and marched across the road. "What's our next move?" Her mind whirled with ideas, her energy returning with her renewed enthusiasm.

"I brought backup." Triple pulled up his jacket to reveal a handgun at his waist.

Holly and Triple probably wondered why neither she nor Tamsin brought no traditional weapons. Why not use a gun and simply shoot the Witch Finder who came to threaten them? That Triple now revealed a gun fit for a normal threat situation spoke to that mindset. If she were a regular, she'd have done the same thing. Nothing normal would happen tonight, and they were not about to face down a regular.

Tamsin put a hand on Triple's arm and shook her head. "It's a good idea in theory, provided it comes as a total surprise. Against a Witch Finder, it's a risky move at best. If she has even a hint you're carrying, it could be turned against you in an instant."

Triple looked confused. "It's locked and loaded, and I'm a damn good shot." His hand rested on the grip. "I can make this thing count, if I have to."

Morrigan backed up Tamsin. "Triple, it doesn't matter how good you are with a gun. This isn't a normal fight. It will have marginal value and high potential for harm to you. All we can reliably count on is magic and the power of the universe to have our backs."

His gaze remained intent. "Bullshit. I'm a crack shot, and I'll use it if I need to. Nobody will threaten us without pushback."

Tamsin patted his arm and his gaze softened. "Trust Morrigan. She's right. We can't take the risk of the Witch Finder anticipating a gun."

"That's messed up." Triple dropped his jacket back over the weapon, but his words no longer held their intensity.

"You need to leave it in the car." Morrigan would try to protect him and Holly as best she could, but with a loaded gun floating around, she worried that things could go sideways in a real big hurry. Neither of them could fully comprehend the kind of battle they prepared to walk into.

"Okay, okay. So, what is the plan then?"

Tamsin stared down the winding road, and Morrigan could follow her train of thought. They were in sync. "Once we have everyone in position, we walk in."

"And then?" Triple put the safety on his handgun and tucked it underneath the front seat of his SUV. The click and beep secured it as much as possible, given their circumstances.

Morrigan swept her gaze over their small platoon. "And then we fight for our lives."

❖

The wind whipped up, sending debris flying through the air. Freddi smiled and ducked as a couple of pinecones whizzed past her head. Perfect. Game on. The Keeper made her approach, and with her came the prize Freddi had been reaching for her whole life. It felt so good to be her. Too bad Franci didn't share in the beauty of it. That intruding thought made a frown flicker across her face, giving her a moment of unease. Franci's cryptic end to the earlier call gave her pause. It would be just like her older sister to throw a wrench into her best-laid plans.

Bitch never tired of screwing with her. She'd been trained as a Witch Finder right along with Freddi, yet big sister's heart had never been in it. A peacemaker at her core, except for her joy in tormenting Freddi, she'd advocated for reconciliation of the two factions from the time she began her formal training. As it had been in the beginning, she'd tried to convince the upper core of the Black Faction. She embraced the why-can't-we-all-just-get-along philosophy. Freddi thought it stupid, and she hadn't been alone.

Much to Franci's disappointment, not a single witch in the Black Faction had bought into her mindset, and her disillusioned sister took the rejection personally. She moved away to live quietly outside the craft. She should have stayed there. Maybe Freddi would have let her live out her life in peace.

The phone call alone, threatening her, changed that plan. Franci would go down right along with the Keeper and the rest of the goody-two-shoes, White Faction witches she so wanted to live all together in bliss with. No bliss for any of them. She would take out every last one who refused to bow at her feet once she leveraged the magic inside the pages of the *Book of Darkness*. Blood would spill and witches would be crushed. She could hardly wait.

Wouldn't be long now. The Keeper and whoever she believed could help her would step into the park any minute. The whispers on the wind let her know that the time grew short. She and Ian were ready. The shadows of the trees and the stones provided excellent cover and a good view for them at the same time. Regardless of how stealthy the coming witches believed they might be, she'd see them, and they'd never know what awaited them in the shadows.

The other little tidbit that gave her comfort, Franci wasn't nearby either. Despite her declaration about not being at her home in France, and the unspoken threat that she might be close by, Freddi would be able to feel her if she were here. It had always been that way, much to Franci's dismay. Freddi reported every move Franci made to their mother. She made sure her sister failed at her attempts to change the world they'd grown up in. For whatever reason, Franci could never grasp why. The fact nobody wanted the world she hoped for had escaped her, and Freddi made sure she crashed in her endeavors to facilitate peace.

"You think she's coming?" Ian's voice wafted softly on the night air.

She glanced up at the full moon. "Oh yes, she's coming."

"I'm ready."

"Don't do anything unless I tell you, and be quiet." He better not go cowboy on her.

"I have a great view."

"I'm warning you, Ian. Zip it and stay right there until I tell you to move."

"Whatever."

She bit her lip and took a deep breath. If she could sew his lips shut, she'd do it because he wasn't getting the keep-your-mouth-shut part. Might be necessary to do this on her own, except it was too early to drop him. She'd wait and see who came with the Keeper.

Depending upon how many approached, she might be forced to rely on his assistance. At least at first. Once it got down to her and the Keeper, she didn't care if he made it or not.

"Just shut up and wait." She tried one more time.

"Aye, aye, Boss."

She slapped her hand over her mouth to keep her own scream inside. And then the Keeper stepped into the clearing.

CHAPTER TWENTY-NINE

Moonlight washed over Tamsin as she stopped on the path leading down to the swinging bridge. Any other night it would have been all darkness and shadows. Not now. The full moon glowed like a beacon, spreading out warm, golden light to show her the way. Her face grew hot, and her fingertips tingled as though she'd just touched a burning flame. The *Book of Darkness* throbbed against her back, the intensity of it growing with each passing minute. Rays of the moon sparkled on the river's surface, making it look beautiful and serene, inviting her to come and stand on its banks. Its beauty undeniable, it presented a façade just the same, for beneath the calm-looking surface, it roiled swift and dangerous. A grim reaper of equal opportunity, with no regard to age, race, sex, or religion. Many had lost their lives when underestimating the power of the river to take what it wanted.

Much like many had underestimated the power of the witches on both sides of the divide. The war had raged century after century over the grimoire snugged up against her back, taking soul after soul. Throughout the ages, guardians gave up the lives near and dear to them in order to protect it against the witches intent on exploiting its power. Now, hiding nearby, another sought to possess it, and though Tamsin would not run, she would never allow it to rest in her hands.

Tamsin presented like the river—easy-going and calm on the outside, powerful and determined on the inside. The grandmothers were right about this place. It sang to her, an internal melody only she could hear, but hear it she did. How she wished Morrigan could share it with her, and if she could, then she'd believe body, mind, and soul. For a moment, she flashed back on Morrigan's face as she'd walked up from the riverbank earlier. In those few minutes she'd lingered there alone something inside her had changed, and it made her believe that whatever it had been, Morrigan now understood why this must happen tonight. Her fingers flexed as she smiled. She wasn't alone anymore.

She also wasn't alone in this place, and she wasn't talking about the companionship of someone she loved. The one hiding in the darkness wouldn't even know how to love. Intense hatred rolled through the wind, slapping her as if the Witch Finder stood in front of her. "Come on out," she invited her. "I'm here." Bitch, she added silently.

With her arms wide, comforted by the knowledge that Morrigan watched from behind her, and soon, Triple and Holly would descend on the other side of the river, she waited. After briefly discussing options, they had decided upon a divide-and-conquer strategy. Tamsin and Morrigan would walk in from the Aubrey White Parkway entrance to the Bowl and Pitcher, the same one where the car bearing California plates had been parked earlier. Holly and Triple would approach from the west side of the river, dropping down to the swinging bridge from the stables-area trailhead, where they'd deposited them ten minutes ago. With both sides of the Bowl and Pitcher covered, the chess pieces were all in place. If she'd spent months planning this battle, it couldn't have come together better. When it was right, it was right.

And then she stepped out into the light and confronted a tiny, slender woman with shiny, dark hair that caught the rays of the moonlight. Beautiful, really, if she ignored the waves of fury directed at her. Nasty little Witch Finder. With that level of hate inside her, she'd make a bet, not a popular witch either.

"You have what's mine." Interestingly deep voice for a woman that petite.

Tamsin took a wide-legged stance, her bare feet connecting with the earth. Her shoes were back at the gate. She'd pay a price for her barefoot approach, and she would without regret. Bruises and cuts would heal. Worth it to absorb every ounce of power she could get from any source, including drawing from the earth. Grace and Georgie and Ella came back again and again to the land, and she respected their guidance.

"Then come and take it from me." She gripped the straps of the backpack, the vibrations flowing through the palms of her hands into the rest of her body.

Her gaze flickered momentarily up the hillside on the opposite side of the bridge. Moonlight dappled the landscape. The shadows moved, and she resisted the urge to smile. Triple and Holly, on the other side of the river where the viewpoint had paths leading down to the water, were slowly making their way toward her.

Out of the corner of her eye, she noticed a glow begin to appear on the stones named Bowl and Pitcher. What it meant, she didn't know yet, but she had faith that she'd be shown when the time came. Another piece of the Prophecy making itself known.

"Oh, I will take it, but I think it would be better if you came to me." Despite her words, the Witch Finder began to move in the direction of the swinging bridge.

Interesting that she chose to move away from her rather than toward her. Silent prayers to the Goddess rushed through her mind as she gathered her powers and readied herself for battle. Her prayers were cut short when her feet were swept out from under her, and she landed with a thud on her back, the backpack digging into her shoulder blades, her hands releasing their grip in an attempt to cushion her fall. Her breath rushed out as she was propelled toward the bridge and the witch who stood in the center of it.

"That's better." The Witch Finder laughed. "Let's get this party going."

❖

Morrigan had accepted her role as backup grudgingly and remained in the shadows of several close-together pine trees. Not normal for her, or any of the highly trained White Faction warriors, to play second fiddle. She typically led the charge, and this wasn't sitting well with her. When the Witch Finder stepped out into the moonlight, her body began to buzz. Critical to take extra care with this one. Everything about her screamed dark power.

On the other side of the bridge, another witch emerged from the cover of darkness and began to walk toward the bridge. A man, no less. Shocked her that they'd sent a male for a job with this level of importance. The energy she'd sensed since they arrived signaled all female. Quite the twist, and she silently urged Holly and Triple to hurry up. Things already felt sideways.

Then she heard the scream. Actually two. On the other side of the river, one of the moving shadows went hurdling down the hill. From the sound of it, Holly had just fallen and tumbled through the rocks and underbrush toward the river's edge. The second scream, the more concerning one, came from Tamsin. Morrigan watched in horror as she flew onto her back, her arms flinging out to her sides as she lost her grip on the backpack, and then, most concerning of all, she began to slide toward the Witch Finder standing in the middle of the bridge. Whatever magic the woman used, it was fucking powerful.

No hesitation. No second thoughts. She raced out of the shadows and toward Tamsin. Imperative to reach her before she slid onto that bridge. The Witch Finder might not be very big, but clear enough, even from here, that she controlled massive power. She could not allow her to get her hands on Tamsin, and she sure as hell would do everything she could to prevent her from taking control of the *Book of Darkness*. She had a horrible feeling all the spells and protections that had kept it safe up until now didn't mean jack in this moment. The witch standing in the middle of that bridge could and would take it and harness its evil power.

"Morrigan!" Tamsin's voice was high and loud. "Stop her! Hurry!"

"On my way." She ran, stumbling on branches and rocks while still managing to stay on her feet. She reached out and caught hold of the backpack. It didn't slow down Tamsin's slide toward the bridge, and they were both dragged to the edge of the river. Her hands on the straps and her heels dug in, she leaned back. Tamsin's arms slid out of the backpack at the same time she rocketed onto the swinging bridge. Vaguely she wondered if she'd just dislocated Tamsin's shoulders when yanking the straps free. No time to give it any meaningful thought as Morrigan tripped and tumbled into the river, her head going under, her grip on the backpack iron-tight. Cold water slapped her skin, pushing her breath out, and still she held on to those straps.

Her head bobbed up, breaking the water's surface, to the sound of screams filling the night. With water rushing all around her, hard to tell where the screams originated. Tamsin? Holly? Or were they her own? One arm flailed as she caught sight of the Bowl and Pitcher, the light coming off them seeming to beckon her. Her other arm pulled the backpack tight to her chest, the grimoire inside pulsing against her. She kicked hard and pulled with a one-arm sidestroke while maintaining her grip on the bag. After all of this, she'd die before she let go of the grimoire. The way it appeared to be going, the die part might come true. If it did, she'd take the *Book of Darkness* down with her.

The sound of struggles, screams, and strikes of light let her know the battles were both physical and magical. She didn't dare waste the focus or energy on what happened on land. She turned inward instead. In her head, she worked her own magic. Hard to think as the currents reached and clawed at her legs, trying their best to pull her under. With every ounce of energy she possessed, she resisted.

Sputtering, she quickly offered up her prayer to the Goddess. "Earth and water, air and flame, light encircle my body and all that I hold. Great Mother, wrap me in your web of power and bring perfect protection unto me. So it shall be."

Her head went under again, and when she surfaced sputtering and gasping, light rained down on her face. The current continued to pull in its unrelenting demand for her acquiescence. She refused its call, drawing on the answer from the Goddess to kick and pull closer to the stones. The answer waited there. She felt it all the way to her soul.

Tightness in her chest made it hard to breathe, and her tears mingled with the fresh river water. She pushed harder, kicked harder, hoped harder. The shoreline loomed shadowy and far away. Were her efforts bringing her any closer? It didn't feel like it. Then her toes touched sand, and this time she heard her own scream.

Someone reached out and grabbed her hand, pulling her farther into the shallows, where she sank to her knees, the backpack crushed close to her chest. "Come out of the water."

She blinked and looked up into a face she hadn't seen since she was eighteen years old. The trauma of the river almost claiming her life must be causing her to hallucinate. The ghost of a long-ago love. "Franci?"

❖

Freddi screamed as the Keeper broke free of her spell and stood up. The way the other one had grabbed onto the backpack right before plunging into the river sent a bad message. It could mean only one thing. The *Book of Darkness* had gone into the river too.

She threw out a punch of magic toward the Keeper, using everything in her arsenal. The fucking bitch continued to try to defy her. That grimoire belonged to her, and the possibility she or her minions could get away with a snatch-and-grab didn't sit well. At least the magic knocked her target down. Again. For the second time and the third. The bitch kept getting up. Nobody should be able to bounce back like that. What kind of magic did she have? She'd anticipated the Keeper would be strong, just not at this level. With everything she'd grabbed over the last few days, nobody should be powerful enough to defy her or shake off her lightning strikes.

Her concentration on the Keeper, at first she ignored the screams coming from behind her. Too much happening in front of her—the Keeper who refused to stay down and the witch with the backpack being carried downstream by the river. She assumed Ian could take care of whatever backup the Keeper had deemed important enough to bring with her. They'd fail, just as everyone would fail when they faced off with her. The universe wouldn't let her down.

Then, she turned. The scream had a decidedly male tone. That she didn't expect. Freddi spun just in time to see Ian rolling down the hillside. He landed with a thud near the bridge and didn't move. Damn it anyway. If anyone killed him, it should be her.

Big surprise that she'd be left to handle this on her own. Her mental count put her opponents at four. The Keeper, the one who had grabbed the pack and plunged into the river, and two behind her. They had no idea the hell she would bring their way, but they'd find out soon enough. They might believe the four-to-one odds put a win in their favor. They'd be quite wrong. A hand raised, she sent magic flying toward the man rushing in her direction. He flew from his feet and tumbled over the bridge rail into the water. The river would do the rest of the work for her. In moments, he'd be dragged down under the surface by the strong currents, the air pushed from his lungs. Not even a challenge. One down. Three to go.

She whirled back around and focused once more on the Keeper. With two in the river and one, from what she could tell from here, who appeared to be limping, the odds of a win shifted firmly back in her favor. Now she had to make sure the Keeper remained immobilized so she could get to the witch in the river and the grimoire she'd stolen from Freddi. The moment came now.

Gathering a storm in the tips of her fingers, she reached out to send its rage into the Keeper. She dropped her hands, the magic falling away, and filled the night air with her scream. That bitch, that fucking bitch, had disappeared. For two seconds, she'd looked away, and now this. No way should this be happening to her.

A light drew her gaze, and she gaped. The stones were glowing like the beacons of a lighthouse. "No, no, no, no!" She raced off the bridge and toward the shoreline. Stumbling on the rocks and sand, she went down hard on her hands and knees. The rocks cut into her skin, warm blood soaking her pants, the pain barely registering. She focused on the two figures nearest to the stones and the sound of the splashes in the river getting closer and closer to shore. How? How could anyone escape the grasp of this river? All of it wrong.

As she pushed to her feet, she tried to turn it all around. She called for more power. "I am a woman of the moon, beneath the dark skies. I am dark and light in shining beauty. In power and magic, I am God and Goddess. So it shall be."

Energy filled her again. She surged to her feet and raced toward the stones, blood flowing down her legs.

CHAPTER THIRTY

The ice-cold water knocked the breath out of Tamsin, and she gasped, taking in a healthy dose of it. No time to pause or to give anything else a thought except for getting to Morrigan and the *Book of Darkness*. The Witch Finder who had attacked her with intense magic gave her only a few seconds to make a move, and she'd done what she'd needed to do to get away. Those few seconds had given her one option for escape, and she'd taken it without pausing to consider the danger. She'd propelled herself up and over the bridge rail, dropping into the cold, moving waters of the river. Her arms reaching up, she pushed, her head breaking the surface, and wonderful, cool air filled her lungs.

Now she kicked and swam with every ounce of strength she possessed, arms burning, heart pounding. Thank goodness for all her work around the farm. The fitness that came from the manual labor provided what she needed to fight the insistent river. Perhaps a bit of assistance from the Goddess too. She'd take anything the universe wanted to send her way.

It registered briefly that Morrigan had made it to shore and stood next to another woman. It wasn't the Witch Finder, and it wasn't Holly. She'd heard her screams and had seen her tumble down the hillside. No way she'd be down by the river, given the pain that had echoed in her voice. She'd been hurt, and hurt bad. It also wasn't Triple, who, like Tamsin, had gone into the river. His efforts to reach shore were loud and directly behind her. At least she knew he hadn't succumbed to the drag of the river currents. Who stood next to Morrigan? Ally or foe?

Reaching the shoreline after what felt like a lifetime of fighting the currents, she stood straight, her legs trembling, and then she slipped on a rock and fell back into the water. Lightning pain shot up her leg. She ignored it and pushed up again, stifling the scream that rose in her throat. "I'm coming," she yelled over the sound of rushing water. Tears gathered in her eyes and slid down her cheeks. "I'm coming." Almost a whisper this time.

From behind, strong arms wrapped around her, lifting her. A minute later, her feet touched dry land. "Come on," Triple said, the cold of his hands seeping through her shirt. "She hasn't given up, and she's getting close."

She didn't bother to look behind her at the approaching Witch Finder. Instead, she focused on getting to Morrigan and the stranger who stood beside her. The nearer they got to the stones, the more they glowed. It hit her then. "The Prophecy," she said quietly.

"Yeah, gotta think you all nailed that one. The second I realized they were on fire, I knew you had it right." Triple glanced over his shoulder. "Come on, let's hurry. The crazy lady is gaining ground, and she's holding out her arm. I'm thinking that's a bad thing."

"Duck," Tamsin yelled right before a bolt whizzed by their heads. They straightened up, and she screamed, "Run." Tears streamed down her face, and her spirit soared. Renewed strength filled her. Triple ran right next to her.

She almost made it to Morrigan before her feet were swept out from under her and she started to slide backward. Not again. Who was this fighter, and where did she get her strength? A first for Tamsin. She'd been around some powerful witches, but nothing like this one. Her power pressed against Tamsin so hard it made her chest hurt. How she wanted to take a swing and knock her out. To feel her hand connecting with her chin.

Squeezing her eyes shut, she concentrated on taking a swing of the more magical variety. The pull lessened, and her movement away from the stones slowed. Suddenly, a warm hand around her ankle pulled her back toward the light and, along with it, came a boost in power. Morrigan's hand. *Thank you, Goddess.*

"Go, go, go," Triple yelled. "The stones are opening, and the fire is rising. I got this bitch." He turned away from her and began to run toward the advancing witch, taking several blows that made him stumble back a few feet. Each time he got back up and pushed closer, refusing to give in to her show of magic. He showed his bravery a thousand times over, no gun required.

As Triple worked to slow the witch, Tamsin scrambled to her feet and, taking Morrigan's hand, ran, or rather limped quickly, to the stones.

The mystery woman nodded as they approached. "Come on, hurry. He won't be able to slow her down very long."

"Who?" Tamsin looked at Morrigan. "Who is she?" Morrigan's energy toward the other woman remained calm, steady, and without threat. Ally.

"No time to explain. We have to take care of this, and quickly." She held out the damp backpack, heavy with both water and the *Book of Darkness.* "You were right. This is the moment. We have one chance to end this, and it's right there, right now." She pointed to the fire rising and falling in the interior of the stones.

She took the backpack, slipped it on once more, and then started to climb the stones, Morrigan at her side, the blood from the cuts on her legs leaving a trail as she ascended. Heat grew more intense as they climbed, and the grimoire thrummed against her back as if it were saying, hurry. A few feet now, and they'd reach the opening that appeared in the largest of the stones. Flames roared inside it, and in that moment, she understood. It all came together in amazing clarity. Her heart pounded even harder, and tears flowed down her cheeks.

❖

The craziness of seeing Franci after all these years almost knocked Morrigan to her knees. A thousand questions raced through her mind, not the least of which was how in the world had Franci showed up here, of all places? It felt like a thousand years and a million miles between them. So much guilt to overcome, and now in this moment that could change everything, Franci shows up and saves her ass. The universe playing a cruel joke on her? Or karma coming due?

"I have your back. I've always had your back. Trust me," Franci whispered into Morrigan's ear just as she started to climb alongside Tamsin. "Your friend is no match for my sister. She'll take him down hard, but I'll give you time. It's the least I owe you."

"Why?" she tossed over her shoulder, staring down into a face little changed after all these years. Still beautiful, with eyes so dark they looked like the night.

"Because it's the right thing to do."

"That can't be all of it." Franci would be putting her own life at risk, and she couldn't wrap her head around a Black Faction witch helping them with the one thing they all wanted to get their hands on.

In her years as a warrior tasked with making sure the Keeper remained safe, she'd never come up against anyone from the Black Faction who worried about doing the right thing. The focus always about power and killing the Keeper. About seizing control of the *Book of Darkness* and using it to control the world. Not once had she ever seen a glimmer of goodness.

Except that wasn't quite true. Her memories of that long-ago summer were filled with sweetness and passion. Of another young woman who, like Morrigan, had been coming into her own and who shared thoughts and dreams with a kindred soul. They came from different worlds, yet their souls spoke the same language. Those very disparate worlds had dragged them apart, but not before she'd seen the goodness that lived inside Franci. She'd often wondered if they'd beaten it out of her.

The answer stared her in the face right now, that same goodness reflected in those gorgeous dark eyes. In the curve of the full, rosy lips that once upon a time she'd kiss every chance she got. Franci's soul remained good and true. "She'll hurt you." Morrigan didn't want anything to happen to Franci.

"She won't."

Morrigan didn't believe it. "How can you be so sure?"

"She's my sister. Now, go."

That the witch hunting Tamsin happened to be Franci's sister almost caused Morrigan to lose her grip and crash back down to the ground. It at least explained Franci's mysterious appearance here. For a moment she considered the possibility she worked with her sister and then cast the thought aside. Kindness remained dominant in Franci's aura. She came to help, but not her sister. How could two sisters be so different? A puzzle for another time. Right now, they had to save the world, and she continued to climb, her fingers searching for purchase as she ascended.

A sharp pain drilled into her back, and one hand came off the rock as she gasped in pain. She slid a foot or so back down the rock face before catching herself again. Franci hadn't been wrong about her sister, and that shot in her back hurt like hell. Refocused, she began to move up the rocks closer and closer to the fire. Her drive to protect Tamsin quadrupled, and that witch's magic would not take her down. Not tonight. Not ever.

"Franci," she called out over her shoulder. "If you ever cared for me, stop her now, please."

"I did, I still do, and I'm on it."

The sound of screams and running feet filled the night, but her eyes remained on Tamsin. "Keep going, Tamsin. We're almost there." The heat grew intense, the surface of the stones hot against her hands.

"Just a few more feet," Tamsin called down. "I'll send it into the fire."

The flames reached to the sky from the opening that yawned wide in the stones. The mouth of a dragon waiting to be fed. The temperature around them kept rising until it felt as though they were in the middle of summer instead of a cool, dark night. Wet hair and clothes dried, the chill of the river swim pushed away.

The grimoire had always before been impervious to destruction by fire or any other means, for that matter. The truth stared at her now with hot, red eyes and a wide, hungry mouth. A fire like no other, born of magic and the spirits of the universe, beckoned above them. The fire that could save them all.

"Keep going." The pain hit her between the shoulders once more. Another one like that and her bones would shatter. Tears welled up in her eyes, but she held on. "Franci, stop her," she screamed again. "We're almost there."

A hand grabbed Morrigan's ankle and pulled. She kicked and connected with flesh. A face that looked a lot like Franci's, but without the kindness, stared up at her. "Nice try, cunt. Not good enough." She yanked Morrigan's leg again. She kicked harder and kept climbing as her muscles screamed and her shoulders felt as though they were dislocated.

A rush of power whizzed by her, and a second later Tamsin screamed. Morrigan watched in horror as Tamsin hurdled past her. "No!" She reached out with one hand and snagged the backpack. Once again, Tamsin's arms slid free of the pack, but she continued to fall. She dropped to the ground with a frightening thud. Their fingers had touched for a second, and the charge hadn't diminished. The energy it filled her with propelled her upward. The hand that held her ankle refused to relinquish its hold, despite kicking again and again in her attempts to free herself. The unrelenting grip of the Witch Finder didn't stop her. She continued upward as fast as she could, even though every fiber of her being screamed at her to go to Tamsin.

❖

God damn it. Franci had been a thorn in her side Freddi's whole life. Leave it to her saintly sister, in the most important moment ever, to show up again to screw her over. She'd have had this thing done if her meddling sister hadn't gone out of her way to help these witches. Just once she wished Franci would butt the hell out. Just once she wished Franci would have her back. She'd been able to keep hold of the witch closest to her while sending up a charge that knocked the Keeper off the stones. She remained down and out in a crumpled heap at the base of the stones. Perfect. Now to stop the one still climbing. That one wasn't giving it up. Well, she'd take care of her shortly.

"No, Freddi." Franci grabbed her pant leg and dragged her down to the ground, causing her to lose her grip on the witch. Her sister stood in front of her, towering over her as she'd always done. The intimidation used to work on her. Franci tall and athletic, Freddi petite and pretty. Everyone gravitated to the tall, athletic sister while making the very wrong assumption that the petite, pretty one wasn't big enough or strong enough to matter.

Given her comment, Franci must have added reading minds to her list of talents. Apparently, she'd been doing more in France than drinking wine and eating pastries. "It's mine." Simple explanation. No time to get into details, and besides, she owed her sister nothing. Well, nothing beyond payback, and she'd get to that later.

She ignored Franci and started to climb again, reaching for the foot of the witch above her as she tried to scramble up the stones at the same time. While so far she hadn't been able to pull her all the way back down, at least her progress had been seriously impeded. She held the pack in one hand, the prize Freddi sought, and she'd grab it one way or the other. She found purchase on the stones and followed the other witch as she climbed.

She didn't get far. Franci grabbed the back of her shirt this time and yanked with enough force that Freddi screamed high and loud as she lost her balance and fell back, hitting her head on the ground. Rocks bit into her scalp, warm blood soaking into her hair. Unacceptable. She curled her fingers around one of the larger rocks at the same time she jumped up to her feet with her arm swinging. A lifetime of being less than Franci, of being compared to her and found wanting time and time again, fueled her rage. The rock connected with Franci's forehead with a satisfying thud, and her sister went down in a heap right next to the motionless Keeper. "Now stay down, you fucking bitches."

Above her on the stones, the other witch, freed from her hampering grasp, climbed fast now. Energized by eliminating the last impediment between her and the prize, Freddi started to climb after her, closing the distance with impressive speed. Heat poured over her, drying the blood in her hair and making it stick to her head. She didn't worry that the witch would have a chance to throw it in, for everyone knew the *Book of Darkness* had been rendered impervious to fire. This would be no different. The flames would spit it out and into her waiting hands.

At the top of the stones, the witch stopped and appeared prepared to drop the pack into the flames. "No!" Freddi caught up to her and reached out. The grimoire might not burn, but she would, and she didn't want to have to dive in after it.

Only then did she notice the witch wasn't alone. How? How did the Keeper make it to the top of the stones? She'd been on the ground, out cold next to Franci, yet here she was, a smile on her face as her eyes met Freddi's. And where had the man come from? She'd wrapped him in unbreakable magic, yet there he was, right next to the Keeper. The three of them, hands linked, dropped the precious bag into the flames.

Freddi screamed again when she saw it catch fire, the flames eating the pages of the grimoire. "NO!" It didn't make sense. It shouldn't, couldn't, burn. She wouldn't let it happen. With arms outstretched, she dove into the fire, the skin on her hands turning red and then black as she reached for the bag that held her destiny.

CHAPTER THIRTY-ONE

Tears streamed down Tamsin's face as silence dropped over them. The stones closed again to conceal the fire with the power to save the world. The power that did save the world. The Witch Finder's screams lasted only seconds as the flames consumed her alongside the *Book of Darkness*. It ended here. Forever.

The air turned cool once more, as though the fire had never been. The stones were almost cold to the touch as she carefully made her way back down, feeling every bump and bruise and cut. She'd be mixing up some hefty batches of salve when she got back to the farm. What a glorious thought: back to the farm.

"That was awesome." Triple slid down the side of the stone until his feet touched the ground and he bounced on his feet. High energy rolled off him, and no one would guess he'd been forced to fight for his life against the currents of the river or been knocked down again and again by a powerful witch. "Did you know that was gonna happen?"

Tamsin joined him beside the stones, groaning as her bare soles connected with the earth. Yup, pretty much everything hurt. "No, I didn't, but I hoped." She'd come here on faith and trust, and neither had let her down. The *Book of Darkness* was no more, the flames destroying what her family had protected for centuries. The world was now safe forever from the evil that had caused the words to be written in blood, page after page.

"What happened to the Witch Finder?" Triple ran his fingers through tangled hair.

Morrigan's feet touched the ground too, and she shrugged. "I think the Prophecy was about more than just destroying the *Book of Darkness*. I think it was also about ending the Black Faction, and it took the epicenter of power with it."

"But where the hell did she go? I mean, I was up there with you guys and saw it all. I'm just having a little trouble getting my head around it. It's like the Bowl and Pitcher ate her. What kind of weird shit is that, even for you witch types?"

Sometimes the regulars missed the magic in magic. It didn't always have a ready explanation and definitely not an advance explanation. What happened surprised her just as much as Triple. In a good way, that was. "I think you've grasped the general idea. The stones took her."

"Where?" Triple still looked confused.

Tamsin shrugged. "I don't know, and I don't need to."

"I'm gonna say it again, some weird shit going on, but wow. I don't think I'll ever look at this place the same again. Glad you invited me to the party."

Tamsin agreed. "I don't think any of us will forget what happened here. One of those life-changing moments."

Morrigan kneeled next to the stranger. "Franci, can you hear me?" She brushed hair off her face. The woman groaned, blinked, and sat up.

"Freddi?" She blinked a few more times and blew out a long breath. "Where is that little brat?"

Brat wasn't the word she'd have used, but then again, not her sister either. "She's gone."

"Good." She almost laughed. So much for sisterly love.

Tamsin put a hand on Morrigan's shoulder. "Ah, you want to introduce us?"

Morrigan actually smiled. "This is Franci. You know." She dipped her head and looked away for a moment before meeting Tamsin's eyes. "The girlfriend I told you about."

At first Tamsin didn't understand, and then it hit her. "Seriously?" "I kid you not. Franci, this is Tamsin, the Keeper."

Franci stood up, swaying for a second and putting a hand to her head. "You're safe." Clearly, she'd been hurt, yet her first thought turned to Tamsin. No wonder Morrigan had been drawn to her. Nothing like the one now captured for eternity inside the stones.

Tamsin nodded. "I am. Thanks to everyone here and to you. I'm curious, though. How did you know to come here and, more important, why?" She'd never known someone from the Black Faction to do anything except hunt a Keeper and kill them if they got the chance. Certainly not protect one as she'd done tonight. More and more it turned out to be a night of wonders.

"She is…was…my sister, and I knew what she was capable of and the deep darkness that lived inside her. I've always watched her, even after I moved away from the order. I couldn't use my magic in that way, much to the dismay of my family. I grew up to be a great disappointment to them."

"But why help me?" Tamsin still didn't understand.

"Because it's time."

Now that, she totally understood. Tamsin smiled and looked to Morrigan. "See. I'm not the only one who thinks it's time for a change."

Morrigan put her hands on her hips. "Really? You think now is the time to say I-told-you-so?"

"No time like the present." She looked around. "Triple, where's Holly?"

❖

Morrigan peered through the darkness, searching for their sister-in-arms. Sort of hard to see very far in the darkness, even with the light of the full moon. Once the stones had closed, all the illumination provided by the fire inside disappeared, and it became a normal dark night. If not for the full moon, it would be impossibly dark. "Holly!"

"Ah, folks, I could use a little help." Her voice came from the direction of the west side of the swinging bridge.

All four of them headed that way, a sad group of tired warriors hobbling after the battle that left them beaten, bloody, and bruised. Damp, too, after the impromptu swim in the river that all of them were lucky to have survived. Anyone who said magic didn't exist hadn't seen three people defeat the rapids of the Spokane River on a dark, moonlit night. Lots of people succumbed to the waters on warm, sun-drenched days. No way that survival would have happened tonight without some serious magic.

Back at the bridge they could see Holly up the hill about a hundred yards, sitting on top of a motionless man. "Hope you're not gonna be mad after you told us no weapons, but I might have tucked this into my pocket." She held out a stun gun. "Worked pretty good on big boy here. He didn't see it coming."

"You did not." Morrigan laughed, and it hurt, tears pricking at the back of her eyes. Worth it though seeing Holly straddling the man and holding out her stun gun as she challenged him to try to make a move.

Franci walked close to lean over and peer into the man's face. "Ian, what the hell were you thinking, helping Freddi?" The man, still twitching slightly, didn't answer. She straightened up and shook her head. "I know this guy, and I'll take care of him. More of a dumb shit than a real threat. Pretty boy, which is probably what saved his life with Freddi. She always did like a pretty toy, boy or girl."

"I don't think I can walk." Holly scooted off the man and over to a downed log. She pulled herself up and sat. "Me and that hill had a little disagreement, and the hill won. Don't know if I broke the ankle, but it's a real possibility. Might have to call in sick to work for a few days, Boss." She chuckled.

Tamsin laughed too. "No worries there. I think a few days of sick leave are on the agenda for all of us. Nobody got out of this one unscathed." She put a hand to the back of her head.

"Anyhoo," Holly said. "A little help would be appreciated. Like a lot."

"I got ya." Triple helped her up. "Lean on me, and I'll get you back to the rig. Holy Family ER is close too, and we'll get you all x-rayed."

Franci put a hand on her arm. Not quite the charge she got whenever Tamsin touched her, but a tiny flutter that reminded her of those long-ago days. "Can I talk to you for a moment?"

Morrigan studied her face. "Of course. We owe you a lot for this."

"I brought you this." She slid something off her wrist and put it into Morrigan's hand.

She stared. "The bracelet of the Elders." Could this night get any more surreal? "I never understood why you took it."

Franci dropped her head and then looked back up to meet her gaze. "I wanted a part of you with me because I knew we could never be together. They wouldn't let us. I didn't realize what I'd done until much later, and I've lived with the guilt ever since. I can't make it right, but I can return what belongs to you. The only amends I can make, even if really late."

Morrigan slipped the bracelet onto her own wrist and gave Franci a hug. "Thank you."

"I'm sorry." Pain echoed in her voice.

"Everything happens for a reason. Even this. Do you think you'd be here tonight to help make the Prophecy became reality if it hadn't? It was all meant to be."

"I like that."

"Just the truth as I see it. Now, come up, let's get out of here."

They started toward the bridge, Morrigan catching up to Tamsin, and were met by about half a dozen bobbing beams of light. It reminded her of a concert in the dark with everyone holding up a lighter as they swayed back and forth to the music.

"Stop," a strong male voice commanded. "Don't move another step."

"Oh yeah." Morrigan took Tamsin's hand, brought it to her lips, and kissed the back of it. "It's entirely possible I called for backup while I was watching you walk straight toward the Witch Finder." A few familiar faces came into view. At least they'd sent in the "A" team. Nice to know they cared, even if they did threaten to toss her out of the order.

Tamsin laughed. "Well, I think they're a little late."

EPILOGUE

How'd it go?" Tamsin kissed Morrigan as soon as she stepped through the door. The week had turned awfully long with her gone. She'd kept herself nice and busy, hoping that she'd miss her less that way. Big fail on that score. She might have missed her even more.

"It was good, all things considered. To bring everyone together after centuries of fighting, it will take a chunk of time. With Franci's help, things are changing, and she'll see it through. The woman has some serious stones."

"About Franci..." Tamsin almost hated to bring up the subject.

Morrigan laughed. "You know, I've thought a lot about that since that night, and it's kind of like you told me all along. Trust. The universe brought me and Franci together for a reason, even way back when. I really believe it was so the night you saved the world, she would be there to help."

Tamsin hugged her. "I love how you see things these days. You're a different woman from the one who charged up onto my porch and demanded I pack my bags and haul ass out of here."

"Yeah, yeah, yeah. You were right all along."

"I never get tired of hearing that." She smiled.

Morrigan hugged her also and whispered in her ear. "I plan to tell you that for the rest of your life."

"Promise?" Tamsin rested her cheek against Morrigan's, breathing in deeply that intoxicating scent so uniquely her.

"Promise." She kissed her again. "And you can take that to the bank."

"All right then. Let's get ready." She glanced out the window at the sound of a roaring engine. Triple heading up the driveway on his shiny, crimson Harley with the ghost flames. "Triple's here, and Holly and the grandmothers should be right behind him."

"Shouldn't I change? Not exactly wearing my finest."

Tamsin looked at Morrigan and shook her head. "You look perfect. Like the first time I saw you." The memory still made her heart flip.

Morrigan grimaced. "I showed up here a road-weary mess."

She took her face between her hands and stared into her eyes. "You were perfect. You are perfect."

"Well, you keep thinking that, and I'll ask you again in about twenty years. See what you think after living with the good, bad, and the ugly."

Tamsin laughed and hugged her. "Deal. For the record, it won't change how I feel."

Together they walked down to the water, the same spot where they'd stood with Holly, Triple, Grace, Ella, and Georgie when they'd called upon the magic of the universe to guide them. Still beautiful. Still magical.

Half an hour later, they stood together holding hands while facing Grace. The others formed a circle around them. The faces that gazed on them reflected joy and hope, exactly what filled her heart. The bruises were gone, the injuries healed, and even Holly's cast removed, her broken ankle mended. With her cancer responding well to treatment, she insisted on being here and continuing to live her life to the fullest, however long it might be. From a night filled with danger, pain, and near loss, they'd all emerged stronger and filled with excitement for a brighter, happier world. For a world that no longer required the protection of a Keeper.

Tamsin's world had grown in the months since. Endless possibilities that had eluded her before stretched out before her, all of it made sweeter by the woman sent to save her. Morrigan brought a shine to a life that before that night had been only an unobtainable dream. Today, it would all come true. Her heart soared.

Grace stepped forward, smiled, and raised her hands to the bright-blue sky. "Let's get this wedding started."

About the Author

Sheri Lewis Wohl lives in NE Washington State where she's surrounded by mountains, rivers, and forests. It's a perfect backdrop for her stories of danger, romance, and all things paranormal. When not writing, Sheri enjoys cycling, running, and training and working with her three German shepherds.

Books Available from Bold Strokes Books

Bones of Boothbay Harbor by Michelle Larkin. Small-town police chief Frankie Stone and FBI Special Agent Eve Huxley must set aside their differences and combine their skills to find a killer after a burial site is discovered in Boothbay Harbor, Maine. (978-1-63679-267-5)

Crush by Ana Hartnett Reichardt. Josie Sanchez worked for years for the opportunity to create her own wine label, and nothing will stand in her way. Not even Mac, the owner's annoyingly beautiful niece Josie's forced to hire as her harvest intern. (978-1-63679-330-6)

Decadence by Piper Jordan, Ronica Black, Renee Roman. You are cordially invited to Decadence, Las Vegas's most talked about invitation-only Masquerade Ball. Come for the entertainment and stay for the erotic indulgence. We guarantee it'll be a party that lives up to its name. (978-1-63679-361-0)

Gimmicks and Glamour by Lauren Melissa Ellzey. Ashly has learned to hide her Sight, but as she speeds toward high school graduation she must protect the classmates she claims to hate from an evil that no one else sees. (978-1-63679-401-3)

Heart of Stone by Sam Ledel. Princess Keeva Glantor meets Maeve, a gorgon forced to live alone thanks to a decades-old lie, and together the two women battle forces they formerly thought to be good in the hopes of leading lives they can finally call their own. (978-1-63679-407-5)

Murder at the Oasis by David S. Pederson. Palm trees, sunshine, and murder await Mason Adler and his friend Walter as they travel from Phoenix to Palm Springs for what was supposed to be a relaxing vacation but ends up being a trip of mystery and intrigue. (978-1-63679-416-7)

Peaches and Cream by Georgia Beers. Adley Purcell is living her dreams owning Get the Scoop ice cream shop until national dessert chain Sweet Heaven opens less than two blocks away and Adley has to compete with the far too heavenly Sabrina James. (978-1-63679-412-9)

The Only Fish in the Sea by Angie Williams. Will love overcome years of bitter rivalry for the daughters of two crab fishing families in this queer modern-day spin on Romeo and Juliet? (978-1-63679-444-0)

Wildflower by Cathleen Collins. When a plane crash leaves eleven-year-old Lily Andrews stranded in the vast wilderness of Arkansas, will she be able to overcome the odds and make it back to civilization and the one person who holds the key to her future? (978-1-63679-621-5)

Witch Finder by Sheri Lewis Wohl. Tasmin, the Keeper of the Book of Darkness, is in terrible danger, and as a Witch Finder, Morrigan must protect her and the secrets she guards even if it costs Morrigan her life. (978-1-63679-335-1)

A Second Chance at Life by Genevieve McCluer. Vampires Dinah and Rachel reconnect, but a string of vampire killings begin and evidence seems to be pointing at Dinah. They must prove her innocence while finding out if the two of them are still compatible after all these years. (978-1-63679-459-4)

Digging for Heaven by Jenna Jarvis. Litz lives for dragons. Kella lives to kill them. The last thing they expect is to find each other attractive. (978-1-63679-453-2)

Forever's Promise by Missouri Vaun. Wesley Holden migrated west disguised as a man for the hope of a better life and with no designs to take a wife, but Charlotte Rose has other ideas. (978-1-63679-221-7)

Here For You by D. Jackson Leigh. A horse trainer must make a difficult business decision that could save her father's ranch from foreclosure but destroy her chance to win the heart of a feisty barrel racer vying for a spot in the National Rodeo Finals. (978-1-63679-299-6)

I Do, I Don't by Joy Argento. Creator of the romance algorithm, Nicole Hart doesn't expect to be starring in her own reality TV dating show, and falling for the show's executive producer Annie Jackson could ruin everything. (978-1-63679-420-4)

It's All in the Details by Dena Blake. Makeup artist Lane Donnelly and wedding planner Helen Trent can't stand each other, but they must set aside their differences to ensure Darcy gets the wedding of her dreams, and make a few of their own dreams come true. (978-1-63679-430-3)

Marigold by Melissa Brayden. Marigold Lavender vows to take down Alexis Wakefield, the harsh food critic who blasts her younger sister's restaurant. If only she wasn't as sexy as she is mean. (978-1-63679-436-5)

The Town that Built Us by Jesse J. Thoma. When her father dies, Grace Cook returns to her hometown and tries to avoid Bonnie Whitlock, the woman who pulverized her heart, only to discover her father's estate has been left to them jointly. (978-1-63679-439-6)

A Degree to Die For by Karis Walsh. A murder at the University of Washington's Classics Department brings Professor Antigone Weston and Sergeant Adriana Kent together—first as opposing forces, and then allies as they fight together to protect their campus from a killer. (978-1-63679-365-8)

A Talent Within by Suzanne Lenoir. Evelyne, born into nobility, and Annika, a peasant girl with a deadly secret, struggle to change their destinies in Valmora, a medieval world controlled by religion, magic, and men. (978-1-63679-423-5)

Finders Keepers by Radclyffe. Roman Ashcroft's past, it seems, is not so easily forgotten when fate brings her and Tally Dewilde together—along with an attraction neither welcomes. (978-1-63679-428-0)

Homeland by Kristin Keppler and Allisa Bahney. Dani and Kate have finally found themselves on the same side of the war, but a new threat from the inside jeopardizes the future of the wasteland. (978-1-63679-405-1)

Just One Dance by Jenny Frame. Will Taylor Spark and her new business to make dating special—the Regency Romance Club—bring sparkle back to Jaq Bailey's lonely world? (978-1-63679-457-0)

On My Way There by Jaycie Morrison. As Max traverses the open road, her journey of impossible love, loss, and courage mirrors her voyage of self-discovery leading to the ultimate question: If she can't have the woman of her dreams, will the woman of real life be enough? (978-1-63679-392-4)

Transitioning Home by Heather K O'Malley. An injured soldier realizes they need to transition to really heal. (978-1-63679-424-2)

Truly Enough by JJ Hale. Chasing the spark of creativity may ignite a burning romance or send a friendship up in flames. (978-1-63679-442-6)

Vintage and Vogue by Kelly and Tana Fireside. When tech whiz Sena Abrigo marches into small-town Owen Station, she turns librarian Hazel Butler's life upside down in the most wonderful of ways, setting off an explosive series of events, threatening their chance at love...and their very lives. (978-1-63679-448-8)

Broken Fences by Jo Hemmingwood. Former army sergeant Seneca Twist has difficulty adjusting to civilian life until she meets psychologist Robyn Mason and has a place to call home. (978-1-63679-414-3)

Never Kiss a Cowgirl by Ali Vali. Asher Evans dreams of winning the National Finals Rodeo in Vegas, and Reagan Wilson wants no part of something that brings back the memory of what killed her father. (978-1-63679-106-7)

Pantheon Girls by Jean Copeland. Cassie Burke never anticipated the detour life was about to take when a meeting with a prospective client reunites her with a past love and reignites the star-crossed passion they shared twenty years earlier. (978-1-63679-337-5)

Roux for Two by Aurora Rey. For TV chef Chelsea Boudreaux and hometown boy Bryce Cormier, love proves as tricky as making a good pot of gumbo. (978-1-63679-376-4)

Starting Over by Nance Sparks. Jennifer has no idea if she can mend Sam's broken soul after the sudden loss of her wife, but it's never too late for starting over. (978-1-63679-409-9)

The Accidental Bride by Jane Walsh. Spinsters Miss Grace Linfield and Miss Thea Martin travel to Gretna Green to prevent a wedding, only to discover a scandalous passion—for each other. (978-1-63679-345-0)

Three Wishes by Anne Shade. A magic lamp, a beautiful Jinni, and a cursed princess make for one unbelievable story. (978-1-63679-349-8)

Undiscovered Treasures by MJ Williamz. For Cyl and her friends Luna and Martinique, life's best treasures often appear when you're not looking. (978-1-63679-449-5)